Praise for Philippe Boulle's
Vampire: A Morbid Initiation:

"It sent shivers down my spine."
—Tim Dedopulos, author of **Hunter: Apocrypha**

"There is a palpable sense of dread and anticipation throughout... Definitely a book to devour...."
—Chris Madsen, *Culture Dose*

"Boulle has weaved an excellent tale.... I heartedly recommend this book."
—Ralph Dula, RPG.net

Vampire: The Masquerade Fiction from White Wolf

The Clan Novel Series

The Clan Tremere Trilogy

The Clan Lasombra Trilogy

The Dark Ages Clan Novel Series

Also by Philippe Boulle

For all these titles and more, visit **www.white-wolf.com/fiction**

The Madness of Priests™

Philippe Boulle

Second Volume in the Victorian Age Trilogy

1554 LITTON DR
STONE MOUNTAIN, GA
30083
USA

WHITE WOLF
PUBLISHING

ISBN 1-58846-829-1
First Edition: February 2003
Printed in Canada

White Wolf Publishing
1554 Litton Drive
Stone Mountain, GA 30083
www.white-wolf.com/fiction

Wherever God erects a house of prayer,
The Devil always builds a chapel there;
And 'twill be found, upon examination,
The latter has the largest congregation.
—Daniel Defoe, *The True-Born Englishman*

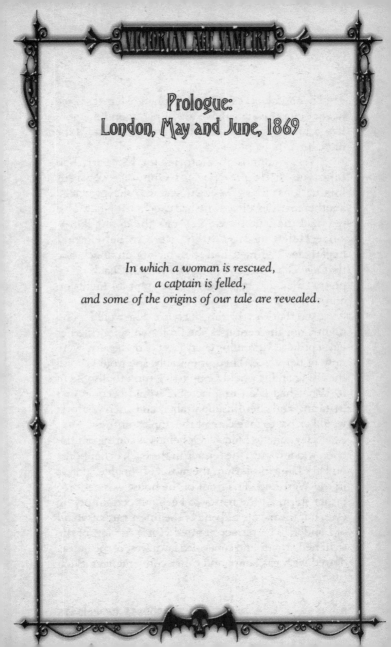

Prologue:
London, May and June, 1869

In which a woman is rescued,
a captain is felled,
and some of the origins of our tale are revealed.

"Beautiful, isn't she?" Lady Ophelia Merritt's voice never quite traveled above a whisper, sounding more like a breeze through silk than anything else. "Like fine china."

"Yes, I suppose." Victoria, for her part, had relatively little patience for Ophelia's constant infatuations. Every week, it seemed, she produced another man or woman who had caught her fancy. This one had the bluest eyes, that one the fairest skin—since Helen of Troy, if you were to believe her hyperbole. The next had the voice of an angel, one that age could never be allowed to spoil. Each one a pretty fancy that kept Lady Merritt rapt for nights on end.

And that was the rub, of course. She would spend nights, not the centuries she professed, admiring her latest protégé, devouring every facet of his beauty, every note of her voice. Then, inevitably, she would tire of the thing and it would be up to Victoria to dispose of it. What had been irreplaceable would become first irritating and then insupportable, and then Victoria would arrive to take care of the unpleasantness.

"Her name is Emma." Ophelia was staring out the open window onto the terrace in the back of her home on Park Lane in Mayfair, the most fashionable address in the West End. The front of the house was perforce rather stern, all the better to keep out certain prying eyes, but the façade hid one of the finest gardens in all of London. The terrace granted visitors a view of the tight hedge maze and concealed lawn west of the house, dotted with gas lamps and other conveniences. Such as shadows deep enough for every kindred in the city to play their games.

"Where did you find her, milady?" Victoria had no real interest in this creature, but her social better expected the question and she had no desire to be petulant tonight. Let the great dame of London's undead have her distractions and let Victoria get on with her business.

"She came with Monsieur Pachard. A bauble he acquired from acquaintances in County Durham, if I understand correctly." Lady Merritt smiled. "Don't be so surprised, dear child, he and I have much in common."

Victoria felt her blood rising, the bitter sting of bile joining it. This would complicate matters when the time came. It took her several seconds of gazing at nothing in particular before she could speak again without betraying herself. She realized, of course, that she could hide very little from Ophelia Merritt—but the key was never to say anything. Feelings were never as important as words. Finally, Victoria felt her voice was sufficiently icy and spoke again. "What can I do for you tonight?"

"Oh, yes." Ophelia's voice took on the sour tone of a child reminded that it had to come in from the garden. "Michael. He's proved tiresome."

Another toy, another grave.

***

"And what do you see for me, holy man?" Prince-Regent Valerius smiled at the blond man, showing only the hint of his fine teeth. "A thousand years of glorious rule?"

Lady Merritt felt a delicious tension bunch in her

innards and, satisfyingly, heard young Emma gasp in the next room. The young woman had tasted her blood only twice and already the bond was strong. The tension she felt, though, had more to do with the implications of the prince-regent's question. A faux pas tonight could be very unpleasant indeed.

Valerius had now sat as London's preeminent vampire for seventy years, ever since Prince Mithras had departed for parts unknown. He'd acted as seneschal before that time , but always in the shadow of the ancient monster who claimed the name of a Persian god. No longer. Under Valerius's regency, the city had weathered an unpleasant outbreak of sectarian violence among its undead twenty years ago and shortly thereafter hosted the Great Exposition that confirmed it as the center of the civilized world. Valerius had helped usher the city into modernity and cemented new and lasting relationships among the sophisticated predators who stalked its nights.

The social gathering tonight, for example, would have been unthinkable under the more backward-looking rule of Prince Mithras. In those nights, the Tremere order was banished from London and the blood-wizards hid in the shadows of County Durham or simply remained out of England altogether. Tonight, Monsieur Pachard, who had first brought darling Emma into this house, was a guest of honor and acted as the representative of his order in Valerius's court. And neither was he the only Tremere present. The insufferable Doctor Bainbridge was about as well, probably stuffing his abnormally tolerant gullet with the pastries and meats set out for those guests best described as entertainment.

"Your Grace, Father Anatole is a practitioner of

mysteries, not political intrigues." Stephen Lenoir stepped forward as he spoke, and Lady Merritt knew that he saw the danger as well. And good that he did, since he had brought this Anatole to London in the first place. Lenoir cut, as always, a dashing figure in his black-as-night evening suit. His hair matched the fabric so well she had to assume the one had been tinted to match the other.

"But Mr. Lenoir," Prince-Regent Valerius said, "surely we are all enlightened enough in this age of reason to listen without judgment to such entertainments. Or do you purport to reintroduce the superstitions of the past into this city?"

Lady Merritt smiled. The prince-regent had a skill at weaving these traps of paradoxical rhetoric. Vampires, creatures who lived without life, who fed on blood and burned to ash by the light of the sun, discussing the merits of reason versus spirituality was an elegant snare indeed. Valerius had built much of his rule on the basis of squarely entering the age of modernity—for Lenoir or his guest to challenge that would be dangerous. But then again, the prince-regent had requested a scrying.

"As you say, Your Grace," Lenoir said with a mild bow. "For the purposes of your amusement, then." He turned to the guest. "If you would oblige, Father Anatole?"

"Bien sûr, mon prince."

The mystic was, as his kind often were, somewhat disheveled. His long blond hair had the unkempt look of a traveler or a colonial and his simple frock looked like that of a Catholic monk. A long string of rosary beads weighted with a brass Egyptian cross hung at his neck, adding to his monastic appearance. His eyes, a deep blue, burned with the light of madness unimagined, a powerful enticement to creatures such as those assembled here tonight, who felt they could imagine it all.

He closed his eyelids for what would have been a heartbeat had any of the players in this little drama had beating hearts. Then he opened them again to reveal eyes gone purely white as his irises turned to look inside. He spouted a bevy of words in languages Lady Merritt could not comprehend—a standard prelude to his predictions, it seemed—and began.

"I see a king… cursed and alone… He wanders alone through trees scented with violets…"

Whispers began already. Could the king be the absent Prince Mithras? Or was it Valerius himself? Or another, perhaps?

"The king enters a room and it is a shambles… Trash and jewels are scattered everywhere… He roars and his lost armies rally to him from the very earth… Together, they battle against the enemy… the pretender…"

All the whispering died with that last word. Was the mad French priest calling Valerius a pretender to his face?

"The king is victorious… But during the battle, he passes by a thorn-bush and is scratched… In the thorn bush, there is a viper and it bites him deeply… The king sits on his throne, but he is sick and the kingdom withers before his eyes…."

Suddenly the cleric's eyes were clear again, blue and piercing, staring straight at Valerius. "This is what I see, my prince."

Well, Lady Merritt thought, *I doubt I shall invite Mr. Lenoir again.*

***

Emma had outlasted the other favorites, thank providence, and so Victoria had had the time to gather information about the girl who would inevitably become hers to dispose of. She'd very quickly grown tired of Lady Merritt's tendency to go through protégés, but had never before thought it worth disobeying her own patron in London for it. Indeed, Ophelia Merritt had welcomed her seven years ago when she'd arrived by transatlantic clipper from Nova Scotia after a harrowing escape from the destructive war consuming the American states she'd nested in for a great deal of time. For that, Victoria owed Lady Merritt a great deal—the Good Lord only knew what her reception might have been had she been forced to try Paris.

Still, the matter of Emma was different. The mildest amount of research had revealed that her birth name was not Emma Druhill, but Emiliana Ducheski. She was the daughter of an inbred clan of misplaced Slavs who had survived under the careful eye of the warlocks of House Tremere for some centuries. Even if Monsieur Pachard, the Tremere envoy in London, had intended Emma as a gift for Lady Merritt, discarding her would be an embarrassment. If, as Victoria believed, the Tremere had plans for young Emma, then it would be significantly more awkward.

Lady Merritt, as one of the grande dames of London's night society, would be hard to attack directly, of course. Victoria would make for a much more palatable target, a way to hurt Merritt without causing a breakdown of the traditions. Victoria was anxious to make sure that did not come to pass.

The gravity of the problem came to light when Victoria uncovered, with the help of her manservant

Cedric, that Emma Ducheski had in fact been married to a Captain James Blake of the 12th Hussars shortly before her introduction to Lady Merritt. Blake had spent the last two months in Africa, as part of an action in Ethiopia, but would surely discover the alarming change in his bride's condition upon his return. Although the union seemed to be one of those not uncommon matches between the heiress of a wealthy commercial family and the son of a less-than-solvent viscount, the letter Cedric had intercepted seemed to be heartfelt. More importantly, there was a good chance that Pachard, in his constant quest to establish legitimacy for his order, had engineered the union in order to gain access to the aristocracy. All the more reason to forestall any unpleasant fate for the girl.

Thus, Victoria put pen to paper. Little Mary-Elizabeth did a fine job of serving as an escritoire, laying bare-backed on the cotton sheets of Victoria's bed in her house on Charlotte Place. The girl, barely into womanhood, was a marvelous creature and she suppressed little giggles as the pen strokes through paper tickled her back and Victoria's hand brushed her bottom. Victoria felt urges more immediate than the safety of Emma Ducheski rise in her, but kept her head about her. First the letter, then there would be time for the pleasures of feeding.

My Dear Capt. Blake, she began. *I have it on good authority that your duty keeps you from your darling wife's side, but I urge you to return....*

***

"Be quiet, you foolish thing!" It was almost July and the time had come. Emma Blake was not making things any easier, however. She was still besotted with Lady Merritt, the woman who'd used her body and soul for nigh on six weeks and then suddenly grown cruel and cold. She was insisting that Victoria return her to the house on Park Lane, confident that her mistress would welcome her back with open arms.

Finally, Victoria had to clamp her hand over the woman's mouth lest her screams alert some Peeler or other bothersome fool. Cedric was guiding their carriage, a heavy black coach, across Blackfriars Bridge and into Southwark, a warren of cutthroats and ne'er-do-wells whom Victoria knew not to trust with the opportunity to make mischief.

Of course , she was coming here to find one of the worst of the lot.

"Think of your husband, girl," Victoria hissed, releasing the pressure on the girl's mouth lest she suffocate. "He is coming for you."

A flicker of confusion passed across the young woman's face. "James? But he died…"

Panic seeped into Victoria's veins, but she kept it from her face. Might James Blake be dead already? If so, all was lost. "Who told you that?"

"Milady."

Victoria relaxed. "She lied. She wanted to have all your attention for herself. James Blake is alive and well."

"No," the girl said stubbornly. "Why should I believe you? You are the liar here."

"Think what you want, girl. The evidence of your own eyes will show you the truth soon enough." Victoria's thoughts completed the sentence for her: *I hope*.

The carriage stopped in what passed for a square in Southwark, namely a tight knot of three streets and four alleys, with an alehouse and a workhouse-cum-brothel facing each other across the way. The carriage took up much of the available muddy space.

Victoria pushed open the shutter on the window by her head and looked out at the workhouse. She waited, listening to the noise from the tavern across the way, and the grunts of a prostitute and her client making use of one of the alleys. In the many years since she had last needed to take a breath, Victoria had discovered that her senses had grown much sharper than those of a mortal woman. Become a nocturnal predator, she could—when she put her mind to it— see with the acuity of an owl and hear like a great cat. Thus, she was not altogether shocked that she saw Samuel coming.

Samuel was new to both the blood and the city. The former condition meant he was still perfecting the compensations that came with damnation. The curse had caused a sort of pestilence in his flesh, making it resemble one of the countless sick who clogged hospices during outbreaks of disease. Most people do their best to ignore such disgusting folk and Samuel had discovered how to enhance that effect. Unless he did something obvious, most people never had any idea he was there.

Victoria Ash, however, was not most people. She had dealt, once upon a time, with a true mistress of this trick, the undead street urchin Clotille who had watched all of Paris's intrigues unseen. That was several lifetimes ago, but Victoria's acute senses still allowed her to see—or at least sense—a novice like Samuel approach. She was aware that the fog and the shadows seemed a little too thick in a corner or down an alley and a deep instinct born of simple survival told her something was within them.

Nevertheless, she let him reveal himself. To his credit, he did so without the usual fanfare of such displays. He did not jump out at Victoria and her charge for the sake of a cheap shock. Instead, he just appeared, like a detail seen but unnoticed up until that point.

"You have it?" he asked.

"Of course," she said. "I always pay my debts." With that she opened the door and pushed Emma Blake bodily into the mud.

The girl screamed. "What? But—"

She was cut off as Samuel dragged her bodily into the whorehouse where he made his nest.

***

James Blake found his wife Emma right where the anonymous correspondent had said he would. It had been a frustrating exercise to receive these letters while stationed on the Red Sea, anonymous notes that first hinted, then outright said that Emma had been the victim of some criminal enterprise. All men of the world knew of stories of white slavery and the fate of young English women who were kidnapped by foreign flesh-peddlers or their domestic accomplices. To have his new bride suffer this misfortune, however, was a shock.

That the correspondent had never shared her identity—Blake had sensed some femininity about the hand—and had delayed the final revelation as to where Blake could find Emma had at first seemed insupportable. It had, he conceded, given him the necessary time to secure a leave of absence from the colonel for himself and his regimental brother Captain Lewis. Add that to the debt Blake owed the old man.

And so, as afternoon gave way to evening, they

had made their way into Southwark and got into the workhouse the correspondent had indicated. It was clearly a brothel now, and probably the base for a veritable network of guttersnipes and pickpockets as well. In the backmost room, there had been—just as he was told—a trap-door toward a cellar and there, curled on cold ground, was Emma.

Blake's heart had sunk when he saw his wife. Despite their separation, and his initial resistance to the proposed marriage, he'd grown genuinely fond of the girl from County Durham. But much of her beauty was gone now, washed away by some terrible disease or abuse. Holding a lantern before him, he saw just how pale and thin she had become. It was as if all the color had been drained from her flesh. Blake had seen a similar aspect among soldiers on campaign deprived of nourishment—had she been starved all these long weeks?

Moving as gently as he could, he carried her up above ground. To do so, he put his lantern on the edge of the floor of the upstairs room, then grabbed Emma under the arms and backed up the steep step-ladder. He still had her in this hug when things went horribly wrong.

A terrible scream from behind Blake was the only warning he had of the impending attack. He glanced over his shoulder and his mind struggled to make sense of what he was seeing. *Something* was rushing his way, covered in rags and rotted flesh, baring teeth that seemed larger than a wolf's.

Lewis, who had been standing by the door, tried to bring his pistol to bear, but the thing was too fast. With a swing of a ragged paw, it pushed the soldier aside and made a line for Blake and his bride. Lewis hit the flimsy wall like a sack of potatoes, his gun discharging with a thunderous noise. The creature didn't stop.

Blake's hand were full supporting the unconscious Emma, so he had no way to reach for his own weapon. Still, Lewis's action did buy him a split second to do one desperate thing. Holding Emma to one side, he gave as strong a kick as he could directly into the oil lantern he'd set on the ground, sending it at the creature. The lantern broke when he kicked it and oil, glass and flame hit the thing like an incendiary wave.

It screamed a deep raspy scream and Blake felt a surge of satisfaction.

The thing—a man surely, the teeth had been a trick of the light, yes?—writhed in a mad panic, clawing at the layers of tatters it wore as clothing. Blake stamped his foot to douse the few licks of flaming oil that had stuck to his heavy cavalry boot and hoisted Emma onto his back as a stevedore would a sack of grain. "Lewis!" he cried.

The other man got up as best he could, and winced in pain as he put weight on his left leg. He'd hit the rotting plaster of the wall with sufficient force to leave a goodly hole in it and crack an underlying beam, and his joints had suffered as well. Still, he hobbled forward as best he could. "Go!" he exclaimed.

Blake moved back the way they had come, down a tight little hallway and into a larger common room, then toward the street and their waiting cab. With Emma over his shoulder he couldn't glance back, but he did take a few opportunities to turn bodily and make sure Lewis was keeping pace. The two men had been friends ever since they met as young cavalry lieutenants and Lewis had stood as Blake's groomsman during his wedding to Emma. He hadn't hesitated to go into danger to save his friend's wife. Blake wouldn't forgive himself if the man's injury kept him out of the saddle.

The first time he turned back was at the end of the first hallway and he was heartened to see Lewis not far behind. He was limping, but bore the determined look Blake knew so well. They were going to make it.

The second time Blake looked back, he had crossed much of the large common room and was near the exit. The commotion had drawn curious whores from the rooms upstairs. It struck Blake as odd that people would have been up there during the daylight and be descending now, but then again these were bawdy girls and other night dwellers. He supposed they must sleep during the day, when the decent world has dominion over the city streets.

These onlookers were in all likelihood drunk or besotted with opium, because they looked on a well-dressed man carrying a wan woman over his shoulder with only mild curiosity. Blake drew his own pistol with his free hand, lest any of these ne'er-do-wells get any urge to detain him. Then, as he approached the exit, there came another withering roar.

Blake turned and saw Lewis coming into the room. Black and gray smoke was curling up from behind him, as the fire spread from the oil to the waiting timbers of the old workhouse. This too did not seem quite to register with the half-dozen onlookers. For a moment, Blake wondered if he'd imagined the wail, but then the thing emerged from the smoky hallway right on Lewis's heels.

There was no doubt in Blake's mind that this was a thing, not a man. It moved with the gait of an animal

THE MADNESS OF PRIESTS

and screamed like a banshee. It had shed its flaming tatters, but smoke clung to its boil-covered hide.

Lewis turned in time to get off another shot with his pistol, this one at point-blank range into the thing's chest. The shot, loud and true, was enough to knock the stupor from at least one of the thing's housemates, a fat woman who let out a scream and dropped the tallow candle she'd been using for light. Lewis, meanwhile, hobbled quickly toward Blake and the waiting exit.

But the shot hadn't felled the creature. Lewis had taken only a few steps before the thing, enraged but seemingly unharmed, was on him. Its hands, like the gray mitts of some freakish beast escaped from a menagerie, clamped onto Blake's truest friend. One covered his face, fingers clawing at eyes and mouth. The other grabbed at his chest, finding purchase in the man's clothing. Blake was sure the thing was going to drag Lewis down like a wolf bringing down a stag, but the truth was worse still. The beast lifted Lewis bodily off the ground, and with a sickeningly wet sound, pulled him apart.

Smoke was filling the room, but Blake still saw with horrible clarity as his groomsman's head separated from his body. Wet gore burst from Lewis's abused torso and the smell of offal joined that of burning wood and linen.

Terror gripped everyone in the room except for Blake and the creature, which buried its maw in Lewis's corpse to feed. The fat woman's dropped candle had rolled still lit under a worn curtain, and more fire and smoke were joining the conflagration that must be growing in the back of the house. Just before it was swallowed in smoke, Blake saw the creature look up and toward the flame now before it. He saw fear there.

The others in the room panicked and ran. Some, in the suicidal way of those acting solely on fear, ran upstairs to escape a growing fire that would surely follow them. The lucky ones pushed past Blake and out to the street, knocking over tables and spilling a variety of materials to feed the flames. Political tracts, penny dreadfuls, a glass of some cheap grain liquor, a half-full oil lamp—all helped push the room toward inferno.

Blake backed out the door, hearing the howls of the maddened creature and the screams of the besotted residents. Beside the door was a variety of detritus, from a pile of rotting garbage to a barrel of waste water and stacks of wooden boards and planks, discarded from some makeshift scaffold or kept around to help draw carts stuck in the mud of the streets.

He made up his mind, put Emma down, and did what needed to be done.

***

Victoria Ash gently stroked Mary-Elizabeth's hair as the girl slept, her head resting on Victoria's lap, in the parlor on Charlotte Place. Victoria had just perused the previous day's press, and was taking the time to think. The reports of the fire in Southwark said several score unfortunates had met their end in the blaze, which had spread to five different buildings before the fire brigade and the local citizenry could beat it back. Many of the dead, it seemed, perished in a former workhouse become (in the poetic license of the newspaperman) a "den of iniquity." The fire was thought to have originated there during one of the violent disputes so common in that section of society. The most unfortunate circumstance was that the only real exit from the building had been blocked by debris, condemning those within to a fiery tomb.

"Good luck, little Emma," Victoria said aloud to no one in particular but waking the girl lying in her lap.

"Mm?" Mary-Elizabeth mumbled sleepily.

"Nothing, my darling." But as she said it, Victoria knew it was a lie. She'd taken a risk to save Emma Blake—and whatever Tremere intrigues she was destined to play a role in—and it would not do to completely let the girl out of her sight.

Perhaps, she thought, looking down at Mary-Elizabeth, *young Emma needs a friend with whom she can share her secrets.*

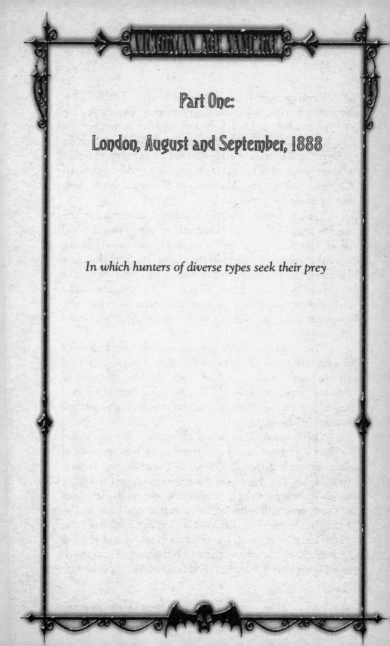

Part One:

London, August and September, 1888

In which hunters of diverse types seek their prey

Chapter One

Tomb robbery, it seemed, came easily to Lt. Malcolm Seward. Indeed, the lock popped open without much effort, and he couldn't help but wonder just what his facility for sacrilege might imply about his character. In light of his activities over the last few months, vandalizing the offices of Pritchett & Sons Undertakers of Coggeshall, Essex should seem only a minor transgression, but he was still nervous.

"Quickly now," said the man with Seward, "before we are seen." Like the lieutenant, this man was dressed in simple, dark-colored country clothes—looking something like a gentleman returning late from the hunt (although it was early in the season). In fact, he was a viscount—James, Lord Blake to be precise—and although the scandal would be far greater were he to be discovered in the midst of such a burglary, it had been his idea.

The two men slipped in through the back door of the undertaker's. That door gave onto a small courtyard whose stone wall they had both clambered over, so Seward hoped they would not be seen. Surely no one would notice the absence of the padlock on the outside latch. He hoped.

The door was a service entrance, and the room behind it was not dressed in the proper, somber ways of deep mourning like the front of the shop surely was. Indeed, Mr. Pritchett would use the examples on display in his storefront to help families decide on the specifics of their service, interment and observances. Instead, the back store was a utilitarian space, where the paraphernalia of death was stacked in rows on shelves or in large boxes. It all seemed much less proper and much more commercial as Seward and Lord Blake crept through the tight rows of mortuary knickknacks. A rack of black broadcloth suits—ready for those who had no proper attire in life but needed it in death—stood opposite shelves filled with box –upon box of cards. The cards were blank save for the pre-printed border designs, ready to receive the details of a service. They would be sent to a printer's shop to have those inscribed upon them. In the corner of the room, on a tall wooden tripod, stood the large box of a photographic camera. Mr. Pritchett must serve several well-to-do clients ready to have daguerreotype mourning cards made of their beloved dead before the interment.

"Through here." Blake pointed at a large set of double doors at the far end of the cluttered space, near the hallway leading to the front of the business. Another padlock dangled from a heavy chain wrapped through iron rings in the wooden doors.

Seward still had the pry bar he'd used on the outside lock, and he brought it to bear anew. The padlock itself was awkwardly placed for the bar's use, but one of the rings in the doors offered better prospects. He slipped the end of the bar through the ring, dug it into the edge of the door and pushed out. As he'd suspected, the wood had suffered some rot and after a few seconds of effort, the ring slowly came out. A small shower of sawdust and the clanging of the chain and lock accompanied its liberation.

The two men froze at the sound, hoping the undertakers sleeping upstairs wouldn't wake. After several minutes of hearing nothing but their own breathing, they relaxed. Opening the door, they headed down the shallow slope into the facility's small, cold cellar.

Like the storage room, this basement was cluttered. In fact, it seemed that supplies from above had migrated down into the cold for want of more room. More boxes crowded along one wall. In the corner were two fresh blocks of ice slowly sweating down into drip pans. That, added to the fact that the room's floor was a full six feet below ground, kept the air positively chilled. After all, this was where they kept the corpses.

There were two of them this night, both sitting in caskets and ready for burial the next day. The first, in a tiny white coffin, was a child. Seward, who'd arrived from London the previous day, had overheard talk of a village girl dead from fever and this was evidently that child. "Rest in peace," he whispered, and turned to the other casket.

This one was full sized, of black-painted oak with brass fittings. Seward himself had helped the deceased's brother Harold choose it. The man inside was Seward's brother-in-law, John Claremont. Three nights previous, Seward and Blake (along with Seward's poor widowed sister, Joanna) had witnessed the man's murder. Now, they were here to guarantee its permanence.

"Are you certain this is necessary, Colonel?" Seward had served in the 12th Hussars under Lord Blake's command and had never lost the habit of referring to him by rank.

"No." Blake signaled for Seward to help him raise the lid of the coffin. "There's very little of which I am certain in these affairs, Seward, but I for one am not ready to take any risks."

"But—"

"Come, boy!" Blake's shout reverberated in the small, cold chamber and brought both men up short. He continued in a harsh whisper. "I've seen my wife fallen to these creatures and perhaps my daughter too. I won't have other innocents damned because I failed to act. Will you?"

That was the question, wasn't it? Just how far would Seward go to protect those he cared for? Or even to succeed in his own ambitions? He'd faced the horrors of the battlefield in Egypt and the Sudan and they had changed him, made him harder. Since his return to England the previous winter, every day had brought another dark truth for him to deal with, another challenge to overcome. His sister's life was destroyed. His lover's soul was in jeopardy. The unthinkable was now not only thinkable, but doable. He lifted the casket's lid.

John Claremont was dressed in the black wool suit Seward and his sister had picked out the day before. His flesh was puffy and wan, covered in a layer of undertaker's makeup. He looked neither rested nor peaceful. He simply looked dead. "What now?"

"Open his jacket, vest and shirt," Blake said. "So we can see his chest." While Seward did so, Lord Blake opened the small tool bag and began fishing around for items.

"Alright," Seward said. His brother-in-law's chest was pale and terrible. A large angry wound, sewn shut with black catgut, showed where the killing blow had emerged. John Claremont had been stabbed in the back, the tip of the long thin blade emerging between two ribs. The wound on his back was surely more dreadful.

"First, the talismans." As Blake fished various items out of the tool bag, Seward wondered just what strange doors had opened in the colonel's mind since tragedy had visited his family. This was the same man, after all, who had railed against superstitions of all sorts for as long as Seward had known him. The lieutenant marveled as he quickly cut the threads keeping Claremont's lips sealed, and drew out the man's tongue. Onto it he placed a dry circle of unleavened bread—a communion wafer. Seward didn't want to know just where he had got that item. Then, onto Claremont's eyes, Lord Blake placed two large copper pennies. Finally, he pried open the man's hand and slipped in a copy of the *Book of Common Prayer*.

"The fifty-first psalm," Blake said, holding up a page obviously taken from that same book. "We will use it to cover the damage of the next stage."

Seward didn't speak as Blake bent over to retrieve other items from the tool bag.

"This," Blake said, "requires a stronger hand than mine." With that he handed a large mallet and a sharpened wooden stake to Seward.

"Good Lord..."

"It is necessary, Seward. It wasn't so long ago those damned souls who killed themselves had this done to their bodies by law. And were buried at a crossroads. That was for the same purpose as ours: so they would stay in their graves."

"Claremont didn't kill himself," Seward said, but he knew the argument was futile. The murderer had been a cursed man, able to heal grievous wounds and endowed with terrible strength, and as far as they could tell, the servant of an even more terrible beast. If there was a chance that John Claremont could be caught in the damned state of undeath, they had to act.

Seward placed to the stake over the man's heart, just adjacent to the place where the knife-blade had protruded, and readied the mallet. While Blake read from the psalm, he drew back.

"Make me a clean heart, O God: and renew a right spirit within me," Blake read. "Cast me not away from thy presence: and take not thy holy Spirit from me."

Seward brought the mallet down once, twice, and three times more.

***

John Claremont's body found its final rest in a small country graveyard in the farmlands just east of Coggeshall. The funeral and interment were dour, simple

THE MADNESS OF PRIESTS

affairs. It was the second week of August but just a touch of the coming autumn decided to visit the skies for the occasion, in the form of banks of gray clouds that dropped a cold mist on the ceremony. The vicar spoke the required words to lead the mourning, and his appreciations of John, a local man who had made good in London and brought respectability to his family, were honest, if rather unmoving. The clergyman made little mention of the circumstances of Mr. Claremont's death, saying only that he had been taken before his time.

In fact, Father Bethel knew very little about how John Claremont had died. All he had been told was that the man was murdered by an intruder in his own home, a fine house in Chelsea. The vicar assumed that it had been a case of burglary, an attempt to steal the receipts of Mr. Claremont's latest business dealing, or to take what plate, jewels and other valuables might be in the house. At the request of Lord Blake, the casket remained closed during the service. Blake had been, it seemed, a friend of the now-widowed Mrs. Claremont during her childhood, when she had lived in Egypt, and he was now present to lend his support to her. He'd communicated to Father Bethel that poor Mrs. Claremont's condition was so fragile that viewing her husband's body was a medical risk. The priest was not wholly comfortable with this limitation on the proprieties of mourning, but Lord Blake was a respected man of station and a veteran of colonial campaigns, so he deferred to him.

The attendance that unseasonably cold afternoon was not numerous. Mrs. Joanna Claremont, the widow, was there in full mourning attire, of course, but she was visibly overwrought. She leaned on her brother, Lt. Malcolm Seward, who stood out in the dashing blue uniform of the Royal Horse Guards, the regiment entrusted with guarding Buckingham Palace. He wore a black armband as a sign of mourning. The other prestigious guest was the aforementioned Lord Blake. Nearby was Dr. Harold Claremont, elder brother of the deceased. He had not been overfond of Lord Blake's request for a closed casket either, but he too had deferred to the viscount's superior station.

Beyond that, all the attendees were women. Mrs. Enid Claremont, the deceased's mother, had been widowed twelve years previously and now laid her youngest son to rest. By her side were her two daughters, Mrs. Margaret Cunningham (whose husband Terrence was first mate on a merchant marine vessel currently sailing the Sea of Japan) and the unmarried Elizabeth Claremont. The latter had charge of Millicent, John and Joanna's infant daughter. Finally, Mrs. Sarah Claremont, wife of Dr. Claremont, stood with her husband. With the exception of Lt. Seward, all wore black from head to toe, many resorting to wool cloaks to stave off the rain and wind.

"Forasmuch as it hath pleased Almighty God of His great mercy," Father Bethel said, not needing to consult his prayer book, "to take unto Himself the soul of our dear brother here departed, we therefore commit his body to the ground."

The men helped lower the closed casket into the hole the gravediggers had prepared, and Joanna Claremont's sobs began to mount in volume. Without her brother to lean on, she swayed.

"Earth to earth, ashes to ashes, dust to dust." As was his practice at such moments, Bethel looked at the small gaggle of mourners before completing the prayer for the dead, hoping to bring a sense of reassurance with his words. "In sure and certain hope of the resurrection to eternal life."

Lt. Seward and Lord Blake exchanged a cold look, and Father Bethel could not shake the intuition that to them, the concept of eternal life had lost its comforting air.

Dr. Gerald Watson Scott opened his asylum near Highgate after returning from India in 1879. He had practiced medicine in Delhi and Bombay during his "colonial adventure," as his sister Elizabeth insisted on calling his attempt to find fortune in the East. That attempt had lasted almost ten years, during which time he had faced hardship after hardship. Despite all the pretense of recreating the gentility of English country life in the tropics, and the fact that in India servants were even more plentiful (and even more invisible) than in the mother country, there simply was less distance in the colonies between the salons of well-heeled Englishmen and the savagery of the natural world. Dr. Scott had once flirted with the Romantic attraction to the natural, with the longing for the purity of experience unfiltered by society or industry. India had cured him of all that. This was a place in which the hinterland crawled right up and into the city; in which a country trip involved tigers and cobras.

As a medical man, Dr. Scott saw firsthand the ravages of tropical life. The diseases that laughed at his science, the infections and ailments that seemed to conspire against his every effort. Colonies of lepers, outbreaks of influenza and malaria, and a heat that addled the brain and rotted the flesh—it was enough to drive a man to madness. And drive him to that it had, during the hellish monsoon season of 1875. There, when the rains were beating down on Bombay with relentless glee day after day and week after week, when the line between air and water seemed as blurry as that between sleep and wakefulness, he'd felt something in his mind give way.

The years of struggle to maintain the decorum expected of a medical man finally ended and a profound sense of release overcame him. The dreary, dank reality of his clinic gave way to the fantastic truth of a world without logic or certainty. He imagined that opium smokers used the poppy to enter this plane, this ecstatic mindscape in which the peeling plaster of a ceiling became a roadmap to the hidden lands, and the screams of a man whose gangrenous foot was being amputated merged with the bars of a divine symphony.

The madness lasted until the rains ended and probably cost the lives of three patients. For when the sole doctor in a private clinic goes mad, who is to tell? How could the Hindu carpenter, sent by his Welsh master to the medicine-*wallah* because of a rusted nail that had embedded itself in his foot, know that Dr. Scott would understand that the man's heart was poisoning his soul and should be removed? Or the gouty baronet know his nightly medicines would involve strychnine in doses made to slay one of the pachyderms so prevalent in this mad land? Or the half-breed child of an unusually decent cavalryman know that his fever would be diagnosed as the result of the traumas of a too-bright world, and cured by the simple method of blinding with a poker?

When the dementia lifted with the first rays of pure sunlight, tinted an almost-green by the humidity still redolent in the air, Dr. Scott realized with full and frank honesty just what he had done. The gaping maw of his madness opened up again at that point, and he teetered on its edge. He refused to fall in, however, and instead decided that he must turn to the ailments of the mind. For if India had done this to him, then it must have done it to others. The next year he opened a small, discreet asylum dedicated to such victims.

The rains returned, of course, and with them Dr. Scott's demons. But this time he had the devils of others' minds to contend with and he found that the work was enough to keep his world in focus through the diluvian

THE MADNESS OF PRIESTS

months. He made plans, however, to return to England and take his work with him. The Duke of Avon's cousin had benefited from Scott's ministrations and so His Grace had seen fit to sponsor the establishment of an asylum in Highgate, with the understanding that patients of high birth required more discreet care than they could receive in Bedlam and other such institutions. Dr. Scott had thus spent the last nine years providing just that sort of care, gaining friends in Whitehall, at Buckingham Palace, and in many of the finest homes on Park Lane. He still refused, however, to go outside in the rain and spent most of London's wet winters and springs holed up in his office with the shades drawn. There was no need to mention that to Lord Blake or Lt. Seward, however, who had come to visit him this August afternoon .

"Her case is not so unusual, milord." Scott glanced at his notes before continuing. "Mrs. Claremont has suffered a very serious shock, after all."

"My sister," Malcolm Seward interrupted, "saw her husband murdered before her very eyes, doctor."

"Yes, quite." Scott closed his leather-bound folder, masking the sheaf of hand-written notations within, and turned his attention on Seward. "All I wish to establish in your minds, Lieutenant,"—he glanced toward Lord Blake—"milord, is that the feminine constitution is susceptible to damage under such conditions. Especially when a woman sees her husband, the man who takes over the place of strong male from her father, slain in such a gruesome manner, it is natural for her to retreat from a reality suddenly become too harsh."

"She must remember, doctor." Lord Blake spoke like a man accustomed to command. His gray hair was cut short and his mustache finely waxed. Despite being in eveningwear, he seemed like a man ready for war.

"I understand your concern for Mrs. Claremont, milord—"

Blake stood and approached Dr. Scott, who sat behind a large desk he'd had shipped back from India. The details of his preliminary evaluation of Mrs. Claremont were in the closed leather folder on the large mahogany surface.

"This goes beyond Mrs. Claremont, Doctor." Blake's voice was cold and hard. "The man who murdered her husband was no random ruffian."

"The details of her case are of course vital…"

Blake waved him to silence. "My own daughter has disappeared, doctor. She is at risk and I must find her. Joanna Claremont knows where she his and whom she is with, but she refuses to speak. All she does is sob!"

"I will of course do my best, milord, but her alienation is extreme. As I said, having seen her husband killed and now buried has reduced her to an infantile state. This is a woman we are speaking of and being closer, from a mental perspective, to infants than we, they are more likely to retreat. We must coax her out of her crib if we are to get the answers you seek, milord."

"Action, not words, Dr. Scott. Joanna Claremont knows something of the whereabouts of my daughter Regina and I will know what, retreat from reality or no."

Dr. Scott felt the tiny muscles around his left eye spasm once, twice. Men of station came here hat-in-hand for the most part, desperate for anyone who could make the taint of madness disappear from their family tree— or at the very least hide it away behind closed doors and absolute discretion. The doctor was not used to such demands. "Treatment takes time, milord. I must beg your patience."

"I cannot afford to be patient, doctor." Blake turned on his heels and stormed out of the office.

Seward approached Scott and spoke quietly. "Take care of Joanna, doctor, please." Then he too left.

***

The ride back to Monroe House, Lord Blake's London residence on Arlington Street, took a good hour. The streets seemed especially crowded and with the parliamentary and social season ending for another year, there was the added bustle of last-minute activity before the peerage made its yearly emigration to the country for hunting and sport. Blake would not be making the journey to his County Durham estate this year.

The two men didn't speak until they had arrived back at the house proper and had the butler lock the door behind them. "I don't trust that witch doctor, Seward."

"He seems earnest enough, Colonel, but if you think there is a better place for Joanna, then—"

"No, no." He waved off Seward's suggestion. "He'll take good care of your sister, but I don't think he understands the importance of her recalling the details of her discussions with my daughter. He is too focused on his own methods of care."

"Begging your pardon, Colonel, but who could rightly understand any of this without having experienced some of it?" Seward followed Blake through to the back of the house. "I don't think I understand it myself."

Neither man spoke for a while after that. They made their way through the kitchen, usually terra incognita for anyone but the servants in such a house. The kitchen maid and cook looked askance at them, but not overly so. Lord Blake had appropriated the cellar for some private matter and the stairs down to it were through the kitchen. Mrs. Miller, the cook, knew not to ask questions of her betters.

Seward, less accustomed to the realities of a grand house with its servants, caught the eyes of the maid Isabel and wondered if she knew anything of the mad world he had entered. Did she suspect that her mistress Lady

Regina, daughter of Lord Blake and his own betrothed, was missing and in the clutches of a creature neither living nor dead? Could she understand that devils in human masquerade had visited this family?

"We are dealing with the undead, Lieutenant." Lord Blake spoke once they were below ground and the door at the top of the kitchen stairs was well closed. He held a hooded lantern in one hand, but didn't look at his young companion despite the light. His voice had little of its usual strength. "Damned things come from the East, who breathe not, who exist outside Almighty God's divine order."

"I'll admit to having seen some strange things since Christmastide last, Colonel, but—"

"Believe what you may, but you saw how that devilish harlot recoiled from fire and daylight." Indeed, they had last seen Regina several days ago in Dover, in the company of a woman of unparalleled beauty whom they knew as Miss Victoria Ash. Faced with fire, she had bared animalistic fangs. Faced with the rising sun, she had fled to the safety of her carriage, taking Regina with her.

"And," Blake continued, laying his hand on the iron knob of a small wooden door at the bottom of the stairs, "you saw what has become of my Emma." Worse still than facing Victoria, they had seen Lady Emma Blake board a ferry for Calais with a small party that included some of the same Slavic relatives who had buried her in County Durham the previous winter.

"I admit that I have little explanation—"

"I was young and foolish once too," Blake interrupted. "I refused to believe in the scope of the evil we face, but do not trick yourself into denying the awful truth, Lieutenant. We both saw Emma lying dead last winter. We saw her cold, still form."

"Yes…"

"Her body has risen from the grave, Lieutenant. The woman whom I married, the woman whom I *loved*, has been damned to Hell by the perversity of her witch-born kin."

The calm soldierly tone Blake had been known for in the regiment was gone now, replaced by a desperate energy more suited to a puritan or a demagogue. Seward felt his confidence failing. "But surely a death can be faked," he said.

"Do you think I would not know of my own wife's death, Lieutenant?" Blake's blood rose, turning his face an angry shade of red. "Do you think me a blind fool?"

"No, of course not, Colonel."

"Then you must face the horrid reality that confronts us." And with that he opened the door into the cellar. There was a man hanging there by a large metal hook through his shoulder. He was laughing.

Chapter Two

Gareth Ducheski did not mind the hook any more. It was a nasty iron thing, and he guessed it had once been used to suspend a huge chandelier. Or perhaps it had hung in the coach house and been used to keep the harness up off the stinking hay and dung-like mud. Now, one end hooked into the wooden rafter of the cellar and the other pierced his back just under the right shoulder blade. Its tip emerged under his clavicle.

He had hung there for seven days and nights now, ever since the damnable Blake and sniveling Seward had managed to overpower him. That, now that still bothered him. How could he, a scion of a family that had served the masters for generations, one of the lucky ones who had drunk the dark blood and been made strong by it— how could he be overwhelmed by such as they? It had been the woman, Joanna Claremont, who had surprised him by recovering from the murder of her husband to hit him over the head with something. That wound alone would not have done him in, but then Blake and Seward were on him and even the black blood in his veins hadn't been enough to hold back unconsciousness. Then they had used fire on him and—to his shame—he had spoken.

There were concessions, of course. From the repeated arguments Blake and Seward had every time they came down to this cellar where they had placed him, Gareth had gathered that not all was well for his captors. Joanna Claremont was locked in an asylum, it seemed. What's more, the master had escaped to the continent with darling Cousin Emma. And little Cousin Regina was missing as well. Gareth had taken to laughing whenever the two men entered the cellar in the hopes of interrogating him. He had precious little to tell them anyway, but it was pleasing to make them ill at ease.

THE MADNESS OF PRIESTS

Laughter came easily, because unlike them, he understood that his condition was improving. As a proper child of the Ducheski line, his blood was laced with the unholy vitae of the masters and that black ichor was growing within him. Already it had strengthened the muscle and tissue around the offending hook, so that the pain he felt there was little more than a mild stinging. The smells were also returning at long last. His nose had been scorched along with much of the rest of his flesh last winter, and he'd existed since then in a damnable state in which the world was a dull and bland place. But now, at long last, he could smell again—the rotting wood of the door, the rat-dung in the muddy floor three inches from his dangling toes, the fear in the house above his head.

Every hour spent here, he knew, brought him closer to freedom and vengeance. Laughing came naturally.

***

It was not altogether unusual for the blood to fail to coagulate, but still it worried Dr. Bainbridge. Although a seasoned thaumaturge—or "blood sorcerer" to use the sensationalistic phrase of some of the more squeamish kindred—his arts did not lend themselves to prophecy and scrying. His attempt to read the fates through the medium of drops of his own blood scattered on a broad copper plate was imprecise at best.

"Well?" The voice was cold and hard, devoid of most of the musical quality it had once enjoyed. This was not a man speaking, but a thing. This was Lord Valerius, once prince-regent of London, who had last drawn breath in the same year William the Conqueror arrived from Normandy. "What does it say?"

"Nothing good, I'm afraid." The droplets continued to flow long after they should have dried, or gravity should have brought them to rest. Instead of pooling, they danced a chaotic dance. "Mr. Wellig's scheme seems to have gone astray."

Valerius closed his eyes and slowly shook his head, as if suddenly feeling the weight of the centuries on his slight shoulders. Neither of the men fit any of the stereotypes of undeath. Going beyond the fact that neither man was especially pale or possessed of semi-decomposed flesh—that was the purview of only the most wretched of their kindred—they still seemed unlikely candidates for undying creatures of the night. Lord Valerius was a handsome man, no doubt, but he dressed in simple eveningwear and his hair was cut short as was proper. Only his economy of movement hinted at the fact that he was more than one of the many gentlemen who made London their home. He could also call upon eldritch powers to overwhelm the mind and the soul, but none of those seemed evident. Bainbridge was an even less likely candidate for the specter of damnation. Positively portly, he had the look of a friendly country gentleman come to town, a man who had discovered a mistress in science and industry, perhaps, but still a jovial and harmless fellow. Certainly not a creature who fed on the blood of the living, much less one who drained that same substance from ritually prepared babes for use in dark incantations like the one he'd undertaken this night.

This, of course, was the whole point of the great masquerade these creatures and their kindred practiced. Who in their right mind would suspect the terrible truth when the comfortable falsehood was so evident?

"You understate, Bainbridge. If your colleague's attempt to poison our honored prince failed, there is considerable trouble on the horizon. All those who might be accused of being complicit in his scheme face very harsh retribution indeed." The former prince-regent did not have to point out that the two of them, one Anton

42   THE MADNESS OF PRIESTS

Wellig's associate in House Tremere, the other the fallen seneschal of that self-same Prince Mithras, would be at the head of that list.

"Perhaps all is not lost, milord." Bainbridge wiped the copper plate clean with a white kerchief. It sopped up the blood and left the copper with a shine. "The augury is hardly precise and I have heard no news of Prince Mithras since the ball at Sydenham. Perhaps the poisoning is in progress."

"I think it behooves us to find out."

***

In Seward's dream, the Essex mortuary where he drove a wooden spike into the heart of his own kinsman merges with the refurbished operating theater he knows exists below the Taurus Club for Gentlemen on Pall Mall. The theater is dressed as a ritual chamber, as it was upon his initiation last month into the Taurine Brotherhood, the secret fraternity of soldiers that is the true heart of the club.

John Claremont's body, that stake already driven through its chest, lies on the ground along with several others. In the dream, Seward walks among them but his point of view often shifts to somewhere above so that he sees the corpses forming a rough star-shape on the ground. On the central altar is the only female, a mythological harlot with the head of a bull but the body of a woman, complete with pert, perfect breasts and an engorged, open sex.

Seward becomes aware, in the way so common in dreams, that he is nude and that his own sex is swollen and aching with desire. A warm, sticky substance covers him— the blood of some unknown creature. Advancing toward the bull-woman, he watches her writhe with both fear and desire, and he feels the eyes of others upon him.

The actual sex act is largely absent from the dream.

One moment he is approaching the bull-woman and the next he is within her, feeling her legs clamped about him. A sudden fear that she will somehow swallow him whole grips him. She can be his conquest but also his conqueror, he realizes. Feeling his own essence surging from his loins to feed her hungry need, weakening him as a leech does a tiger, he reaches desperately for any way to defend himself from the beast-whore. His hand settles on the stake embedded in John Claremont's dead heart, somehow now at hand. He yanks it free and it becomes a knife, sharp and deadly, the weapon of soldiers from the time of Noah and Abraham. He plunges it into the bull-woman's flesh.

A torrent of blood wells from the gash across the woman's neck and the bull-head, now and suddenly always a mask, slips off her head to reveal a face. That of Regina, his fiancée.

Seward woke with a start, his body beaded with sweat under the linen covers that his own thrashing had wound around him. He'd had the dream, in one way or another ever since they had buried John Claremont, but tonight it was stronger.

The glow of the gas lamps along Pall Mall painted the ceiling of his small apartment a dull yellow. These quarters, adjacent to the Taurus Club and reserved for members without their own homes in the city, were a blessing, but he did not sleep well here. The echoes of Regina's murdered face still in his mind, he tried to shake the horror from himself. His breathing returned to normal and use of the chamber pot and wash basin made him feel more like his own self. Dreams, he told himself, were nothing to be worried about.

With wakefulness, however, came the awareness of which memories were true. John Claremont's fate was one such truth, but more horrible still was the ceremony that had indeed initiated him into the Taurine Brotherhood. The silver bull-head pendant hanging from his neck marked that membership. He remembered the bull-woman now, a masked prostitute his brothers had offered him as a "soldier's right." He remembered taking her on that altar. He remembered raising the sword—never a stake in reality, just a ceremonial blade. And he remembered slicing her throat to complete the ceremony.

Nightmare had become reality. He was a murderer.

***

Joanna Claremont hadn't spoken a single word since her initial outburst upon her admission to the Highgate Asylum. That night, when Lord Blake and Mrs. Claremont's bother Malcolm Seward had brought her in, she'd been in hysterics, sobbing about the murder of her husband John. As Dr. Scott understood it, that ghastly crime had occurred right before Mrs. Claremont's eyes and she had been inconsolable and largely incomprehensible ever since.

The asylum—which, after all, was intended as a shelter from the world at large—had apparently done its primary task and calmed her addled mind. Indeed, hysteria had been replaced by silence, stoic and total. Mrs. Claremont responded to stimuli, be it food spooned into her mouth or her clothes lifted over her head by the nurse, but she would not speak and her eyes had no focus in them. Dr. Scott had seen silence as a step in the right direction at first, but with his patient's muteness now approaching a week in duration, he wondered if it might not be a permanent condition.

In an effort to better understand this walking catatonia, Dr. Scott undertook a second thorough examination of Mrs. Claremont. He made it a practice to put newly admitted patients through a complete medical inspection, searching for signs of any physical ailment that might contribute to their madness. He could hardly count the number of deranged noblemen he'd examined only to find swelling on the head, indicating a powerful blow, or signs of an infection of the blood. There was much work to be done, Dr. Scott felt, in the field of physiological causes of dementia and other mental disorders. His first examination of Mrs. Claremont, however, had occurred during her manic phase, and had required her to be strapped to an operating table. Even a generous observer would have called Scott's exam that night hurried.

On this night, things were much easier. The nurse, an Irish girl named Allie, disrobed Joanna Claremont with only mild difficulty and led her to the examining table. There, the madwoman responded to the nurse's slight touch and lay down.

"Thank you, nurse. Please stand aside, but be ready in case the patient relapses into mania." Dr. Scott approached and before doing anything, observed. His conclusion that Joanna Claremont was in retreat from the harshness of reality, fully alienated as it were, seemed confirmed by her even breathing. Utterly nude, her chest rose in the quiet rhythm of breath, and her legs were just slightly parted in a comfortable pose with concern for neither prudery nor wantonness. The reality of medical practice was that doctors had to put aside some of the moral standards of the quality in order to execute their duties. One learned to look at naked female flesh as a thing disconnected from the woman one was examining. Patients, however, rarely achieved such detachment— the shame of exposing their most intimate organs to a man not their husband was too real to be forgotten. For Joanna Claremont to lie before him without any of that shame, then, meant she was either unaware of what was going on or that her madness had remade her into an

Eve before the apple, unaware of shame itself.

Scott proceeded to a careful, methodical examination. He listened to her calm breathing and healthy heart. He drew blood and examined the often-telltale tissues of the gums, palms and labia. He tested reflexes with a small mallet and a needle. She responded automatically to stimuli—withdrawing from pinpricks, for example—but without the conviction of either man or beast. The simplest constriction with an easy hand kept her from withdrawing from a syringe and the characteristic muscular contractions of pain faded quickly. It was, Dr. Scott decided, as if Joanna Claremont had been shut off like some industrial machine.

He only found the scars by chance. He decided to draw more blood and bound her left arm to allow the veins to swell for easy extraction. As the flesh grew slightly flush from the swollen capillaries, he noted a fine pale line in the webbing of flesh between her index and middle finger. Releasing the tourniquet, he watched the scar fade almost completely from view as her natural pallor returned. Using a magnifying glass to painstakingly reexamine her body inch by inch, he found more of the tiny scars. They were all in sensitive, hidden areas of her flesh—behind both knees, in back of her right ear, under her right breast, between all her fingers, and the toes of the left foot. The thinness and precision of the incision indicated the use of a scalpel or a razor in especially deft hands.

Dr. Scott was certain the cuts had caused a great deal of pain. He also knew he had seen such work before.

***

Returning to London was not what Beckett would call sound strategy. A mere six months ago, he had been in Queen Victoria's capital in an attempt to procure a rare document and things had gotten somewhat out of hand. One of the other bidders in the little auction held in a warehouse on the Isle of Dogs had ended up truly and fully dead with his blood quite literally on Beckett's hands. A scholar and a vampire both, Beckett's research into the origins of vampirism often took him into dangerous situations, but that did not make him foolhardy. Or at least not as foolhardy as some made him out to be. Seeing as he had entered London without proper deference to the resident vampiric authorities, he doubted destroying one of the city's respectable monsters would win him any friends. Despite their pretense of familial bonds—the vampires of this city and many others referred to one another as "kindred"—the laws of the undead were suitably draconian. Unwarranted destruction, most especially by an uninvited interloper, invariably resulted in a sentence of final death. Beckett had, wisely he thought, sought immediate passage out of London, intending not to return for a healthy interval. Among creatures who could very well live to see the next millennium, six months was not a healthy interval.

Yet, here he was, sailing across the Mediterranean in a cargo ship headed for Marseilles. From there, they would transfer to a train, cut across France, and then complete their journey in yet another ship. Soon enough, he would be back in London, and in company that would do nothing to repair his reputation in the city. *Ah well*, he thought, *danger is what keeps the blood moving*.

"Is the city as marvelous as they say, *effendi?*" cried one of Beckett's two companions, from his place at the sole porthole in the small cabin they all shared. An Arab named Fahd, he'd never been outside of his native Cairo, and marveled at the prospect of a trip as far away as famed London. "Will we see the Britisher queen?"

"No, Fahd," answered Hesha Ruhadze, "I very much doubt it." Ruhadze was a vampire, although one hailing from Nubian roots. Those of his line, known properly as Followers of Set (and derisively as serpents), were considered a disreputable lot among the vampires of London. Firmly pagan in their beliefs, they claimed to be descended from the ancient Egyptian deity Set, and were said to still worship that storm god. Beckett, who had seen a great deal in his one hundred and fifty years of undeath, could neither entirely confirm nor deny the stories other vampires told about the Setites. He had found, however, that Ruhadze at least knew a great deal about the ancient past and was very skilled at avoiding entanglements with authorities. That made him a good vampire to know.

"Tell me again about this Kemintiri," Beckett said.

Fahd jumped from his post at the porthole and debased himself before Ruhadze. "Allow me, great one!" The man, already a toad-like creature with an arm rendered useless by grievous injury, had become a true sycophant of Hesha's during the time at sea. The Setite nodded and Fahd launched into his description.

"In the nights before night, Great Set stood against his brother Osiris the Tyrant. The Tyrant, conspiring with their father Ra and their sister Isis, sought to enslave the world. Great Set, however, knew that freedom was the destiny of man and sought to overthrow those who would put us all in chains.

"In order to stand against the Tyrant," Fahd continued, relishing the tale, "Great Set crossed the desert to the shores of the river between life and death. There, he drank deeply of those waters and freed himself. The waters became his very blood and he stood free from the lash of the sun, held by his senile father, and the shackles of death, held by his mad brother."

Beckett raised an eyebrow in Hesha's direction. This part of the story was in fact the most interesting to him as it spoke of the origins of vampirism in uniquely

Egyptian terms. In Europe, the most widely held belief was that kindred were descended from Caine, the biblical first murderer, who somehow found he could pass on his accursed state. The story of Set and Osiris bore more than a passing resemblance to that of Caine and Abel—rivalry between brothers, the progenitor as outcast—but it also had some key differences. Most importantly, vampirism here was no curse, but a liberation.

Beckett had reason to doubt some of the details, however. For one thing, as far as he knew, Followers of Set were no more free of the "lash of the sun" than any other vampire. If anything, they were more vulnerable to its effects, and many of them (Hesha Ruhadze included) affected tinted glasses to shield themselves from even the wan light of torches and gas lamps. He'd had no opportunity to see a Setite exposed to actual sunlight, of course, but he guessed their flesh would burn as readily as his. If Ruhadze had lied about this to Fahd, how much of the rest was true?

"The Great One was not satisfied, however," Fahd continued after a sufficiently dramatic pause, "for the world was still in chains. Thus he sought out those able to stand against the Tyrant and gifted them with water from his veins. They became his followers, blessed be their names.

"Among them were the Maiden of Plagues, who brought ruin to the slave-camps and barracks of the enemy; the Dark Serpent, who moved through the night and struck at the enemy's heels; the Mother of Priests, who birthed the thirteen hierophants and founded the path of serpents; Seterpenre the Sorcerer, who built the city of Tinnis as a snare for the weak; and last was the Many-Faced Goddess, Kemintiri."

Fahd looked at his master, seeking further permission to continue the tale. Beckett had the impression that the man was about to reveal a deep secret of the Setite sect, already known for keeping its truths hidden. Of course, in all likelihood, that impression was intentional, the result of this dramatic recitation arranged for his benefit. Ruhadze nodded assent.

"The goddess was a proud woman. Born into the slavery of Osiris, she became a high priestess among his people, an overseer in the slave-camp. But the more men she ruled, the more clearly she understood her own bondage. One night, when Osiris was sleeping, she traveled into the desert and sought out the Great One. She had expected a great battle or a trial of sorts—after all, she was the high priestess of Great Set's enemy. Instead, he simply appeared and ordered her to kneel before him.

"'No,' she said, 'I will respect you as the first of the free, but I am no slave of man or god.' The Great One smiled his fanged smile and gave her the gift of his veins. For a time, the goddess stayed with Set as his consort, lying with him and sharing great plans. Great Set's destiny was a lonely one, and he welcomed her touch and marveled at her skills. Like a snake shedding its skin, she could become those he desired most. She became Kemintiri, She of the Thousand Faces.

"'You must return to my brother's lands,' Set said one night and found that his lover had already prepared herself for the journey. 'Yes,' she said, 'I will live in his camp and undo his works from within.' And so she did, taking on a new countenance and quickly finding her way into Osiris's bed. There she was the perfect spy for our cause and she worked to enslave the slave-master.

"But as ever, danger lurked among the enemy. Isis the Witch, lover to both her brother Osiris and to their son Horus, grew jealous of this former priestess who had become her rival. She too knew the ways of illusion and dressed herself in the raiment of her second brother Set and slipped into Osiris's bedchamber when the Tyrant was away. Kemintiri, thinking the Great One had arrived to complete the overthrow of his siblings, threw herself into his arms and showered him with adoration. Isis, pleased to uncover her rival's secret and aroused by this secret encounter, allowed Kemintiri to please her. Then, she spoke in the Great One's thunderous voice:

"'I reject you as a temple harlot,' the false Set said. 'You have betrayed me for my brother's seed and I condemn you.'

"'But my lord,' Kemintiri pleaded for she loved the Great One who had freed her, 'I have done only what you asked.'

"'You are unworthy of my gifts and I curse you!' the false Set thundered.

"'Then,' said Kemintiri, rising defiantly in her nakedness, 'you are no god but a seedless fool!' The Thousand-Faced One was proud after all, and thinking herself cast out, she spat vitriol at the one who'd loved and forsaken her. She turned and left.

"Isis smiled at this and took on her own shape again. Then she found her brother Osiris and revealed Kemintiri's love for Set to him. Osiris raged, and called into the heavens: 'I reject and condemn you, Thousand-Faced Harlot! Begone from my sight!'

"And in the desert, Kemintiri heard him and went mad. Rejected, or so she thought, by both Set and Osiris, she determined to love no god but herself. With her gift of a thousand faces, she would walk the world, seducing and destroying those who had seduced and destroyed her.

"This is the story of Kemintiri, the Thousand-Faced Daughter of Set." Fahd had a faraway look in his eyes, as if simply recounting the story had transported him into an ecstatic state. It probably had, Beckett realized.

"Very good, Fahd," Hesha Ruhadze said and extended his left hand. There was a black bead of blood in the palm, welling from a small puncture wound in the fleshy pad below the thumb. "Well told."

The man leaped to his master's hand and cupped

his lips around the dark vitae. Although Beckett had abandoned the practice some time ago, many vampires enslaved mortals by feeding them quantities of their unholy blood. This had several effects on the drinker, or ghoul: It formed a bond of unnatural love or even worship for the vampire in the mortal's heart; it granted him a portion of the vampire's preternatural strength; and it even extended his life. Vampires used ghouls as retainers and assistants, for they could guard the undead during the day and help them deal with the daylit world. That the process damned the mortal's soul seemed a small price to pay for most.

Beckett returned to the matters at hand. "What do you hope from this journey then, Ruhadze? To destroy an enemy?"

The Setite smiled. "Nothing so simple, Mr. Beckett. The progenitor of my line never rejected his daughter, at least not in any way as drastic as she seems to believe. Were she to understand that… Well, that would be a great service to us."

"I suppose it would." Beckett found it interesting that Hesha never talked in the religious terms he encouraged in his ghoul. Did that reflect a lack of faith or hide a depth of it?

"Indeed. Kemintiri is said to have been the most widely traveled of Set's children. She has been a thousand people in a thousand lands, according to the poets. She could mean the recovery of a wealth of lost lore for us."

And there it was. Like a master angler, Ruhadze was showing him the hook, confident he would bite anyway. Beckett had traveled the four corners of the Earth trying to uncover the origin of vampirism—it was the one, all-consuming passion that kept him going night after night. He was certain the Setite was using him for some other end, but still, the chance to uncover an ancient like Kemintiri… He couldn't pass it up.

Two years ago, Beckett had broken up a ritual in Cairo, dispatching a Setite priest named Anwar al-Beshi in the process. Al-Beshi had been, he'd later discovered, a worshipper of Kemintiri. His destruction had left behind only his two ghouls as people who might know just how this had begun and what al-Beshi had planned. The first ghoul was Fahd, who knew precious little and was now "converted" to their cause. The second had been an Englishwoman named Emma Blake. And her trail led to London.

Chapter Three

There were to be no performances at the Royal Albert Hall this night. With the season now over and the nobility abandoning London in droves, the entertainments for the high-born were on a much reduced schedule. The comic operettas and other low-brow performances would be starting up soon for the joy of the middle classes, but that would be in other, less posh sections of London. The Albert was reserved for activities of an altogether higher caliber. All this made it an attractive meeting place for the undead court of London.

Five of them were gathered in the royal box, a huge space with a perfect view of the darkened stage. There were others in the hall, of course—lesser kindred, as well as ghouls and other thralls acting as guardians—but these few represented the crown of bones on the city itself. But that crown was missing its greatest and blackest jewel, the prince.

"His Royal Highness is in seclusion for the time being." The speaker was Lady Anne Bowesley, his seneschal. A beautiful creature with hair of the finest chestnut, she had the natural bearing of one born to rule. "He asks us all, however, to uncover the conspiracy that led to the debacle in Sydenham."

"Debacle" was a genuinely restrained way of putting it, the assembled worthies agreed. Lady Anne had organized a grand ball at the Crystal Palace in Sydenham, south of London. A great number of the city's undead, essentially all those who euphemistically referred to one another as their kindred, had come to mark the anniversary of His Royal Highness Prince Mithras's return from a century of travel abroad. It had seemed to be great success at first. The palace was decorated for the occasion and shone like a glass beacon in the night. Lady Anne and several of the more prominent guests had ensured that pliant mortals were also invited, fetching young things who would willingly give of their blood in private rooms curtained off from the main gathering halls. A few deaths could be expected, but those invited knew to restrain the hunger enough to sip lightly.

In the middle of receiving guests, however, the prince had suddenly left for one of these feeding areas. Mithras was a truly ancient creature and sometimes had less tolerance for the social niceties of modern life, so this was not entirely out of character, but he had been about to hear Captain Nathaniel Ellijay, one of his trusted aides, formally request the right to bring a protégé into undeath, and leaving at that point was a surprising snub. That soon faded from the assembled minds when the smell of burning fabric filled the space, with smoke and flames on its heels. The long silken drapes hiding the feeding areas burst into bright orange and green fire and chaos ensued.

Kindred do not age in any normal way and their unliving blood allows them to accomplish a great many eldritch feats, but their condition comes with a few glaring weaknesses. One is a distinct vulnerability to fire. Such open flames in a large group of undead thus created a panic of epic proportions. Indeed, the fear of fire is so overwhelming in most kindred that they become mad, slavering beasts stampeding to safety. A mortal fire brigade, readied ahead of time just in case, had brought the conflagration under control, but not before the assemblage had fled and a goodly number of the mortal feeding stock had died in the flames. Lady Anne's display of the prince's uncontested rule of London was ruined.

"I've had a devil of a time determining just where the fire started, Mary Anne." The speaker was General Sir Arthur Halesworth, a broad man in military uniform who was one of two vampires formally charged with maintaining order in the prince's name. A sheriff of the undead, as it were. His use of Lady Anne's Christian name was a testament to how close the two were, although it still raised eyebrows. "The fear it inspired has muddled memories and only led to baseless accusation after baseless accusation."

"That hardly inspires confidence, General." Lady Anne's tone was hard, and although few at this assembly had ever seen her lose her composure, the beastly nature that lurked in all kindred raged in her undead heart too. "I assume you have more to report."

"Yes, yes," he said, his anger significantly closer to the surface than his mistress's. "I have several reliable sources who saw Miss Victoria Ash enter the feeding rooms mere moments before the fire started."

"Miss Ash is under your protection, is she not?"

The seneschal's question targeted another woman in attendance. Blonde hair in ringlets framed an ashen white face drawn in thin, alluring lines. Her full bosom was raised and wrapped by a wasp-waisted corset that lived up to its name. Lady Ophelia Merritt's hips and torso seemed to be linked by an articulation no thicker than her swan-like neck. She flitted a fan of emerald green embroidered with black roses in a quick motion that seemed to dismiss the question, or rather its subject.

"She follows no counsel but her own, that one." Another flick. "But she is no insurgent. This attack smacks of the barbarian enemy, I would think."

"The Sabbat, you mean." General Halesworth had very little tolerance for couched language when it came to matters he considered his bailiwick. "We've kept those curs out of the city since the prince's return. It was the regent who let them run loose."

"That, my dear sheriff,"—flick—"sounds a great deal like motive for just such an attack."

"Perhaps, but jumping to conclusions isn't the way we do things, milady," put in Juliet Parr, the third woman in the assemblage. The contrast between Miss Parr and Lady Merritt could not have been greater. Where the grande dame of London's kindred scene wore fashions that spoke of legions of tailors and not a single concession to comfort over style, Miss Parr's attire was pragmatic and simple. Her gown was a simple country dress and coat, made of tweed in a pale brown that almost matched her hazel hair. She had the body of a slight girl but the bearing of a man who'd faced the charge of cavalry and lived to tell the tale. In fact, in less formal occasions, Miss Parr was often seen in distinctly masculine clothing, an eccentricity most tolerated because of her reputation. Like General Halesworth, Juliet Parr served as a sheriff for the undead of London, specifically responsible for the better-lived neighborhoods north of the Thames. Her specialty, however, was information—it was said there was nowhere in the City or West End where Juliet Parr did not have her ear. Among a hidden society of creatures feeding on the blood of an unknowing mortal mass, information translated very readily into power.

"My own investigations," she continued, "have revealed a few interesting facts. It seems that Miss Ash has already departed the capital in the company of her coachman and guardian Cedric and her protégée, Lady Regina."

"Lord Blake's daughter, yes. She was presented to me on the Embankment last month." Lady Anne was known for her peerless memory for the kindred of the huge city. It was an important asset as seneschal. "Her departure is not necessarily indicative, however. Many of our kindred have left for the country with their chosen prey."

"Indeed," Miss Parr continued, "but there are other elements that point at a connection. It seems that Lady

THE MADNESS OF PRIESTS

Regina's entry into our world was motivated by a desire to find her mother, the supposedly late Lady Blake."

Lady Anne cocked her head ever so slightly in question.

"I'm as yet unsure who claimed Lady Blake, or even if she has been Embraced or not. The Blake estate is in County Durham and my connections there are limited." Juliet ignored the reproachful fan-flick from Lady Merritt. "But it has come to my attention that Emma, Lady Blake was born one Emiliana Ducheski and was known to our night society."

Juliet had the satisfaction of seeing Lady Merritt's latest fan movement falter mid-flick. "Emma?"

"Yes, milady," Juliet answered. "I believe she was a protégée of yours for a few months in 1869."

"Might I suggest that you enquire more precisely as to Miss Ash's whereabouts, then?" Lady Anne's tone still had steel in it. "It would be most unfortunate if an oversight of yours drew further unwanted attention."

Lady Merritt left without another word, or another flick.

***

"Have you seen His Royal Highness since the fire, General?" Captain Nathaniel Ellijay, who'd been the silent fifth in the royal box, had left his position at Lady Anne's side as the evening wore on. The seneschal's business was never quite finished and with the shock of the events at the Crystal Palace still fresh, she would be receiving visitors until close to dawn. Ellijay, as was proper, had awaited her leave and then sought those who shared his love for her and for their prince. General Halesworth was at the head of that list. The two military men had retreated to one of the boxes stage left at Royal Albert Hall.

"Yes. The prince is not himself." Halesworth's hard features, barely hidden by his well-trimmed mustache and beard, were a study in restraint. There was boiling anger there, held carefully in check. "I like this not one bit, Ellijay."

The younger officer, both in appearance and years of unlife, leaned in a touch closer than was entirely proper. Albert Hall was sacrosanct, especially with the city's worthies assembled, but a ban on violence did not prevent eavesdropping. The ball at the Crystal Palace had also supposedly been safe. "He left me mid-sentence, General. Without a word. I've never seen him do such."

"Don't turn into a prattling child, Captain. Do you understand that the prince was here before Hadrian built his wall? Our entire existence is an eyeblink to him. Don't presume to understand his ways, much less express concern."

Ellijay took a step back as if slapped, the blood beginning to boil within him. His eyes—pale gray things placed just a touch too close together—locked onto the general's and he saw the beast there. A fine sheen of sweat, tinted pink with the blood that kept him from his grave, rose to the back of his neck and the line of his brow. The general seemed like the coil wound tight in a mantrap, and Ellijay felt he had just tripped the wire.

"No, of course not," he said, the urges to run and to strike first competing for his unbeating heart. Like a living man might turn to the Our Father, he spoke in the musical voice of prayer and reached for the silver bull-head medal pinned to his uniform. "Like our brothers in Persia and Rome, we bear arms for Mithras the Golden. We sacrifice to him and he brings us victory over death itself."

"Praise be," Halesworth answered in the same reverential tone, touching the gold bull-head on his own chest. "See that you don't forget that, Captain."

Malcolm Seward was not sure just what form the pursuit of so-called undead devils would take, but given his experiences in the last several months, he had not expected a nunnery. The roundabout path of the makeshift investigation that led them to the convent had started a few days previous, when Lord Blake had finally given up on interrogating the laughing degenerate in the basement of Monroe House. Without any firm lead as to where Regina might be—other than perhaps France, and from there who knew—and with Dr. Scott still reporting utter silence from Joanna, Seward had suggested that they gather their thoughts anew. He had always been fond of puzzles and deductions, and if Dr. Conan Doyle's *Study in Scarlet*, which he'd enjoyed earlier in the spring in the most recent *Beeton's Christmas Annual*, was to be believed, then criminal detection was just an especially complex puzzle.

"How did Miss Ash come to be at Bernan House for Lady Blake's funeral?" he'd asked. Indeed, Victoria Ash had appeared suddenly a few days—no, a few nights—after Emma Blake had breathed her last. Seward was not about to share that she had discovered him with Regina in a most scandalous position, but still her appearance was strange. "Had you seen her before that night?"

"No—" Colonel Blake had answered quickly as if by instinct, but then stopped to consider. "Although she did seem familiar to me, as if it were natural for her to be there."

"She was, that is, she had that effect on me as well, Colonel." In fact, she'd had quite a more arduous effect on Seward, but he kept that to himself as well. "It is perhaps one of her dark gifts?"

"So you accept her nature, then, Lieutenant?"

"For the time being. But that still leaves the question of how she knew. Did anyone ask her?"

"No. She said she knew my wife through a friend in London." There, Blake had paused. Both men were aware that the next step might depend on that name, but it seemed a struggle to resuscitate it from its grave in memory. After all, it had been months and...

"Oh, it was that insufferable woman, what was her name... Winthrope!" The colonel stood bolt upright, lifted by the light in his memory. "Baroness Winthrope!"

That had led to a search through various listings of the peerage as well as calls to friends of Lord Blake's. They'd quickly discovered that Baron Winthrope had died of a fever three years before. A distinct amount of social pressure applied to Sir Gordon Sterling, younger brother of Lady Winthrope, added to a promise to introduce the man to the Duke of Avon, revealed that messages for the baroness should be sent to the Convent of St. Cecilia near Amberley, Sussex. They'd taken the first train and had now ridden by hackney carriage out to the discreet stone and timber cloister hiding between pastoral fields.

"I suppose," Seward said after they'd been sitting in the carriage at the top of the small drive for nearly ten minutes, "there's nothing to do but to go knock."

Colonel Blake didn't give much more response than a grunt, but clearly an affirmative one, because he was soon walking along the gravel path and up the broad steps to the heavy oak door. He grasped the iron knocker and gave it two heavy raps.

Long moments of pregnant silence crept along. It was past noon and the heavy August sunshine beat down on their heads. The door was on a southern facing and so the convent gave them no shelter. Blake had reached for the knocker to give it another rap when a small peeping hatch opened in the door facing Seward.

The wizened lines of an old woman's face floated in the gloom behind the lattice of thin iron bars in the peephole. "Yes?"

"Um, yes," Seward said, "forgive us, Sister. We are here to inquire about Lady Winthrope."

"There are no baronesses here, sir."

"But this address was given to us by her brother and—"

Blake forced his way between the door and Seward, coming face to face with the anonymous nun within. "My wife knew Lady Winthrope in Egypt, madam. It's imperative that I talk to her."

"Be that as it may—"

"Tell her Lord Blake wishes to discuss Miss Victoria Ash," Blake said.

"But," the nun began, "there is no Lady Winthrope—"

"Tell her," Blake barked. "It's imperative. Imperative."

The nun's face backed away from the small opening in the door as if bitten, then she closed the shutter with a sharp snap of wood on wood.

"She is in hiding, do you think?" Seward asked. "That nun knew she was a baroness, so she must be."

"Most likely." Blake turned from the door and looked back at the hackney. "Now we wait."

And so they did, for almost a half-hour. Both men felt sweat and heat building under their woolen clothes and had reason to wish for a canteen of water. They'd both served in Egypt and the Sudan, however, and knew heat and thirst could be much worse. Part of the soldier's skill is to be able to remain immobile, inactive but alert, and so they did. Neither man said a word until they heard the latch of the door opening.

One of the huge oaken doors swung inward to reveal the wizened face of thirty minutes previous. The nun's face was all that was visible of her body, every other inch of her covered by her black and white habit. "This way," she said in a whisper. "Please do not speak."

They entered into the dark structure, their eyes struggling to adjust from the glare of the high sun outside. The massive crucified Christ overlooking the large entrance foyer seemed ghost-like, hidden in the shadows. From there the sister led them through the hushed halls of the convent, one claustrophobic nook at a time. There must have been other sisters, certainly, but Seward saw none of them. He had relatively little experience with Roman Catholic practice, but given that religion's checkered history in England it seemed right to him somehow that these nuns remain hidden from prying eyes. For their own protection, certainly, and also to let others get on with the business of the Empire.

I sound like Captain Ellijay, he thought, his mind drifting to his sponsor in the Taurus Club and—he reminded himself—in Her Majesty's Own Horse Guards. He owed Colonel Blake a great deal dating back from his service in Egypt, but in a few short months he'd come to owe Captain Ellijay even more. He thought of what chance he would have had, as the son of a ruined gentleman farmer, to enter into the most prestigious cavalry regiment in the Empire and gave a little laugh.

"Shh," the old nun hissed, bring Seward out of his reverie. She led Blake and he into a small room that appeared to be an unused cell. There was a simple bed and a small wooden desk by the thin window with a frame of tightly crossed iron holding panes of frosted glass. A wooden crucifix, with a small carving of the Savior nailed there, hung high on the wall. The nun ushered them in and then signaled wordlessly for them to wait. She left and closed the door behind her.

Seward made his way to the small window and noted it was hinged. He pushed it out and saw a view of the pastoral fields that spread out to the east of the convent. Sheep gnawed at tough grasses in an enclosure a quarter-mile away. The bucolic scene was a counterpoint to the darker realities peeling back before him and he could not help but draw contrasts. His mind called up images of battle in the 12th Hussars' ill-fated raid in the Sudan last year—parched savannah and black-skinned native insurgents suddenly superimposed themselves over the Sussex panorama. *But at least those Arabs were soldiers of a sort*, he thought, and it was true. Although wrong-headed and backward, they still fought like devils, and he respected that. The undead and eldritch things he'd discovered in England proper were another matter entirely. Inbred Slavic pagans and erotic succubi had revealed themselves, and ensnared Regina in their web. Now more than ever, he understood the need for groups like the Taurus Club, secret associations come together to defend, preserve and expand the Empire in a hostile world. He reached for the silver bull's head hanging around his neck—the symbol of his membership—and was proud.

"Lord Blake."

The voice was quiet, feminine and close at hand. Seward turned around to see they'd been joined by a different nun. This sister stood taller than her elder, but was significantly thinner. Her face was unlined and teetered on the edge of gauntness. Nevertheless Seward couldn't help but guess that under her habit, she was quite beautiful.

"Lady Winthrope?" Blake asked.

"Sister Mary-Elizabeth now," she answered and closed the door. Seward noted that she held a small Bible in one hand, and a rosary dangled from her neck. "It has been so for some time," she said.

The room, austere even for one person committed to a life of quiet contemplation as a bride of Christ, was positively claustrophobic for three. The slight breeze that had been coming through the window at Seward's back died when the door was closed and he began to sense sweat building up again under his collar. If the heat bothered Sister Mary-Elizabeth, covered head to toe, or Colonel Blake, neither of them showed it.

"Tell me about Victoria Ash, Lady Winthrope," Colonel Blake said.

A weak sigh escaped the nun as she sat down on the simple bed. "Is Emma well?" Her tone indicated she could guess the answer.

"No. And neither is my daughter, Regina." He took a seat next to her on the bed. "Please, tell me about Victoria Ash."

"She is a devil, Lord Blake," she said. "A devil dressed as a rose."

The story rolled out of the former Lady Winthrope in a quiet, confessional style. She had made some sort of peace with the sins of the past, it seemed, and neither of the two military men in her audience could hold any shame over her. Seward guessed that the only judgment with which she was concerned was that of the final day.

"I first met Victoria when I was but thirteen years of age, gentlemen." Her gaze locked on Blake as she spoke. "I was very much concerned then with the transition to womanhood and when I saw her, I was entranced. In the realm of the physical, she was—she still is, I dare say— the most beautiful creature I have seen."

Seward's mind traveled back to the cold days of last December, when he too had come into the sphere of that beauty. He could not fault the sister on her aesthetic judgment. His breath still shortened with the memory of the woman. Or the thing.

"You understand that age, age has no effect on creatures of her sort, yes? Once the grave yawns wide, it does not easily reclaim them. So you must know that the Victoria Ash I first glimpsed almost three decades ago is the same you may have seen more recently."

"But you," Seward interrupted, making a quick calculation. "That is, sister you cannot be…"

"You will find, Lieutenant, that very little 'cannot be' amongst their kind." She returned to Blake. "The meeting was perhaps coincidental or Victoria and her cohorts may have arranged for the mothers and daughters cotillion that evening so that they might see and sample the young girls on their way into society. Their kind feed on the living in many ways, not only draining the blood of innocents, but also skimming the cream of entire generations to be their playthings."

"I do not understand," Blake said. "Blood?"

The nun smiled and barely a line creased her porcelain visage. "These damned souls flout the grave, but not without a price. To pursue their mockery of life, they consume innocent blood. 'For the blood is the life,' says the Book of Deuteronomy."

"And the cream of generations?" Seward asked.

"As playthings, companions, protégés. They use social events to review innocents as a breeder does mares and studs, seeking the special characteristics that please them. Those they fancy, they seduce, enrapture and ensorcel."

Seward felt a tingling beat of sweat run down his spine and realized his breathing was shallow. He left Blake to ask, "How?"

"You cannot underestimate the devilish power of their kind, Lord Blake. All that is forbidden by decent folk is not only allowed by them, but it becomes currency. They can bend the will of the bravest man with a few words and overpower the strongest man effortlessly." She swallowed and looked, disquietingly, directly at Seward. "Or inflame the passions of a chaste girl with a glance."

"As she did to you?" Seward hadn't meant to voice the question, but he did.

"Yes." She kept his gaze. "It was only a few weeks

after first laying eyes on her, that I was sneaking out of my father's house to find Victoria. At first, she pretended to reject me, which of course forced me to extremes to prove my desire. To earn her touch, I lied to my family, cursed my father, forsook my God, and declared myself a slave to her.

"She was like a master horticulturalist, nurturing and pruning the shoots of original sin within me until they bloomed like the blood-red roses she loved so much. In my fourteenth year my father became aware of some of my escapades, but by no means all. Still, bless him, he tried to return me to the path of virtue and show me the wages of sin. But it was too late and punishments were now rewards for me. Every lash of my father's cane sent no agony, but a vile ecstasy, through me." She paused, and tears welled at the memory, although her gaze remained fixed on Seward. "I cursed him to Hell, my darling father, as he beat me. I exposed myself to him and urged him to take me for his second wife. For the crime of trying to save me, I lured him into darkest sin."

Seward felt the creeping, tingly heat of revulsion and arousal fighting over his heart and loins. The cell seemed to sway slightly and he was aware of only three things: the pins and needles playing across the back of his head, the beautiful face of the nun before him, and the aching between his legs.

Blake seemed less impressed. "And Emma?"

"Victoria had an interest in Emma that I think went back before my time. Victoria asked me to befriend her, to watch over her."

"So you were a spy for this creature when you visited our home," Blake said. A statement, not a question. "Either in London or later in Cairo."

The former Lady Winthrope looked down into the black expanse of her habit. "To my shame, yes."

"How do we find this Victoria Ash?" Blake asked.

"And how do we kill her once and for all? Is fire the only way?"

"Kill?" The nun swallowed audibly. "Yes, yes of course. To free Emma. Or your daughter."

"As you say."

"Fire yes, she fears fire and the light of the sun." Another swallow. "But most of all she fears the light of God, Lord Blake. And the righteous few."

"The Lord has not seen fit to save any of us from her kind yet, sister."

A wan smile crossed her face. "He has brought you here, milord, and I feel I do his work by seeing you. Perhaps, if I can undo some of the sins I've committed, I might find redemption."

"The condition of your soul aside," Seward said, "so far we have only heard words. Nothing that helps us find Lady Regina or her mother."

She looked back at Seward. "Go to Charlotte Place in Bloomsbury, Lieutenant. Victoria keeps a home there. Number forty-nine." She turned to Blake and handed him her small Bible. "And take this, milord. Let it guide you."

Blake opened the small, leather-bound tome in his hands and a puzzled expression crossed his face. He seemed about to speak, but instead snapped the book closed and rose from beside the nun. "Thank you."

"When the time comes, milord," she said, "tell them you walk with St. Eustace."

"I will," he answered and headed for the door. Seward, puzzled, followed him out.

***

"Are you going to tell me what happened back there, Colonel?" Seward had held his tongue during the trip back to the train station and much of the rail trip back toward London. He'd hoped Colonel Blake would simply share whatever information he'd gleaned from Sister Mary-Elizabeth. Now, his patience had eroded. "We could have learned more about Miss Ash's home on Charlotte Place. As it is we—"

"She'd told us all she was going to, Lieutenant," Blake interrupted. He reached into his vest pocket and pulled out a folded yellow telegram. "Read this."

As was his habit, Seward glanced at the provenance and address of the telegram. Wire messages were common for soldiers in colonial postings and it was a good practice to know who was sending a message along. This one, addressed to James Blake, Monroe House, St. James, was from Cairo and sent by a certain Othman al-Masri. It read:

James—It saddens me that dark times visit you anew—Remember Cairo and the creatures your lady wife knew—Seek out the company of righteous men—I make my way to London via Paris to provide assistance— There are Christians there who know the truth as I do—They wear the sign of Leopold— Contact me at the Maison de Tunis with news—God be Praised—Othman

"Who is this man?" Seward asked. "An Arab?"

"I knew him in Egypt. He was, or is I suppose, a holy man among the Mohammedans. He helped me recover Emma from the clutches of these… things, once before."

Seward was mute for a full minute. He'd believed this had all started last Christmastide, but now that seemed an innocent fancy. The Blakes' dealings with the undead went further back. "What happened?"

"You heard Lady Winthrope. Emma was ensnared and cursed, made into a servant of one of their kind. Even after we freed her, she was never the same again."

"Regina had spoken of her mother having a fever…"

"A convenient lie. One of many." The colonel, whom Seward had always known to be made of iron, seemed a withered old man, weighed down by the tragedies of his life.

"How did this Arab become involved?"

"He entered our house as a tutor for the children. You know Regina has always been fascinated by history and the classics, and Daniel—" Blake stopped short. Mention of his son, his eldest child, had been forbidden around the colonel ever since they left Cairo and Daniel Blake had refused to come along. Up until this very minute, Lord Blake had pretended Daniel had never existed and to hear his son's name on his own lips was obviously a painful and bitter experience. Nevertheless, he carried on, although in a weaker tone still. "Daniel was fascinated by astronomy. Othman was very well read in both subjects."

It was another minute before the colonel continued. "One evening, in April of our last year in Egypt, Othman asked to see me in private. I expected to hear concerns about Regina's behavior or some other child-rearing matter best dealt with by my wife, but instead he brought dark tidings. 'Your lady wife is possessed by an evil spirit,' he said. 'She steals from your home to perform dark acts of sorcery.' I was of course scandalized, but he spoke with conviction and, truth be told, I had felt at a great distance from Lady Blake over the past year."

"What did you do?"

"We followed her when she made her way by night into the quarter the Arabs call Bab al-Khalq. She was very careful and we lost her several times, but eventually, in May, we found the abandoned house where the vile thing entrancing her nested."

"Was it," Seward's mouth strained around the words, "an undead creature?"

"I don't rightly know. We arrived to find some ritual

underway. There was chanting and the most terrible laughter. Othman urged caution, and I deferred to his experience in such matters, but I wonder if I might have done more by acting more quickly. We only approached when we heard screams and the sound of a growling thing. By the time we got there, we only caught brief sight of a man fleeing and found Emma, bleeding and collapsed on the floor of some ritual chamber. I think she was to be some sort of pagan sacrifice."

"Good Lord," Seward whispered. Dream-like memories of his own hand performing the sacrifice of the bull-woman floated before him and he felt a wave of nausea. He should confess the truth of the Taurus Club to Colonel Blake. He should, but he would not. Instead, he pushed aside thoughts of his own sins—or were they virtues?—and focused on the colonel's story. "What do you mean by his 'experience in such matters'? Surely your years as a military man outweighed anything he could offer."

Blake responded with a very slight smile. "That is kind of you, Lieutenant, but Othman revealed to me that he served in an entirely different army. He is what the Arabs call a *sayyad*, a slayer of devils. A witch-hunter."

"There exists such a thing? This sounds like stories of the Crusades."

"You will find, Lieutenant," Blake said, echoing Sister Mary-Elizabeth, "that what is possible…"

"Point well taken."

"Othman claims to have faced several varieties of devils during travels in Persia and the Sudan—"

"If ever there was a land where I'd expect to find devils, that is it."

"Yes," Blake said. "I know you faced terrible things there and perhaps the locals have had the help of darker things."

"The telegram mentions something about others like

him." He looked down at the typed words. "Christians who wear the sign of Leopold…"

"That is why this is so interesting," Blake said and handed Lieutenant Seward the Bible Sister Mary-Elizabeth had given him.

On close inspection, it revealed itself to be more than a Vulgate Bible. Although the Scripture was in between those leather covers, so were several other texts, one being—translated from the Latin—*The Testimony of Leopold of Murnau Before His Eminence Cardinal Battista Marzone on the Subject of the Devil's Agents on Earth*. The covers themselves were hard instead of the soft leather of most Bibles and upon examination proved to have leaves of their own glued to them. Opening these revealed a logbook of sorts, bearing the printed title *Record of Membership in the Society of Leopold, Being the Successor of the Holy Inquisition*.

Seward scanned the log, which recorded the membership of one John Saxton of Kent, made a brother inquisitor in March of 1870. The various entries served as a sort of travelogue, recording Saxton's visits to diverse chapter houses, including the one in Dublin (which made him a member), another in Rome, a house in the French town of Avignon, and one in Vienna. Each entry was primarily in the same strong hand, save for the signatures and seals of the diverse houses. That same hand—surely the man's own—noted Saxton's decision to form a London chapter house in December of 1884 along with three fellow brothers. A note in a delicate hand that Seward imagined to be Sister Mary-Elizabeth's was the only other entry, noting John Saxton's death by hanging in March of 1885, executed at Highgate Prison along with three accomplices for conspiracy to overthrow the Crown. *These were no Fenians* exclaimed a final note, *but righteous men of God*.

Chapter Four

"Dr. Scott to see you, Dr. Herringbone." Mrs. Holden had spent a life in service and long ago mastered the art of appearing as if by magic. Her employer, Dr. Nathaniel Herringbone of Doris Street, Lambeth, never noticed her unless she had need of him to. As such, he was often startled as he was on this late August morning.

"What?" He looked up from the stacks of notes he had been reviewing for the last several hours. Herringbone was a compulsive note-taker, a habit that guaranteed a life full of bound diaries and unbound files, but that also made his medical practice doubly valuable. Through constant review of his meticulous records, he uncovered patterns of disease and injury that others missed. Treating the sick was his profession, but tracing the sickness was his passion.

"Dr. Scott, sir. He is in the downstairs library. He was expected."

"Yes, thank you, Mrs. Holden." Herringbone returned to his most recent diary and completed the notations on the dock worker he had spent the morning examining. His research had pushed him into charitable practice, providing medical assistance to London's popular classes who seemed to fall victim to disease much more easily than the well-born. This morning's patient had exhibited a terrible rash, his skin gone raw and bloody across much of his inner thigh. Fascinating , really. Herringbone had seen a similar case in—

"Nathaniel?"

Herringbone looked up to see Gerald Watson Scott peering into his office. He stood up immediately. "Gerald! Have I been making you wait again?"

Scott entered the office and the two shook hands heartily. "No more than you ever did when we studied at

St. Bartholomew's. Still 'Natty the Note' I see."

"Ha! Yes, I must plead guilty to that charge, old boy." He turned toward a cabinet against a wall, overlooking two leather chairs—only one of which was piled high with notebooks and memoranda. "A drink, then?"

"Surely." Scott took the empty chair, while Herringbone first cleared the other—carefully placing the pile near his desk—and moved to the cabinet, where he removed a decanter and two tumblers.

"You must forgive me, I am in the midst of a review of certain cases."

"I believe that review has been ongoing for much of the decade, my friend." Scott raised his glass in toast. "Better days."

"Better days. Yes, quite." Herringbone took a hefty swig of the amber liquid. "Now, your letter said you wished to inquire about some patients of mine?"

Scott drank the whiskey down as well. "Yes. Some months ago, you consulted me on a case. It was a coachman, if I remember, with some fine scarring…"

"Mr. Tinwick! Yes, yes." Herringbone got up and practically raced to one of the large bookcases that surrounded his desk, pleased to put his compulsion to work. "A consultation on the state of mind of the patient, yes? I am so pleased that you have gone into the field of the mind, Gerald! It speaks well of you to bring a measure of science to a field that has for so long been—"

"The patient, Nathaniel?"

"Of course! Of course!" He pulled out a leather diary that seemed indistinguishable from all its companions, although Scott knew Herringbone had devised his own system of cataloging. "Here we are, Mr. Arthur Tinwick, currently of Soho, originally of Cardiff, Wales."

Herringbone returned to the leather chair he'd been in and flipped through the diary. "Came to the clinic upon the insistence of his wife whom I had treated for a recurrent case of palsy. He complained of a persistent headaches and occasional lapses of memory. I asked for your consultation because upon careful examination, I discovered that the man had suffered numerous incisions. You concluded—"

"That they were probably not self-inflicted." Scott lifted his glass to drain the last drops of the whiskey from it. "I've come across another patient who exhibits the same scarring."

"Let me guess," Herringbone said, hardly able to contain his glee. "Another coachman! You see, I've uncovered another one as well, a certain Garnet Codger who runs a stagecoach into the north of the city."

"My patient is a woman, Nathaniel. A certain Mrs. Joanna Claremont of Sydney Mews."

Herringbone was crestfallen. "Not a coachman, then? No, obviously not. But I was certain… I had thought this was perhaps the work of a criminal extorting money from these fellows, or perhaps even some initiation ritual into one of the occult societies making such press these days."

"If so, it goes beyond coachmen."

Herringbone served them both another whiskey. "Indeed. Tell me about Mrs. Claremont and I will tell you about my coachmen."

**

Malcolm Seward found Anthony Pool in drawing room of the Taurus Club for Gentlemen. Pool had served with Seward in the 12th Hussars and been his sponsor in the Taurus Club, so he felt a strong kinship with the man. Among other things, the two had accompanied Regina Blake (along with Lieutenant Easton, also of the Hussars) into the crypts at Lion's Green last winter. That small estate in County Durham, owned by the family of Emma

Blake (née Ducheski), had reserved a deadly welcome for them. They had discovered that Emma Blake's body, supposedly interred there, was in fact missing. They had found this out after fighting a desperate battle against several of her relatives. Lion's Green was, in Seward's experience, cursed ground.

But then again, so too might the Taurus Club seem to some.

"You look like hell, Seward." Pool's jovial nature shone through the rebuke and he passed his fellow solider a stiff drink of whiskey. "Drink up."

Seward did and the liquor left a woody burning sensation in his gullet. "Thank you. Lord Blake and I have been, well, searching I suppose. And I, well, that is…"

"My goodness, man." He laughed. "You're becoming incoherent. Spit it out!"

"There are some terrible things out there, Tony." He sat heavily in one of the high-backed leather chairs. "You remember that business last winter? Well, it's continued. I've seen Lady Blake, walking."

"Alive?" Neither shock nor disbelief tinged his voice, only casual interest.

"Yes, that is, no." He finished his drink and placed his glass near the decanter Pool had apparently appropriated from one of the valets. "Lord Blake speaks of the undead, and witch-hunters, and it would all seem madness, but…"

"You don't have to tell me there are horrible things out there. That's why this club, this brotherhood, is so necessary."

"But that's just it, Tony. This club, what I did to that woman. That was *murder*." The last word was spoken in whisper. "At the time, it seemed, well, not exactly right, but…"

"The word you are looking for," came a voice from

…nd one of the nearby chairs, "is 'necessary.'" Captain Ellijay, whom Seward thought of as the head of the Taurus Club, rose from that seat and took another facing the two lieutenants.

Seward's pulse raced and he could not escape the conviction that the seat Ellijay had apparently occupied had been empty a minute ago. "Yes," he said, although he wasn't sure why.

"Necessity is the critical part of sacrifice, Lieutenant," Ellijay said. "A murderer kills for pleasure, for profit, for hate. He wishes to kill. A practitioner of sacrifice kills not only despite his own misgivings, but because of them. He acts to give something up to a higher power. You sacrificed the bull-woman to Mithras and in so doing sealed a compact with that warrior-spirit. You said, 'I will do anything for the sake of Empire and my brothers, just as they will do anything for me.' Your sympathy for the prostitute who acted as the bull-woman is laudable, but have no regrets. You have acted and must accept the consequences of those actions."

"Yes, but—" Seward began.

"Are you a soldier?" Ellijay asked. His tone was calm but his voice felt like that of a screaming officer. Seward responded in kind, practically leaping from his chair to stand at attention.

"Yes, sir!"

"And what place does regret have in a soldier's life?"

"None, sir!"

"Very good, Lieutenant. Now, I could not help but overhear your worries about Lord Blake and his misadventures." Ellijay's unflinching eyes focused on Seward like a pointer on its prey. "I feel I must remind you of the oath of secrecy of the Taurine Brotherhood."

No other words were spoken, but Seward felt *something*, like a slight pressure on his very soul. The urge to share his worries about the death of a woman in a bull-head mask during his initiation into the brotherhood evaporated and a steel trap seemed to close around those events. These were holy secrets, he realized, and to share them with the uninitiated would be sacrilege against his God.

Seward didn't even notice Ellijay leave the room.

***

Gareth was almost ready, but not quite. He still needed a few more nights, perhaps just a single one, before he could make his escape from this damnable house and be reunited with the master. His strength was building.

In the meanwhile, he still had to put up with the constant prattling of the old man. He'd always believed Cousin Emma had chosen a truly worthless Briton as a husband, and Lord Blake's pitiful interrogations only confirmed his view. The man had managed once, earlier in the month to elicit a few facts from Gareth, but he had been weak then. No longer.

"For the last time," the aging nobleman bellowed impotently, "where is my daughter?"

Gareth chuckled. Would this fool never stop asking fruitless questions about little Regina? Although a delicious flower, that one was off gallivanting with the harlot Victoria Ash. Gareth had no inkling why and Blake had wasted weeks of effort trying to get him to speak on the subject.

"Your women are lost to you forever, you know," he said as a sort of answer. "Perhaps you should resign yourself to that fact once and for all."

The old man's face turned the red of a ripened cherry, so enraged did he become. His fists clenched around the cavalryman's crop he held there and he suddenly swung with it, lashing across the calloused and blistered flesh of Gareth's face.

"Oh please," Gareth said in a mocking voice, "don't mar my beautiful face." His face had been something akin beautiful once upon a time, a lithe and lean cap to a serpentine body. That was before his dear cousin Thomas—traitor to his own blood—had doused him in sorcerous flame in order to protect that brat Regina. Thomas had paid for it with his life, but his magical arts had remade Gareth's skin into a leathery surface of scars and boils. A few lashes were not going to worsen his situation any.

"Do you want me to fetch the fire, you bastard son of an inbred line?" Blake's only success in questioning had come with the help of flames, but Gareth was stronger now.

"If you are cold, old man, perhaps you should."

Blake fumed and lashed out again with the crop. Gareth inhaled deeply and over the smell of his own blood and waste, he could smell the desperation in his erstwhile torturer. Blake's world was crumbling into a horrific tragedy that Gareth found especially delicious.

***

Gerald Albin had been a servant at Monroe House for just over twelve years. First hired on as a stable hand, he'd become the house's principal coachman seven years ago. Much of that time had been relatively easy, as far as servants' lives go, what with Lord and Lady Blake living in Egypt and only coming to London on occasion. They gave him a living stipend and he had had time to hire himself out to others in need of occasional service. For two years, Master Luke, a nephew of Lord Blake's, had taken residence in the house and been something of a boor to work for, but that hardly qualified as hardship when compared to the life Gerald could expect on the factory floor were he to leave service.

He knew the Monroe House stables and much of the rest of the building better than any other, seeing as how Mr. Goosehound had replaced much of the staff three years ago after a rash of pilfering. Thus, he knew well that the knocking coming from the larder under the kitchens was unusual. He doubted anyone else would have heard the sound, since the only adjacent room was a storage cellar under the stables. It was there that Gerald kept supplies for repairs to the coach as well as those private possessions he did not want whoever Mr. Goosehound hired on as butler or housekeeper to inspect while "tidying up" his quarters. As a boy, he'd been beaten for possessing a collection of pornographic prints depicting women being pleasured by various types of horses and so he knew to keep such things hidden.

The wall between the larder and the cellar was brick, but the mortar was old and sound traveled through several holes. It was late at night and by blowing out his own candle, Gerald could note the spots of light leaking through between the rotted bricks. The pounding was like that of a crop on horseflesh, a sharp cracking dulled by the mass of the target.

Gerald's curiosity won out over his not insubstantial discretion when he heard faint chuckling between two of the blows. What was going on behind that rotted wall? He made his way back up to the stables, patted Nick the sleeping horse on the side, and proceeded out the back and toward the kitchen. As expected, it was dark. Mrs. Lorrie, the head cook of Monroe House (and, Gerald reckoned, the perpetrator of the pilfering that had got most of the staff fired), was a notoriously sound sleeper, so entering her domain was not hard. Gerald noted light coming from under the door leading down to the larder, and made his way there on cat's feet.

He stuck his head down the tight stairs and saw the shadows playing at the bottom, revealing the presence of at least two men. His master's voice came up at him from below.

"Where—is—she?" Lord Blake demanded, each word punctuated by another blow.

"Your women are gone, Blake, far from here."

"Where!" Another blow.

"Where they belong."

Gerald closed the door and fled to his own quarters, shaking.

Chapter Five

By the time Dr. Gerald Scott had finished a long evening of discussions with Nathaniel Herringbone, he was convinced that someone was effecting some dastardly plot on several London coachmen, his patient Mrs. Claremont, and who knew how many other people. Nathaniel had kept meticulous notes—as always—including diagrams of the fine scars he'd found on his patients. The sketch for Tinwick, the first case, had been quite general, but with Codger, once Herringbone had suspected a pattern, the diagram was meticulous in the extreme. He had an overall sketch showing placement on the anatomy and then several detailed drawings, showing some of the particularities of individual scars. Scott had commented that Herringbone had a second career as a portraitist, but the other doctor had laughed off the compliment. It was all part of the necessary skills of an anatomist, he insisted.

In any case, the drawings had erased any doubt in the men's minds that Joanna Claremont had suffered by the same hand. Both the overall pattern of wounds—once they allowed for differences in gender—and the individual scars were very similar. The incisions on the underside of Mrs. Claremont's foot had reminded him of the calligraphied Hebrew script he'd studied in school, not in that it formed actual characters, but it had some of the same swirls and lines. He was convinced that the unknown assailant had at one time studied at university or followed other studies that included the Hebraic language. Herringbone's sketch of the underside of Codger's foot showed the same script-like cuts, which the good doctor indicated linked tender clusters of nerves. "To walk on such a wounded foot," he had said, "must have been agonizing."

The questions of who and why remained unanswered, of course. Herringbone's theories were somewhat pedestrian and Scott dismissed them. Having never left civilized England, Herringbone had no real understanding of the uncivilized and fractured mind. Where he saw criminality, Scott perceived the taint of a mind altered from the natural course, a method of thinking divorced from the dictates both of science and Almighty God. Herringbone's idea of some occult ritual did have some interest, but neither Arthur Tinwick nor Joanna Scott had been initiates in some Theosophist circle. Codger he could not attest to, having not—yet!—interviewed the man, but neither of those who had come under his care had been of occult or irreligious character.

The pseudo-textual script of the wounds, however, spoke of secret and mad rites. Not only the nonsense letters engraved in the feet, but the overall pattern of fine white lines that marred all the hidden sensitive tissues, that framed Joanna Claremont's labia and marred the coachmen's glans. These seemed to Scott to be subtle brandings, as if saying in the language of the mad *These people are mine*. No, not people, but things. *These things are mine*.

Dr. Scott was determined to uncover the identity of the mad author of these gruesome messages. He had, however, no real conception of how to go about doing that. Over the ensuing weeks, he flirted with the idea of releasing Mrs. Claremont from his care and then following her, but that seemed only a viable option if she were to rise from her near-catatonic state of withdrawal. In her current condition, he doubted very much that she would even know to walk as far as the front door of the asylum, much less lead him anywhere. He experimented with discussing the idea of freedom before her, in the hopes that hearing the words might somehow pierce the veil of her state, but to no avail.

What's more, Lord Blake and Lt. Seward's visits grew rarer, and Scott could only assume this had something to do with the fate of Lady Regina. Although their absence gave Dr. Scott greater leeway in the remedies he might administer—he no longer had to worry about overly squeamish relatives appearing unannounced—it also made detailed interviews with them difficult. If Lord Blake or the lieutenant were somehow responsible, or knew who was, he would have to convince them to tell him.

It seemed an impossible conundrum, to reconstruct the past of a woman who refused all communication. Thus it came as something of a shock when the madman, or rather the madwoman, in question appeared in Dr. Scott's office. "Appeared" was very much the right term, for one minute the good doctor was once again poring over the meticulous notes Herringbone had sent—copies and summations of his diaries, made in his own hand—and the next he had the distinct impression that he was not alone.

"Good evening, Dr. Scott." The intruder's voice was light, almost friendly, but not quite. Definitely feminine, but with an iron spine run through it—a rose with more thorns than petals.

Scott looked up from his notes and spied her in the gloom. It was late at night and only his desk-lantern cast light in the room. She was sitting in one of the chairs near the small, rolltop secretary's desk that his assistant used when transcribing Scott's notes. Although he was certain he had been alone in the room, he had the disconcerting impression that this woman had been in that chair for quite some time.

"Yes, um…" He swallowed, took just a second to collect himself and rose from his chair. "Yes, good evening. May I be of some assistance?"

"Please, doctor, do sit."

The thorns in her melodious voice somehow stabbed at him then and before he quite realized it, he'd fallen back into his chair. She herself rose and approached, shedding the gloom of the corner like a cloak. She was young, a woman of no more than eighteen or nineteen years, with ringlets of brown hair tied loosely with a bow. She was also dressed like a man.

"I hear tell that you have been asking questions of Dr. Herringbone," she said, smiling without mirth. She wore the black waistcoat and tails of a gentleman ready for dinner, although somehow tailored perfectly fro her girlish form. The vest and shirt suppressed but somehow did not quite eliminate the curve of her slight bust or the flare of her hips. "Questions about acquaintances of mine."

"Yes. I have." Scott spoke clearly and carefully, although his mind was racing. Calm was an important tactic when dealing with the mad, especially the violently so. He had no doubt that this woman was the author of the ghoulish script he had uncovered, and her attire had much to do with his certainty. Scott had, in fact, come across several cases of what he termed "anti-sexed dementia," a condition by which an insane person reverses their perception of gender. In most cases, it was a projected madness—it was his contention that sodomites saw their mates as women—but there were instances of it as an internalized condition. There was even a chap in the asylum at this very moment who was convinced he was Mary, Queen of Scots. Female-to-male dementia was much rarer and that rarity implied that the other symptoms of the dementia (or of the underlying madness) would be all the more extreme—even murderous. He had to proceed with caution, but he also had to establish grounds for communication with this woman.

"I'm honored that you know my name," he said,

omitting the *sir* or *miss* he would have used in a less ambiguous situation. "May I ask yours?"

"Juliet Parr, doctor."

She answered easily and without hesitation, and Scott had to suppress his astonishment that she used a clearly feminine name. Was she even aware that she dressed and acted as a man? He wished to ask more but held his tongue when she placed a slim leather case on the desk before him.

"Open that, would you, doctor?"

He looked up at her. "May I first—"

"No, you may not."

And just like that he could not. The very notion of asking the question he had been pondering simply erased itself from his will. It still floated in his mind—*May I ask where you learned Hebrew?*—but he had no desire to ask it any more. He had only the desire to listen carefully to instructions, to open the case. He undid the copper clasp on the leather tie that kept the two folded halves of the thing together and opened them. The right side of the case held several instruments that were not unknown to a man of medicine—scalpels, clamps, syringes. The left held a fine ivory-handled razor.

"You have stumbled into a place where your inquisitive mind is not very welcome, doctor. Mrs. Claremont, Mr. Tinwick, Mr. Codger, and even good Dr. Herringbone—they have all been very useful to me in keeping abreast of the conversations among the masses here in the capital. Hand me the razor, would you, please?"

Questions formed in his mind, but the volition to ask them was absent. *Useful in what ways? For what purpose?* He handed her the razor.

"Some of my kindred would simply have me kill you, doctor." She opened the blade and it caught the light with a cold glint. "There is an argument to made for the simplicity of that solution, I suppose, but it lacks elegance and foresight. Please remove your clothing."

This was a case of mesmerism, Scott concluded as he shed his clothes, folding each piece carefully because he somehow sensed Miss Parr liked order in all things. His inquiries into the use of hypnotic methods, however, had always suggested that a great deal of preparation was necessary. Here, without preamble, Miss Parr had simply appeared and overwhelmed parts of his will. What's more, he was utterly aware of it, fully conscious that he was in the process of fully disrobing before a madwoman armed with a very sharp blade, and still he had absolutely no ability to stop himself from doing so.

"You see, doctor," she continued once he was completely naked, "it is my responsibility both to ensure the safety of my kindred from inquiries such as yours and to prevent them from undertaking behaviors that might draw undue attention to us. To perform these twin duties it is essential that I have—aides, shall we say?—placed throughout this great metropolis to report when troublesome rumors begin to spread. I've found that coachmen and cabbies make for ideal agents in this regard. They also provide a convenient way for me to travel about town." She said the last with an incongruous smile that spoke of the mania within her soul.

"I will admit," she continued, "that it is something of a personal embarrassment that the very instrument I use to pursue my duties has resulted in precisely the type of inquiry I strive to prevent. Be that as it may, I believe that you may ultimately be a useful addition to my little network. Your asylum would make for a convenient shelter—and larder, I suppose."

Larder? Scott felt the faintest glimmer of alarm, just enough to cause a chill to run up his bare spine. It was enough to draw her attention and she walked straight up to him, fixing him with eyes as cold and dead as marbles.

"You have a strong spirit, doctor. I admire that, truly I do." Her hand moved with lightning-like speed and he felt the trickle of blood flowing down his chest. "Do look down, please."

He did and saw that her razor had left crescent-shaped incisions in both his nipples. Red blood was welling from them and dribbling down the hair on his chest and stomach. *There should be pain*, he thought, but there wasn't.

"Yes, the pain," she said, seemingly reading his mind. "You won't feel it now. Not even a little." She set the sharp tip of the razor's blade at the top of his sternum and proceed to draw it down in a curving, script-like wiggle. It should have been agonizing, but it wasn't.

"My good doctor, you will not remember any of this in the morning. Your mind will recall absolutely nothing of your return, but you will cease your inquiries and report anyone else who might pursue them. And in future you will grant me, and anyone who might come here in my name, full access to your facilities and your person. Do you understand?"

His throat was desert-dry and his chest covered in his own blood. "No... I... I don't understand at all...."

"Of course not. Please forgive me." She smiled and he noticed her upper canines were longer and more pointed than was natural. "Before returning to more elaborate directives, let me be straightforward and direct: You will serve me. If, at any time, you consider not doing so, you shall remember the pain of your wounds. Remember, doctor."

The agony hit him like a thousand blows. Where there had been only the sensation of warm blood, he now felt the cold blade draw across his bone and through his nerves. He screamed and collapsed, sending blood across the Persian carpeting.

"Do you understand?"

He could barely form words. "Y… yes…" And just like that the pain stopped. He rolled onto his back, trying to catch his breath.

"Excellent." She knelt down beside him. Her left hand, still gloved, traveled up his leg toward his exposed and blood-soaked sex. It responded immediately to her rough caress, straining into a painful erection that made him moan aloud.

"Silence, doctor," she said, tightly pinching the base of his member and sending pulses of terrified pleasure into his animal brain. She still held the razor in her right hand and she brought that to bear, placing its cold metal against his straining organ. "Now, doctor, there is something else I want of you."

Scott could barely think, but he knew he would give anything for the horrific pleasure this man-woman had sent into the hard core of his being. Summoned by some urge of hers, he lifted his head to look down at her and saw her expertly flick her blade, and open the large vein on the side of his sex. The blood shot out in a climactic stream, splashing her girlish face and eliciting a terrible smile from her.

Urges darker than even his own overtook her then, as she threw the razor across the room, reared her head back and opened her fanged mouth wide. An eternal instant later she clamped her jaw onto his mutilated shaft and he felt the chilling ecstasy of his life flowing into this creature.

He slipped into unconsciousness knowing he would obey her forever.

***

Both Malcolm Seward and Colonel Blake had spent some time thinking what exactly would be the best approach when entering the home of a creature they thought to be risen from her grave. Seward remembered his harrowing visit to Lion's Green last winter. Blake thought back to his confrontation, nineteen years earlier, with the wretched thing that had taken his new wife as its pet. Both these experiences led the men to believe that this endeavor was likely to be both violent and horrifying. Sister Mary-Elizabeth's warnings did nothing to alter these impressions.

They thus arrived at Charlotte Place well armed on the afternoon of August 30th. The day was clouded and announced autumn, and the citizenry of London seemed to take no notice of one more carriage ambling through Bloomsbury. Gerald, recovered from his discovery of the prisoner hanging in the larder at Monroe House, was at the reins and stopped, as he had with Lady Regina, just around the corner from Number 49, the home of Victoria Ash.

"She might be in there. Or another of her kind." Seward was mostly speaking to himself, trying to visualize just what he might be facing while he checked, not for the first time, that the chambers of his Wembley revolver were full.

"If they are looking for Emma," Lord Blake answered anyway, "I have to believe they are still on the Continent. That maggot Ducheski practically said as much."

Seward made a sound that might or might not have signified agreement, tucked his pistol in the holster under the cloak he'd chosen for the afternoon, and moved to open carriage door. "As agreed?"

They'd settled on a simple, direct plan because they'd rapidly concluded that anything more complicated was foolishness without gathering more information, which seemed largely impossible. They never admitted it, but their plan developed on the assumption that Ash and her kind could clearly bewitch them if given time to do so—an assumption based in Seward's case on personal experience. Thus, the key was to move forcefully.

Seward proceeded without hesitation to the door of Number 49 and knocked. He waited a beat and was preparing to commit burglary when he heard the latch click and a pretty maid opened the door.

"Yes, may I help you, sir?" Seward had never seen the girl—about eighteen by the looks of her. Fetching, with brown hair in a simple bun.

"Lt. Seward to see Miss Ash."

"I'm sorry, sir, but Miss Ash is away on—"

The maid stopped her polite explanation when Seward pushed his way past the stoop. He'd expected to make it all the way into the vestibule or even the hall before the slight girl could react, but he was very much mistaken. As planned, he caught her off guard when he pushed past her, but against all sense she proved to be very, very strong. The moment she regained her balance, the maid pushed out and hit Seward in the stomach with her open palm. He staggered as if hit by a man thrice as big as the girl, all the breath knocked out of him.

She should have immediately followed that blow with a series of others, but instead she moved to close the door. That concession to propriety—or at least to not displaying preternatural vigor to the neighbors—cost her dearly, betraying her in two ways. First, it gave Seward, a trained cavalryman entering a situation he knew to be dangerous, the small moment he needed to recover. Second, the door refused to close and instead stopped on the well-placed boot of Colonel Blake. Distracted by the appearance of a second assailant, she didn't see Seward draw his weapon until its butt was already coming down toward her head. Turning only allowed him to impact her temple rather than the base of her skull.

She tumbled to her knees and Seward did not make

the same mistake she had. His gun came down twice more, the combination of steel and wood of the butt making wet impacts in the maid's skull. Her face hit the thin carpet of the vestibule just as Blake closed the door behind him.

"Quickly," the colonel said. "Inside."

If they had expected some ghoulish den beyond the front door of 49 Charlotte Place, the two men were disappointed. Instead, they found a well-appointed and stylish home. Built on three stories, with only a couple of rooms per floor, the house was nevertheless ingeniously made and full of a variety of elegant touches. Its size (as a home rather than a mansion) and location (in Bloomsbury instead of St. James or Mayfair) may have indicated placement in the middle classes, but the attention to detail and the rich appointments spoke of a woman of station used to entertaining.

Hints that this was no normal house emerged slowly, as the two men explored. They did so after gagging the unconscious maid and tying her securely to the wooden banister of the main stairs. The first floor, mainly made up of the kitchen and other service quarters, they bypassed for the upper apartments, which they took to be the quarters of Miss Ash. They proceeded with caution, expecting another servant or creature to appear at any moment, but they relaxed enough to observe their surroundings.

In the second-floor parlor, the country scene that adorned one wall showed not the traditional grouse or pheasant hunting of the English nobility, but a scene of plantation life in what Seward took to be the southern portion of the United States before that region had exploded into civil war several decades ago. The white Georgian architecture of the main house in the background of the scene, the colorful hoop-skirts and parasols of the ladies walking in the foreground, and the black-skinned field hands glimpsed in secondary positions, all seemed to corroborate that impression. "An odd choice," he concluded in a whisper.

The third floor and its sleeping quarters were even odder. The main room was a bedchamber, which was placed according to some strange architectural fancy in the middle of the building instead of to one end. The effect was to make it very gloomy because heavy shutter-like doors isolated it from the small adjoining rooms and any daylight.

"She fears the sun." Blake emphasized his point by pushing open the shutters at the southern facing of the chamber, which opened onto a small sewing room. The daylight, although weakened by newly arrived autumn and dimmed by the clouds covering the sky, still coursed into the bedchamber and the huge bed in its middle.

"Good Lord," said Seward, as he approached the bed. The linens were a mess, torn and shredded as if they had been attacked by a wild animal. Large sewing shears were still planted in the mattress, amidst the downy filling littering the rose-patterned bedspread. Seward picked them up and aped the stabbing motions that had caused such damage. "The maid?" he asked, rhetorically.

They returned to the ground level. The maid was still propped against the banister in the front hall, her head resting against her shoulder at an uncomfortable angle. Seward and Blake proceeded to her small room, behind a door at the back of the hall, opposite the kitchen. At first glance, there seemed very little to see. The room included a simple bed—well made and undefaced—a wooden desk and a thin armoire, with a small mirror on the door. A wash basin and pitcher rested on the table, alongside a hairbrush.

Closer inspection, however, revealed signs of the same madness they'd seen evidence of upstairs. The surface of the desk, a lacquered oak, bore countless scars from some blade or point. Large gashes, small cuts, even half-formed words and letters had been dug into it. A crude shape recurred and it took Seward a few moments to identify it as the petals of a flower, possibly a rose. Lifting the blanket on the small bed tucked against the wall, he exposed sheets stained by sweat, blood and urine. A smell of mold and offal lingered in the air from that point on.

The armoire, opened, revealed a jumble of clothes piled at its bottom and a single gown hanging from a hook. This last, a black bombazine mourning dress, had received the same treatment as the bed upstairs. Removing it from the hook and holding it up, Colonel Blake exposed the long gashes torn in the fabric and the strips of cloth that hung willy-nilly from its bodice. What had once been a delicate dyed-lace collar was little more than shreds, although the pattern of lacework was still recognizable. And recognize it, Seward did.

"That gown," he said with a lump in his throat. "I think it was Regina's."

Blake laid it over the small chair at the desk, as gently as he could. He then reached under the desk and pulled open its drawer. No bigger than a cigar box, the drawer was still jammed full of papers.

"Listen," Blake said, picking up the first scrawl-covered sheet to read. "'I hate her. Hate, hate, hate, hate. Forever I hate her.'" He picked up another sheet. "'Just because she's a viscount's daughter, she becomes the favorite. I hate her.' The rest of the sheet is filled with the word 'hate' over and over again."

Seward picked up other papers and found more of the same. "Nothing but invectives, Colonel, all on the same blue note paper."

"The house's supply, no doubt," said Blake. Then he pulled out a pink-tinted sheet, crumpled and stuffed in an ivory-colored envelope. "Save this one."

"What is it?"

"A letter," Blake said, "from my daughter."

"What?" Seward turned so that he could look over the colonel's shoulder to read the letter. Blake laid the paper down on the desk and flattened it as best he could. Regina's fine script was visible, but it had been marred by countless rips and the maid's invectives scrawled across it.

"Let's see," Blake said, and he read what he could. "'My darling Jo,'—addressed to your sister, then—'we have… in Paris… seeking—'"

A muffled scream interrupted Blake, along with the sharp crack of shattering wood. The two men turned to face the hall, only to see the maid rushing their way. The colonel rapidly realized she'd broken the heavy oak banister to which they'd tied her using the same preternatural strength that had flattened Seward. She was charging toward them, her blood-smeared face contorted with rage and her gag reducing her scream to a moan of fury. She looked like one of the enraged bulls he had seen in a corrida while visiting Spain. Three steps down the hall, she fully dislodged her hands from the shreds of rope still binding them. Her arms shot forth like claws. Blake swallowed and willed his limbs to act.

A shot rang out and a plume of blood and bone exploded out the back of the madwoman's head. She spun on her leading foot before collapsing on the threshold of her quarters, not more than two paces from Malcolm Seward's smoking pistol, which had felled her. He pulled the hammer back, took a step forward, and fired again, squarely into the maid's shocked face.

Seward then turned to face Blake, who noted both the young lieutenant's steely gaze and the bits of bone and blood on his coat. "We had better go."

"Agreed." Gunshots would not go unnoticed on Charlotte Place, even if the neighbors had learned to avoid paying too close attention to Number 49.

As Seward moved toward the front door and their waiting carriage, Colonel Blake stole into the kitchen and emerged with long matchsticks and a quantity of used frying oil. He doused the small bed and desk in the fat and then struck a match. Stepping over the prone body of the maid, he tossed the match and started a blaze.

By the time the carriage was off Charlotte Place, thick plumes of smoke were rising into the air and neighbors were screaming in alarm.

Chapter Six

"This is the place." Arlington Street, St. James, was just one more house of wealth and privilege in London's West End, as far as Beckett could tell. Ruhadze and he were sitting in a hansom cab as it moved slowly down the street. The houses, large but tightly packed together in the way of over-congested London, were all the residences of the aristocracy or the very upper echelons of the middle-classes. Monroe House, which stood toward the end of the street, had little to distinguish it from the neighboring structures. It was, however, the home of their prey Lady Emma Blake—or at least it had been.

Halim Bey, their London contact and another Follower of Set, had been quietly apologetic. They had wired him from Marseilles, when their vessel went to port there, asking for all information about Emma Blake. He'd done his job well: She was a viscountess, married to Lord James Blake, formerly commander of a regiment in Egypt. They had two main residences: a country estate in the north of England, and a London residence on Arlington Street called Monroe House.

"Unfortunately," Halim Bey said in his richly accented English, "the Lady Blake seems to have succumbed to a fever this past December. She was buried in County Durham." He presented them with a copy of the *Times* from the previous January, which announced the death of several prominent aristocrats, including Emma, Lady Blake.

"Damn." Beckett had hoped this part would be relatively easy, but it didn't seem that way. "Well, is her husband still in London or has he headed north with the rest of the counts and dukes to spend the fall shooting grouse?" London emptied itself of aristocrats after the middle of August and through the winter as they retreated to the country.

"He is still in London, I believe. But there is other interesting news."

"Yes?" It was Ruhadze who spoke this time. He'd been very quiet since they arrived at his clanmate's shop in the Southwark Borough.

"It seems Lord Blake's daughter, the Lady Regina, has been frequenting kindred circles. A customer of mine has seen her on several occasions." The portly Setite smiled. Beyond his own agendas—whatever they were— he acted as a broker in antiquities and other rare items for the vampires of London. Although he was not officially sanctioned by the local vampiric hierarchy, he was tolerated and very well connected. Beckett had used his services several times. If he said Regina Blake was consorting with vampires, Beckett was inclined to believe him.

"Has she been presented to the prince?" Beckett asked. By tradition, all vampires had to appear before the city's prince in order to exist under his rule. Neither he nor Hesha had done so, of course.

"She met him at a ball held earlier this month in Sydenham, but I do not think she is kindred. A ghoul, more likely."

"Of whom?" Ghouls were considered property among vampires. Dependent on their master's blood, they were never independent actors.

"A certain Miss Victoria Ash. A courtesan of sorts in London." Before either of them could ask her whereabouts, Halim Bey raised his hand. "She is an habituée of a mixed parlor operated by Lady Ophelia Merritt, a prominent kindred, but my informants feel that Miss Ash must have left the city. She hasn't been seen since the ball in Sydenham, at least not by my client."

"Monroe House it is, then," Hesha had said to the news. And here they were.

They signaled the cabbie—one of Halim Bey's men—to stop at the end of the street and Beckett got out. "I'll make my own way in," he said as he was alighting to the hay-strewn street.

Hesha just smiled. "As you see fit, my friend."

Beckett cut down a small passage into an interior courtyard shared by two of the buildings down the street from Monroe House. It was an unseasonably warm autumn evening and windows were open up and down the street, so he should be able to get into Monroe House without difficulty. Still, London streets were never without peering eyes and while the metropolis encouraged a helpful tendency to mind one's own business, the sight of a brown-haired man in traveling clothes scurrying up the façade of Monroe House to enter through an upstairs window had more than a passing chance of attracting unwanted attention. Some vampires, Beckett knew, could cloud the minds of observers so that they failed to notice them at all, but such was not his way. Beckett's blood tended toward the animal rather than the cerebral.

Sticking to the shadows along the brick-and-plaster walls of the Arlington Street apartment homes, he was reasonably sure he was unobserved, and so he turned his senses within. Vampires, in their more philosophical moments, spoke of "the Beast," that savage and destructive part of their damned souls that cared for blood and nothing more. Beckett visualized that roiling mass of hunger and rage and gave it a shape. At first it was just a huge maw and two bright red eyes, but he willed it to take on definition. Its head shrank until it had a small, rodent-like jaw and its eyes were small and beady. Large ears the shape of devil-horns sprouted, as did a furred body and large leathery wings. The Beast was a bat, benighted portent of evil, and suddenly so was he.

The actual transformation was effectively

instantaneous. A sudden sense of falling and his body collapsed into the form of a flapping night-flyer. The world became one of sound and smell rather than sight, and he rose in jerky motions into the air. His senses were attuned to the flight of insects, but he knew they would satisfy him no more than kidney pie would in his man-form—only human blood would do. He put the hunger out of his mind as best he could and searched for the roof of Monroe House.

Gifted with the instincts of a predator and the experience of a man who'd been traveling for several human lifetimes, Beckett's sense of direction was impressive even under normal circumstances. In his animal-skin, it was infallible. He found Monroe House with ease and sensed the open window in one of the servants' rooms that lurked in the attic. Perfect.

A natural bat flying in through an open window would panic and flutter about making a great deal of noise. Beckett felt an instinct inside him to do just that, but he suppressed it and instead glided to the wooden floor of the small room. Like releasing a held breath (something he had not had to do in a very long time), he let go of the bat-shape and swelled back into the shape of a man. He was fully clothed, but spared that no second thought—he'd long since stopped wondering just how that occurred. The floor creaked slightly as it took on his full weight, but the portly woman snoring in the small bed didn't wake.

Beckett took in his environs with his newly man-like eyes. The room was small and simple, as were most servants' quarters. The walls were papered in a matte mustard color, and the furnishing consisted of a wooden bed, an armoire that took up most of one small wall, and a matching dresser. A porcelain basin and pitcher sat atop the dresser and Beckett's nose told him a used bedpan lurked somewhere unseen. A few personal touches added to the scene, including a finely printed card propped against the backboard of the dresser. Beckett's eyes beat back the night's gloom without effort and he read the fine, printed script:

In Memoriam

Her Ladyship Emma, Viscountess Blake

Buried on this Thursday, December 29, 1887

in County Durham

Such a mourning cards, Beckett knew, were often sent to those touched by a death but unable to attend the funeral proper. Among the well-born, however, they also usually included a daguerreotype of the deceased at rest, a final image of the beloved man or woman. That the card didn't include a place of interment also seemed odd to him. These were the signs of a death irregular in some way, of a burial meant to hide something, and given Emma Blake's past involvement with the undead—and her daughter's current entanglements, if Halim Bey was to be believed—Beckett thought he knew just what that was. There was a new vampire in town.

He replaced the card and continued his silent survey of the small room. On a hook by the low door was the greatest prize: a ring of keys. This must either be the housekeeper or a well-trusted maid. Careful not to clink the three long keys together, he lifted the ring from its hook and held it fast.

Now, he thought, *to find the master of the house.*

***

"I cannot say, Lieutenant, that I am entirely pleased with your announcement." Captain Ellijay sat in a heavily upholstered chair in the library of the Taurus Club for Gentlemen. He wore the characteristic blue uniform of Her Majesty's Own Horse Guards, the same uniform the tailors had delivered to Lieutenant Seward's residence last month. The uniform he'd worn only once—at his sister's funeral.

"Appointment to the Horse Guards is not something one simply turns down," Ellijay said.

"I understand, sir, and I do not intend to refuse it." Seward was still standing, and his eyes caught the night traffic on Pall Mall outside the window behind Ellijay. Even in the late evening, the posh street was busy.

"To leave behind your regimental duties for parts unknown, barely a month into service, seems tantamount to a refusal, Lieutenant."

Seward looked down at his boots. They were scuffed. "Yes, sir, I can see that. But I have an obligation to Colonel Blake and his daughter Lady Regina that I cannot dispense of. Lady Regina, whom I had hoped— whom I *still* hope—to make my wife, has disappeared in the company of a most dangerous sort. A… that is…" Seward felt as if his tongue were suddenly made of lead. How could he explain to Captain Ellijay just how much trouble Regina had got herself into? Could he actually tell an officer in the 1st Horse Guards that his beloved was in the hands of a blood-drinking devil?

"Out with it, Lieutenant."

"Yes, sir. I believe—that is, Colonel Blake and I believe—that Lady Regina has been abducted by a woman with some monstrous agenda. She goes by the name of Miss Victoria Ash, but that may be some sort of pseudonym. I hardly know how to explain the strange things I have seen, but I have uncovered evidence that she and Lady Regina are in Paris and I cannot forgo the chance to come to my beloved's aid. Colonel Blake is to join me—"

"Lieutenant." Ellijay's voice, always strong, took on an additional layer of importance, like a soldier donning his arms.

It was the same tone Ellijay had used weeks ago when he'd overhead Seward and Lt. Pool, and it had a similarly powerful effect. Looking down into the captain's cold eyes, Seward felt a slight wave of vertigo. He could not look away.

"You are a brother of ours," Ellijay said, "a journeyman in the Taurine Brotherhood. You have taken an irrevocable step into the life of a soldier of the Empire. You understand this, do you not?"

"Yes, sir. I do."

"Your oath was sealed in blood, Lieutenant, was it not?"

"Yes, sir. It was." Images of his ceremony of initiation danced before his mind's eye, of a bowl of ox's blood, of a woman in a mask, of a knife in his hand, of a throat slit. He realized he hadn't given that ceremony much thought since the captain had last spoken to him.

"Then you understand the bond between us. Between brothers-in-arms."

"Yes, sir."

"Then listen to me." Ellijay's voice was calm and even, but there was steel in it. "You will go to Paris after Colonel Blake's daughter and this Miss Ash. You will not stop until you have found what you are looking for, unless you receive the order to from another brother."

"Yes, sir."

"And you will report. Cable me here at the club with updates as to your search. You will exercise the utmost discretion in this matter, however."

"Yes, sir. Of course, sir."

"Very well." Ellijay turned his gaze aside, and Seward felt a great weight lift from him. He had his orders. He would obey.

***

Gareth Ducheski would, in later nights, decide that

he had been the victim of a cruel twist of fate. Indeed, what was the likelihood that the benighted intruder would choose that particular early September evening to invade Monroe House? Had he come the previous night, he might have provided a beneficial distraction that would have allowed Gareth to make a stealthy escape and seek vengeance at some later date. Had the stranger chosen the next night, Gareth would have already been gone and the master of the house, the damnable James, Lord Blake, would have been rotting away, his skin flayed off by Gareth's skilled hands.

No, that the intruder chose the one night in which his presence made a critical difference, was clear evidence that the Fates had an especial cruelty when it came to Gareth. Of course, when he lifted himself from the large hook he'd been suspended on for over a month, he had no reason to suspect just what those three mythic harlots had in mind.

His senses had grown sharper than they had ever been, as if honed by his travails over the last year. Indeed, despite the burning his dear, dear Cousin Thomas—may he rot in Hades!—had inflicted, and the subsequent tortures at the hands of Lord Blake, Gareth now felt unstoppable. Two nights ago, when Blake and his lickspittle Seward had last come to interrogate him, he'd found the pain refreshing. He knew then that he would make good both escape and vengeance the next time.

Thus, he heard the old viscount fiddling with the heavy lock at the top of the stairs in plenty of time to prepare himself. He'd released himself from the hook several times over the last week, and found that the puncture through his shoulder had healed around the metal, forming a large shunt through his flesh. He could easily replace himself on the hook without opening any new wounds. That such a healing was profoundly abnormal never even occurred to him—the twisting of the human form was part of the Ducheski heritage. So he had no difficulty lifting himself off again simply by reaching up, grasping the large iron ring from which the hook dangled and pulling himself up. His physical strength had returned as well.

He deduced that Blake was alone from the sound of his steps. The boy Seward would have to be dealt with later, of course, but his absence only made what came next easier. Gareth stood just slightly to the side of where he should have been dangling and waited. His heart beat the warm blood of life and the cold blood of his family line through his veins.

The door opened and, just as expected, Blake's eyes went to the empty space where he expected his prisoner to be. Gareth could smell the familiar odor of whiskey on the old man's breath. "What?"

"Here, dear cousin," Gareth said as he stepped out of the shadows. That this rotted-out old viscount had married Cousin Emma was another outrage for which he would have to pay.

Blake tried to fight back, but it was no use. Gareth clamped one hand on the man's throat, cutting off air into his lungs. With the other, he grabbed the hand with which Blake held a small oil lamp. Gareth had been felled by fire too many times and knew the old man's fascination with it. He squeezed and felt the man's finger-bones break. He then slammed him against the wall and his gray-haired head made a hollow noise as it hit the wooden doorframe.

Gareth extinguished the lamp, then dragged Blake's unconscious body none too gently up the tight stairs and into the kitchens of Monroe House. It was not, to his way of thinking, any surprise that a servant like the house's cook would make the best showing of defending her master. Aristocrats were, in his experience, a universally weak lot whose only skill was in tricking stronger people into believing they should serve them. Still, Gareth had spent a great deal of time listening to the cook's bemoaning in the kitchens over the last month, so when she came at him with a cast-iron frypan his sympathy for her was limited.

She got in one good solid blow, but Gareth managed to turn his body so that his right shoulder took the impact. Grown hard and inflexible because of the hook, its pain threshold was prodigious and the impact felt like a mild tap. Dropping the unconscious viscount, he retaliated, using his good left hand to deliver a full-force open-handed blow. The slap caught the woman on the right temple and he felt bone crack under it. She collapsed in a heap and he smelled the coppery odor of her blood. He kicked her for good measure and the smell of piss joined the aroma of the kitchens.

He gathered a few implements and then made his way into the house, dragging the old man all the way. He hadn't walked more than a few steps in his previous experiments with liberty from the hook and was dismayed to find that his left knee seemed to have become creaky and ill-suited to regular movement. He laughed aloud at his own condition. Scab-covered, hunchbacked and limping, he was a true scion of the deformed Ducheski line.

Gareth placed the viscount in a chair in the main parlor and bound him there with the golden-threaded ropes meant to tie open the heavy velvet drapes. He would kill him, of course, but not yet. First, vengeance. He splashed a decanter full of whiskey into the man's face.

Blake sputtered, coughed and came to, the liquor burning his eyes. "What?" His voice was raspy, his voice-box damaged from Gareth's compression of his throat.

"Can you say anything else, old man?" Gareth smiled down at him. "Perhaps you could scream." With that,

Gareth plunged a carving knife into the old man's thigh.

Scream he did.

"You never asked the right questions, old man," Gareth said. "So much concern for your harlot daughter and none for your dear wife."

"Emma... dead..." Blake coughed out.

"You don't know very much about your dear wife's heritage, do you Blake?"

"...un...dead...she's gone..."

"Ah, I see." Gareth smiled. "You do understand a few things, at least. Our family has lived alongside the masters—the 'undead' as you call them—for centuries. We are their eyes and ears in the daylight and they gift us with their power. Your dear wife thought to escape that heritage, as if the wolf could somehow become a poodle just by willing it."

"...gone..."

"Even this spring, she still thought she could save you and your daughter, you know. Her quaint feeling of love was still there."

"...where... is she...?"

"Finally, fatally late, a question I might have answered! Do you think I keep tabs on that little harlot of a daughter, her precious blood already so diluted she cannot truly be numbered in our family? Emma was ever my charge and that they left for Vienna without me is your fault." Another twist of the knife, another scream.

It was a full minute before Blake could cough out another question. "Vienna?"

"Surely you've heard of it?" Gareth said jokingly. "The Hapsburg jewel on the Danube? To see Forstschritt, the high house of the great order, that—"

A sound. Gareth's senses had detected a sound from further down the hall. "Please wait," he said to his prisoner in an incongruously pleasant tone. "I must deal with another of your staff. You do have a knack for employing foolishly loyal servants."

Beckett was listening from a study near the downstairs parlor. Emma Blake was in the Tremere father house in Vienna? That complicated matters substantially. In a benighted world positively choking on conspiracy, Beckett found the Tremere blood-sorcerers to be among the most troubling. They were hoarders of secrets, so he had dealt with them on several occasions and each time he had felt that somehow they got the better of the deal. Most worrisome was that, for vampires, the Tremere were frighteningly well organized. Undeath was a selfish condition, one in which personal survival and the call for blood most often overwhelmed other concerns. It was something of a miracle that the vampires who nested in a single city like London or Paris could even cooperate enough to agree on the preeminence of a single prince and his council of advisors.

The Tremere, however, enforced a pyramidal structure that kept them tightly organized, even across great distances. In secret chantries, meeting halls, and libraries across the civilized world (and even beyond, as Beckett had discovered twenty years ago in Macao) they managed to cooperate for grander agendas. If Emma Blake was bound to them, did that mean they had set their resources on Kemintiri's trail?

Beckett shook his head and made slight *tsk* of disdain. He should not have asked that question. Now, his own curiosity would leave him no choice but to answer it.

The ghoul who'd been ranting in the next room must have heard the sound because he came to investigate. From his rambling, and the confidence that wafted off him, the man expected to face a valet or a washerwoman, some mortal he could easily overpower. Indeed, he entered the study where Beckett had been sheltering with a meat cleaver brandished as if it were a saber.

"What have we here?" The deformed ghoul swung the cleaver, intending to gut his opponent.

Beckett took a quick step back to avoid the swing and then stepped forward with a snarl. Fangs extended from his gums and long wolf-like talons from his hands. The ghoul came up short, surprised to find an enraged vampire in the study, and that hesitation was more than enough to doom him.

Beckett used one clawed hand to grasp the ghoul's overextended left arm, tearing into the tender flesh and muscle, making the cleaver fall to the ground. The freakish man did have some presence of mind, however, and managed to use his free hand to clasp Beckett's other arm, preventing him from bringing that second set of claws to bear. Beckett had decided the man was a ghoul from his comments about serving the undead, and his guess was confirmed by the preternatural strength the ghoul exhibited. Beckett's arm was held fast.

That did not prevent him from slamming his head forward into the ghoul's face, breaking his nose and causing blood to run down his features. The ghoul weakened his grip. Beckett pushed him away, then plunged both clawed hands into the man's belly, extricating his entrails with a swift pull. The looping cords of organs were coated in black ichor, like yards of blood sausage.

The ghoul collapsed and Beckett quickly left the study. The hunger was rising in him and the smell of blood was eroding his will to resist. To drink the stolen blood of a ghoul was probably unwise, however. He proceeded into the parlor to find a face from the past awaiting him.

"Lord Blake," Beckett said, looking down at the man tied in one of the parlor's chairs, blood running down from an injured thigh. He'd seen this man before, two and some years ago, when Lord Blake had come to save his lady wife from the same ritual Beckett had so fortuitously interrupted. Recognition flashed across the man's bleary eyes as well.

Beckett tried his best to ignore the coppery blood-smell coming from the man. *He would make a fine meal*, some deep, primal part of him said. He ignored it and his talons and fangs slipped back into their fleshy sheathes.

He used a piece of cloth to bind Blake's wound, then used the bloody knife to cut the ropes tying him to the chair. The man tried to get up, but couldn't.

"Stay out of this, Lord Blake," Beckett said before leaving. "For your own good."

Somehow he doubted the man would.

Chapter Seven

The mansion on Piccadilly had the unremarkable name of Trenton House. It was a grand house among many other grand houses, and although of some note for a few architectural flourishes on its façade, few people passing by would guess that it was any more significant than the various other mansions and clubs on this particular thoroughfare. This was the West End, where influence, wealth and social position converged, after all.

Still, over the last month especially, many of those walking down Piccadilly—or riding in fashionable barouches or hansom cabs, for that matter—had felt something. Very few could put a name to this vague unease, but an especially keen observer might have seen that no one lingered in front of Trenton House. Walkers quickened their pace and horses moved and twitched as if suddenly set upon by large quantities of stinging flies. Moods darkened, patience eroded and tempers flared around the house.

On August 31st there had been an unfortunate lock directly in front of Trenton House. A carter moving wares eastward toward the City proper had suddenly become irate at the nag pulling him down the street and whipped it savagely. The beast, usually docile, had reared and pulled. The cart, poorly made and even more poorly loaded, had overturned, spilling produce across the street. This had startled the horses pulling an omnibus, forcing the driver to fight to hold the train together. Pedestrians began shouting at the carter, who continued to beat his fallen nag bloody, and a row soon began. It took an hour to clear the mess and for carriage and cart traffic, hopelessly clogged, to resume. Sixteen men were arrested by the Peelers who responded to the disturbance, and

THE MADNESS OF PRIESTS

three more were sent to hospital to be treated for the lashes they took from the enraged carter. No one thought to associate the unusual level of violence with the quiet, mundane presence of Trenton House.

What none of these various passersby knew, what in fact only a handful of people and none of them living knew, was that Trenton House was one of the residences of Mithras, prince of London's undead. On a street full of tradition, there lurked a creature—for he had long stopped being anything one could describe as a man— who was old when England was young, who had come to these shores with Roman legions after lurking in the shadows of the classical world for still more centuries.

Lady Anne Bowesley was one of the few who knew the truth. Acting as the prince's seneschal, she had now spent a good month covering for her liege's absence from the various nocturnal gatherings, and the strain was beginning to wear on her. Those responsible for the attack—if attack it was—that had ruined the ball at the Crystal Palace in Sydenham had yet to be found, having fled London directly after the debacle. Captain Ellijay said he had a lead on that young rose Victoria Ash and Miss Parr had resources of her own, but Lady Anne needed more than assurances if she was going to preserve order.

Enough, she scolded herself. She was falling victim to the same aura that affected the mortals in the street outside. Ever since the ball Prince Mithras had been in the grips of some dark humor and his mood was leaking into the very ether around him. His rages and ranting were almost constant now and it was wearing even her indomitable will down. For much of the last few weeks he had been nearly catatonic, speaking only of something called the "hand of glory."

We will find out, in time, what happened, she told herself, imposing calm on the roiling emotions echoing within her. *If anyone has the luxury of time, then surely we who are immortal do.*

"Anne!" Mithras cried suddenly from the sealed, underground room where he'd been "resting" for the past weeks. She heard the call despite being two stories above in the library, because it reverberated in her very mind.

"Yes, Your Highness?" She answered in a whisper, confident that Mithras could hear her.

"Another. Bring me another."

Anne tried her very best to suppress a shudder. She'd brought him the last one only three nights ago—at this rate, London would be devoid of kindred by this Christmastide.

***

"Are you sure you don't wish to accompany me, Ruhadze?"

The Egyptian smiled his serpent smile. "There's no need for us to be coy, Mr. Beckett. We both know the rules of our game and the realities of our natures. We are solitary creatures by nature, not cooperative sorts."

Beckett acknowledged truth of that with a nod. "Still, you sought my help in determining the fate of Lady Blake and now that I have…"

"I thank you for that, of course, but I fear that the stronghold of Tremere blood wizards is one place I do not wish to storm at this time. I am, shall we say, *unwelcome* in Hapsburg Vienna."

"Much as I am in London?" Beckett asked.

"Yes, yes," Hesha Ruhadze answered, dismissively. "But I felt confident Halim Bey and I could guarantee your safety in the metropolis. I realize you are a man of many acquaintances, but could you do the same for one such as I in Vienna?"

"I'd assumed you could care for yourself, Ruhadze."

Hesha smiled again. "And I thank you for that consideration, but I believe I have other avenues to investigate in London. That Lady Blake's own daughter has become embroiled in the affairs of kindred strikes me as less than coincidental."

"Agreed, but we know her mother is in Vienna, and she might be able to answer your questions about Kemintiri. It seems…"—Beckett almost said "foolish" but held it back, skirting the edge of insult—"…careless to leave her be."

"Then careless I will be, in this at least." Hesha moved to the door of Halim Bey's shop, where they were discussing matters. "As the first repayment of the debt I owe you, however, please allow us to arrange safe transport to the Austrian border. Halim Bey knows a man who runs a fine train route from Holland through Germany."

"I can make my own way, thank you."

"Well then," Hesha said, opening the door, "I remain in your debt."

Beckett didn't say anything else, lest he be drawn into another such dance of favors, innuendo and suggestions. He should have left the Egyptian waiting for him outside Monroe House and gone out across the rooftops. Fewer entanglements that way.

Ah well, he thought as he moved toward the Thames and the docks where his ship awaited, *I may have reason to call on that debt one of these nights.*

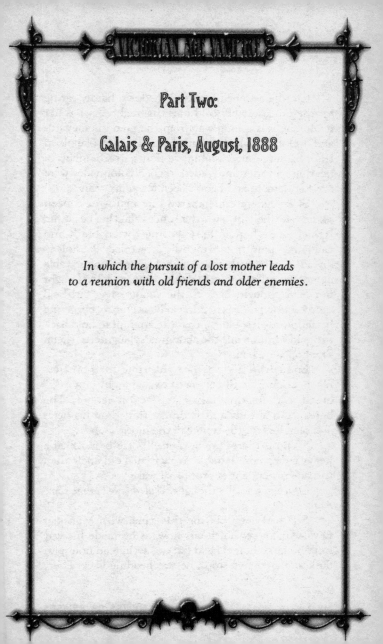

Part Two:

Calais & Paris, August, 1888

*In which the pursuit of a lost mother leads
to a reunion with old friends and older enemies.*

Chapter Eight

Clotille watched from the shadows, hardly caring for the unseasonably cold rain this night. As was her habit, she was a long way from the grand boulevards and ostentatious monuments left to Paris by Napoleon III or his more successful uncle Bonaparte. Symbols of fleeting victories and gilded, rococo colonnades were not her domain and hadn't been for many years.

She vaguely remembered one man—he'd been soldier, she thought—who had once called her beautiful. It had made her smile, exposing rotten teeth and cankered gums, from which he'd recoiled. Pausing to savor the memory that came unbidden from unknowable depths, Clotille wondered if that nameless soldier might not have thought back to the young street girl he'd spurned when he was freezing in New France, buggering his fellow royal soldiers in a futile attempt to hold back the cold winter while the aboriginals slaughtered them. She hoped he had.

Enough! This was not the time for pointless recollections. Clotille allowed herself a phlegmy "tsk" of self-recrimination. It had an effect on her prey. The bureaucrat, already a little drunk, turned on his heels and searched for the source of the moist sound.

"Who is there? Show yourself!" He brandished a heavy cane, more suitable to a wizened old uncle than the superintendent of prisons. "I warn you…"

Of what, Clotille thought. *Will you yell at me some more?*

She had been playing this game with Monsieur Levasseur for several hours now, as he made his way from home to home. He'd left the asylum an hour past dusk and after five stops, he was heading back. Every one of his waylays had been residences—two squalid apartments, two semi-bourgeois houses and a *pension* once run by Ursuline Sisters. In each, he visited the loved one (or ones) of a prisoner in his care. In each, he brought vague news and accepted (or demanded) payment. From the bourgeois, he took money. From one of the poor girls he took the use of her loins, and from the other that of her mouth. The boarder at the last stop had apparently not had anything of worth to trade and so had received three blows from Levasseur's cane and the promise that he would extract "compensation" from the man's incarcerated wife.

Clotille had been with him the entire way, an unseen companion lurking in the plentiful shadows. The mist, rain, grime, and tight alleys of the eastern boroughs were her allies in this, conspiring to keep her from view unless she wished to be seen. And Clotille rarely wished to be seen.

Instead, every once in a while, she gifted her prey with the barest hint of her presence. A sound—like the throaty one that had just drawn his attention—or a sudden hint of movement in the corner of his eye, or even a whiff of rotten breath on his neck. Each time, he started slightly and searched for the stimulus's source. *A sign of a fractured conscience, that. Of a man who spends too much time with condemned innocents.*

Levasseur, frustrated again by the night's unwillingness to give up its secrets, headed off at a fast clip. The soles of his boots made wet slapping noises on the cobblestones and he was close to breaking into a run.

She smiled her crooked-toothed smile and headed off after him. He would lead her into his cloistered world and she would show him the same tender mercy he did his charges.

"He is not for you," said the voice. It was a man's—musical, educated, ecclesiastical almost—and it came from a shadow Clotille knew to be empty. But no, when she looked again there he was, a tall, blond man in the pale robes of a penitent priest. "The prison is mine, little fly."

***

By the time they made it to Paris, Regina Blake and Victoria Ash had been in France for over a week. They'd spent most of that time in Calais, holed up in a private home with a view of the beaches and the Channel waters. Very little information had been forthcoming, but Regina had determined the house to be the property of one Monsieur Alphonse, a pale-skinned gentleman who was, it seemed, older and more weathered than the stones of the seaside. Monsieur Alphonse dressed exclusively in black woolen suits and wore a matching top hat, which he removed in Victoria's presence but not in Regina's.

Victoria wrote a series of letters from the private office handed over to her by their host, which he personally carried into Calais proper to have posted to their recipients. At no point did Monsieur Alphonse address Regina in conversation or in any way offer to provide for her comfort. Those tasks were reserved for the manservant Pierre, a rough sort of butler who was only slightly removed from the stevedores and ferrymen who made their livings on the trade between the port and that of Dover across the strait. Pierre's French was heavily accented and his manner was rough in the extreme when out of the presence of his master and of Victoria.

Regina, although worldly and well-traveled for her age and sex, was still the daughter of a viscount and it took some time for her to understand that in this house she was roughly of the same status as a maid. A visitor's maid at that.

That week was a maddeningly dreary period for her. Over the last eight months, a shadowed world of unknown horrors had exposed itself to her and action had been the only way she had to deal with it. When her mother Emma, Lady Blake, had died last Christmastide, she'd prodded and poked at the strange and inconsistent stories surrounding her mother's death until she exposed the machinations of her cousins, the family Ducheski. Then, this last summer in London, she had drawn back layer upon layer of an entire nocturnal society that nested alongside the world of day. She'd visited balls and dances where creatures without heartbeats drank the blood of the living.

She'd uncovered the unpleasant truth that a dark cabal of these creatures, an occult society known as House Tremere, had its claws in the Ducheski family and had made her mother one of their own. Victoria, her patron in this benighted world of the undead, had pledged to help her find her mother and that quest had brought them to France. Indeed, only a few nights before their arrival, they'd seen Lady Blake and her Tremere murderer escape Dover by ferry and been unable to stop them because of the intervention of Regina's father, Lord James, and her lover, Malcolm Seward.

They'd returned to London for safety, but then quickly made arrangements to cross to France, and Regina had expected the chase to rescue her mother to begin anew. Instead, they had come to Monsieur Alphonse's dreary house and waited.

Regina went over this infuriating litany of disappointments every moment she was left to her own devices, which was virtually every daylight hour. At night, she stayed by Victoria Ash's side, watching her draft yet another letter or simply sit there. There was rarely any talk.

In the early nights of their relationship, Victoria had been coy with Regina about the necessities of her existence. They had sipped each other's blood from crystal snifters under the guise of pledges of secrecy and protection, while Regina slowly discovered that Victoria not only moved in different social circles than she, but was a different order of creature altogether.

The full extent of that terrible difference became clear on the night when Regina had been grievously wounded—mortally so—after infiltrating the ritual that initiated her lover Malcolm into a secretive brotherhood she knew to have ties to the night society. Seward, in the grip of some terrible passion, had roughly deflowered Regina and then slit her throat, never bothering to lift the bovine mask that covered her face and hid her identity from him. That wound should, of course, have been the death of Lady Regina Blake, but it wasn't. Instead, Victoria had opened her own veins and brought them to Regina's lips for her to drink. That cold, black blood had healed wounds no surgeon could hope to mend. It had also forged an uncanny bond between the two women, so much so that Regina often felt echoes of Victoria's feelings.

The two women had been inseparable since that night, but the nature of their bond was fluid. Victoria referred to Regina as her protégée, but seemed to mean it more in its root form of a "protected one" than as an apprentice or successor. Regina thought of Victoria as her guide and protector. But such rational, proper terms couldn't cover up the rawer, darker tint to their relations. A tint Regina feared might damn her soul.

To call Victoria beautiful was a laughable understatement. Hers was a face that, in Marlowe's words, might launch a thousand ships. But beauty was too innocent a term: a flower might be beautiful. Victoria was intoxicating, gifted with a siren's voice and a nymph's form. Regina was distracted in her presence and petulant in her absence. The woman spawned in her a Sapphic passion that, when it bloomed, eclipsed everything else.

That passion was never greater than at the point of feeding. Regina, unable to sleep through the long French days anymore, couldn't help but remember the last time she'd felt the full flame of that attraction. It had been their second night in Calais and Victoria had sent Monsieur Alphonse into the city with the first batch of correspondence. Regina still thought they were to leave at any moment, and was full of nervous energy. They were in pursuit and she felt she could not stand still for even a moment. She'd been pacing the hall outside the adjoining rooms that she, Victoria, and her coachman Cedric shared, when her energy had been diverted.

"Regina," Victoria's lilting voice called. "Come here, please." Now, days later, Regina realized that she could not have heard the voice so clearly through walls and down the hall. The compulsion must have been carried through some other medium than sound—like the blood they shared—but at the time no such thought had occurred to her. She had just responded and entered her protector's room.

Victoria's sense of fashion skirted and often frankly crossed the lines of propriety as dictated by Queen Victoria and her entourage. Still, when she opened the door, Regina felt a heat rise through her and feared she might faint. Victoria was sitting on the large bed that dominated the room, wearing only a sheer dressing gown made from silk so transparent it seemed like gauze, and unsashed to reveal her form. Her hair, fiery red in defiance of the standards for blond and brown, was released from its usual elaborate pinning and cascaded over her alabaster shoulders. Its color matched the delicate down just visible where her thighs met.

Regina, trembling and fearful that if she blinked, this apparition would vanish, reached behind her to close the door. She took three faltering steps, her eyes focusing on the ruby of Victoria's lips.

"I need you, Regina." The words caused those lips to part, revealing sharp canines that protruded like a cat's. Regina had never seen anything so beautiful.

She made it to the bedside and collapsed as much as sat beside Victoria. The proximity was overwhelming and as Victoria shifted to look her in the eyes, the silky veneer slipped off one shoulder, exposing the fleshy orb of her breast. Regina, feeling suffocated by the layers of cotton, crinoline and satin, brought her hands to her throat and tried, inexpertly to undo the knot binding the topmost layer of her clothing. After an infinite instant, the dark capelet fell to the ground beside the bed.

"I need you," Victoria repeated in a whisper so soft it felt like rose petals on skin. She placed her hand on Regina's throat, still covered by the high collar of her traveling gown, and smiled. "This ensemble does not suit you, I think."

Regina felt a chill run through her, thinking herself frumpy and unappealing before this sensuous creature. That quickly became a burst of heat as Victoria raised a long steel hairpin before her eyes. These metallic pins, nine inches long and sharpened to a needle point, were as deadly as any dagger, but at that moment Regina longed to feel it against her skin. She didn't have long to wait. Victoria placed its tip at the top of Regina's sternum, at the point where it met her clavicle. Then, with a swiftness and strength that should have seemed impossible, she cut down, tearing apart the fabric of Regina's top.

Putting down the pin, she then placed her hands along the edges of the tear and pulled apart. It seemed like a gentle movement, so relaxed were her muscles, but the fabric tore apart like rotten lace. Only the tight bind of Regina's corset resisted the cut, leaving her torso constrained but her upper chest and neck suddenly and starkly bare.

"Beautiful," Victoria said, looking down.

Regina followed her glance and saw, despite the harsh angle, beads of her own blood welling up along the line of the scratch left in her skin by the needle point. Victoria bent down and Regina sighed at the feel of the cold, slick flesh of the woman's tongue running up the gash. She knew without looking that the skin was binding itself shut behind that deliciously wet touch.

Victoria raised her head when she reached Regina's neck and continued up so that their faces were less than an inch apart. Regina looked deeply into the green of Victoria's eyes and counted her own shallow breaths, in a vain effort to hold back the wants screaming through her flesh. Victoria did not breathe at all. On the count of four, Regina's resistance faltered and she leaned slowly forward so that her lips touched Victoria's, which parted like a flower. Regina's tongue, acting of its own accord, slipped past her own teeth and into Victoria's mouth. There, it found the dagger-point of the woman's fangs and, wanting nothing more than to be a part of this dark, seductive creature, pressed along the point of them. Victoria's responded with a dart and Regina's tongue came back to her mouth with the copper taste of blood, but no cut.

"More," Victoria whispered as Regina withdrew slightly, moving her head a fraction to the left. Victoria found the artery running up her neck and kissed Regina there. Then she bit down and the pleasure overwhelmed every other sense Regina might have.

But that night had not repeated itself. Regina had slept the length of the day and much of the next night, and since then her protector had been cold and distant. Last night, she hadn't spoken a single word to Regina, and had even left her in the room while she visited the port city herself. Jealousy had almost overwhelmed Regina, so certain she'd been that Victoria had found another who would share her blood.

During the days, when she couldn't sleep and was left only with her memories, things got even worse. With Victoria slumbering, cold and immobile as a corpse, and the memories of her touch growing more distant by the minute, darker thoughts couldn't be held at bay. Thoughts of her father, who had forbidden her to enter this dark world; of her fiancé, who had seemingly been drawn into it; and most of all, of the consequences of her deeds with Victoria. Her sins. Could damnation have so delicious a countenance? Could it have any other?

So it was with a small measure of joy (and a more substantial one of relief) that, the following night, Regina received the news that they would be departing from the coast and heading for Paris. "I had hoped to avoid this," Victoria said, "but it seems to be our only choice."

Regina sensed that she should keep her tongue, but that was all she had been doing for the past days and nights. Giving of her very blood to the unliving creature and getting only physical pleasures that left her spent and guilt-ridden in return. So she spoke. "Is Mother there?"

"Monsieur Alphonse informed me that they took the train there from the coast, but I doubt that it is their final destination." Victoria's voice was dismissive. She had other matters on her mind.

"Informed you when?"

"Excuse me?"

"When did Monsieur Alphonse inform you of Mother's departure for Paris?"

"The night of our own arrival." She seemed ready to say more, but Regina's pent up frustrations would not be contained any longer.

"That was a week ago!" she exclaimed. "We have been caught in this dreary place while that fiend Wellig takes Mother to God knows where when we could have been but a day behind them! I can't believe this! I thought you were going to help me! This is—"

"What," Victoria put in with a tone colder than her own unliving flesh, "precisely, do you think this is, Lady Regina?" Victoria's use of her companion's proper title sounded odd after weeks of intimacy. "Are you suggesting that we chase directly into Paris? Do you have any idea precisely what that entails?"

Regina's blood rose, but she had no retort to give and the breath caught in her throat.

"I thought not," Victoria said. "Do you imagine that London's is the only night society that exists? Well, it is not. Paris has intrigues and secrets all its own, and if anything that city guards its secrets more jealously than its cousin on the Thames. I have not been exchanging empty pleasantries with fawning countesses this past week, girl. I have been arranging for passage and making introductions."

"But surely, we could have… that is, upon arrival—"

"Oh, do learn to speak in complete sentences or to

remain quiet." Victoria took three steps across the room and caught Regina by the wrist. "If you are unsatisfied with my guidance, then by all means, *proceed alone*."

The last was said in a cold, quiet whisper, Victoria's face mere inches from Regina's own, and carried the full weight of the beautiful redhead's scorn. Regina had the sudden feeling of vertigo, as if the floor were slanting back and gravity was pulling her away from this strange, intoxicating woman. This was rejection, and she understood, in that infinite instant, the depths of her own longing for Victoria. At the end of last year, when her mother's death had cast a pall over her family, she'd felt something similar to this with her father—a gaping distance between previously close minds and souls, a chasm of secrecy and resentment driving them apart. This time it was far worse, and instead of feeling anger at being pushed away, she had the mad desire to leap into the chasm in the desperate hope that she might cross it, or barring that, at least end the suffering of separation.

Then, it was over. A slight but unmistakable smile cracked Victoria's lips and the world was set right anew. "It's all right, my dear," she said and released the other woman's wrist.

Regina immediately collapsed into her, trying and failing to suppress her sobs.

"I understand," Victoria continued, enveloping Regina in her long, gloved arms. "I understand. It was unkind of me not to tell you Emma had headed for Paris. I apologize."

Regina caught herself before forgiving by rote. She had never been a lilting flower of a girl and she could not bear to sound like one now. She straightened up and was relieved that Victoria released her embrace without resistance. All too aware of the still-wet tears on her cheeks, Regina did her best to meet Victoria's gaze. "Thank you," she said. "I am very much grateful for your help, but being cast aside is difficult when it is my own mother's fate we are discussing."

"Of course." Victoria sat on the bed and with only a slight gesture invited Regina to do the same. "I should have explained it all more clearly. You yourself noted in London that there was a hierarchy among the night society."

"Yes," Regina said, her hand going unconsciously to the black-rose cameo at her neck, which almost matched that on the frill of Victoria's bodice. "I understand that you are a kindred in their number and I am not, but…"

"But I did not treat you as a servant in London and I shouldn't have here?"

"Um, quite." In fact Regina hadn't exactly felt like a servant, more like an irrelevance, but she held her tongue.

"Do you imagine that Monsieur Alphonse is a friend of mine? Well, he is not. He is useful, certainly, but he has made his place among our kind by providing services to those passing through his chosen port of entry. He exists because many of us rely on him for shelter and information."

"A hosteler, then," Regina said.

"Yes, or something of the sort. But payment is in favors and information from abroad as often as it is in sterling or gold. Under this roof, I am very much aware that my privacy is up for sale. If I treat you as a servant here, it is because that is what I wish Alphonse—and whomever he might be reporting to—to believe."

"I see." Regina didn't have to force the smile of relief out, she so wanted to believe this. Actual belief and the desire for it, however, remained separated.

"But I have treated you shabbily, my dear." Victoria reached to the nightstand and picked up a long ivory letter opener she had draped across the most recent of her correspondence. "It is well past time that I rewarded your patience."

Regina knew she should look away, but did not. She watched as Victoria pressed the needle-sharp point of the ivory blade to her exposed throat. The collar of her gown was low and revealing, shockingly so for the properly dowdy styles of traveling wear, which left her thin neck exposed. The letter opener traveled down along one of the major veins or arteries, leaving a delicate scratch of crimson behind it.

The smell was delicate at first, but grew into a meaty musk as Regina inhaled deeply despite her attempts at restraint. This, she knew, was her passage into the hidden worlds that had swallowed her mother whole. If giving her own blood to Victoria was to give pennies to the ferryman, to drink hers in return was to step boldly onto the barge across the River Styx. That was not, she knew, a journey from which many returned.

None of these thoughts prevented her from leaning in, from touching the welling droplets with her lips and then her tongue, from following Victoria down onto the mattress, or from drinking deeply of the coppery product of undeath.

They were to leave for Paris and would do so together, inseparable.

***

The Maison de Tunis was deep in Paris's Left Bank, in a neighborhood of foreigners and industrial workers, where life was often cheaper than a roof over one's head. Built in the first half of the century by a veteran of Napoleon Bonaparte's North African adventures, it had suffered during the uprising of 1848 and its southern façade still bore scars of fire and patchwork repairs.

For the last thirty years it had been under the proprietorship of Etienne Bisaam, a man of mixed European and Arab descent who had been houseboy to the original proprietor and the beneficiary of the man's will. Bisaam had transformed the ramshackle mansion into a ramshackle boarding house for travelers from the lands in which Mohammed was recognized as the greatest prophet. Algerians, Libyans, Moroccans, Turks and Egyptians rubbed shoulders in the tight halls and shared space in the dormitories (unless they could afford a private room). That most were Muslim men did not always guarantee peaceful coexistence, of course—just last year an Albanian man had murdered a visitor from Damascus over a game of dice—but in the bustling sea of Christians that was Paris, the Maison de Tunis was a welcome refuge.

Othman ibn Saleh al-Masri had visited the Maison once before as a young man, before the Franco-Prussian War and France's subsequent return to Republicanism. The city had done nothing but continue to grow since then, and he was honestly excited to explore the new marvels that awaited him this time. Still, he was not here for tourism.

"*As-salam alaykum*," said the portly man behind the counter, a red fez capping his thinning head of hair.

"*Alaykumu salam*." Othman took two steps forward and put down the canvas satchel that carried his few possessions. "I have need of a room, sir," he said in a precise and refined Arabic that spoke of years in the madrasa.

"But of course," the clerk answered, his own accent rougher and distinctly Mahgrebi. "You can pay?"

Othman's father had been a spice merchant in Cairo and he had to suppress a grin at the clerk's tactless ways. Instead he simply lowered his hand to touch the purse he had slung under his white cotton *galabiyya* robe. The jangle of coins—a mixture of Turkish lire, English shillings and pennies, and a few French francs—seemed to have the right timbre, because the clerk hoisted his girth from the stool he'd been perched upon behind his counter and came around.

"Follow me, good sir." Without glancing back, the clerk then led Othman deep into the rooming house. The sun cast a ruby light through the dingy west-facing windows of the hall and Othman wondered if his guide would even bother with the evening prayer. "This is a good place," the man said, seeming to read a completely different intention. "No one will bother you here."

They climbed a wide staircase to the second-floor mezzanine and then a much tighter one up into the upper stories. The hall at the very top was a tight corridor with bare walls, marked with small, unnumbered doors every few yards. Othman wondered just how the clerk knew which room was his, but he decided not to inquire.

They finally stopped at the second-to-last door on the left side of the corridor. The clerk drew out a heavy ring of keys and attempted first one, then another, and then a third, before settling on the right one. The lock clicked audibly and the man pushed in the flimsy door. He motioned for Othman to enter the room.

When he did, he noted that the single window face north, giving him a wonderful view of the towers of Notre-Dame peeking from the Ile de la Cité and the great hill of Montmartre further on.

"This will do nicely. Thank you."

***

Victoria stood by the window overlooking the Rue des Archives. The light of the gas lamps from below and the crescent moon above bathed her flesh in alabaster. Regina, still lying on the bed in the apartment they had so recently acquired, didn't quite dare speak lest this one perfect moment end.

"They were going to tear this whole area down, you know." Victoria didn't turn when she spoke. "Haussmann and his ideas of perfect imperial architecture would have turned all of Paris into boulevards and esplanades. It's only his patron's fall that allowed the Marais to escape his plans."

Regina swallowed and held her tongue. From what she had seen in the past few nights, the renovations of Paris during the reign of Napoleon III, supervised by his master planner Baron Haussmann, had been a great success. Beautiful avenues cut through the city, opening it up in a way very much unlike the claustrophobia of London. The Marais, the neighborhood that housed the Hôtel de Guénégaud where they had taken an upstairs apartment, seemed a throwback to twisting medieval alleys with a patina of small manufactures crammed into courtyards and gutted old homes. In London, Victoria had once spoken to Regina with great wonder of the course of modernization of the city, but here she seemed nostalgic for the Paris of old.

"If only Jove would restore those bygone years…," Regina said, turning to Virgil to fill the silence in the small room.

"Alas, that is the one thing he never does." Victoria turned from the window and smiled, but wearily. A slight ruby tinge colored the light on her shoulders now, the very first hint of the coming dawn. "It is time for sleep."

She reached outside to close the heavy shutters, sealing them and the windows as well. She then pulled the heavy drapes to block out even the slightest bit of the coming daylight. Regina, still lying on the bed they shared, was plunged into pitch blackness and only vaguely thought of it as strange or troubling. Victoria was a being of the night and as long as Regina was by her side, so was she.

Victoria crossed the room to the bed in a few silent steps. Regina was only aware of her movement because of the slight silk-on-skin rustle of the other woman's gown falling away. Then, a sudden and delicious proximity, as Victoria's marble-cool and feather-soft flesh settled into hers.

The sun, Regina knew, was about to peek up over the eastern horizon and she felt Victoria slip into inanimate slumber. She followed a heartbeat later.

In the dream, Regina is but an observer. She watches, unable to act, as Victoria runs down the Rue du Temple, past the commandery of the Knights of Malta and deeper into the Marais. She is wearing the clothes of a bourgeoise, the wife of a merchant perhaps, but that is merely a cover, allowing her to move through the crowds of frondeurs *who have once again barricaded the streets.*

She has to get to Maximilien and bring him the news. Condé is undone, or soon to be, and Mazarin's soldiers will make them all pay. She cuts into an alley and heads toward the place where he has been lairing, within yards of the Hôtel de Ville. A knot of people appears down one street and she slips into the entry of a home to escape their view. Pressing herself against the wall, her breath comes in shallow gulps and her heart pounds a staccato rhythm.

Somehow Regina, observing without being present, realizes that Victoria breathing or having a heartbeat at all, is significant. Just why, however, she cannot remember right now.

Victoria makes a series of other turns, losing herself in the warren of alleys and streets until she finds the lair of the man she loves. It is down a tight spiral of stairs and into a cellar, where he is always safe from the sun and the risk of fire. The Fronde, the great revolt against the king and his ministers, has forced them into such cramped quarters for the duration, but it is a small price to pay.

"We shall be as kings and queens once our plans reach fruition," Maximilien had said, and she, the fool, had believed him.

Now, those plans and that safety are gone. Cardinal Mazarin's troops are counterattacking and, more terrible still, the Parisian night society is reestablishing its preeminence. Maximilien had said Prince Villon would either side with the Fronde or fall, but neither has occurred. The allies and patrons who were to abandon Villon did not, and his ghouls and loyalists are now making their way through the city eliminating all those who broke covenant with him. First among those to be set out for the sun is Maximilien d'Orsay, the once-kindred who schemed to overthrow his prince.

Victoria makes it all the way to the bottom of the stairs before she realizes that she may be too late. The door, always locked, is ajar. Without thinking she rushes in and takes in the scene: Maximilien lies prone on the ground, a large wooden shaft driven through his chest. Beside him, one man sits dead against the stone wall of the cellar, having apparently failed to keep his entrails from escaping through a gaping wound cut through his belly. Another man stands near her lover, his left arm hanging loose at his side, and his right clasped at his own neck. When he turns to see Victoria, she notes that it is pressing against a grievous wound; the left side of him is drenched in his own blood.

Victoria moves faster than she ever has before, the blood of her undead lover coursing through her living veins and giving her impossible strength and speed. Before the attacker can do more than gape, she crosses the space be-

tween them and plants his own blade into his gut. In shock, he drops his right hand from his neck and a stream of purplish blood flows from the torn vein there. Then he falls dead.

Victoria quickly moves to her lover and with a great pull, yanks the wooden stake from his heart. Regina, watching from some unseen place, is shocked to see him sit up. Victoria cradles him with one arm while she loosens the laces of her gown's bodice and frees her left breast. Maximilien's sharp teeth pierce the white flesh and draw in warm blood.

"Clotille says the prince knows all, my love. We must flee," she says.

"I... fought them off, Victorine," he says raising his mouth from her flesh. "We still have tasks ahead."

"There will be more of them, my love. There is a carter who will smuggle us out of the city. We can make for Holland. Luther will shelter us."

"But Martin," he says, his voice weak from the wounds that refuse to heal. "He is waiting on me."

"We have no choice, my love. You must escape. Anything is worth that."

Sometime in the afternoon, Regina woke from her diurnal slumber. Victoria was cold and dead beside her, a corpse stealing her warmth, but she loved her still.

This was not the first time she'd dreamt dreams that somehow belonged to the undead woman whose blood she had supped upon, but they had never been so clear before. Lying back in the bed, staring into the darkness that sheltered her, she fought to remember the details. Maximilien, who had been to Victoria as Victoria was to Regina herself. Victoria living, breathing, heart pounding, before her own undeath. How long ago?

Regina was no scholar of French history, but somehow the necessary information came to her, as if gleaned from the creature who shared her bed and had lived those nights. The Fronde. A revolt against the Cardinal Mazarin, chief minister of the French Sun King before he rose to manhood. A contemporary of the Stuart King Charles, who'd ruled England over two centuries ago.

"My God," Regina whispered, realizing that the creature beside her had last drawn breath before the Restoration. The cold grip of despair clutched her heart. God, she felt, was very far away indeed.

Chapter Nine

"Tout frais! Tout frais!"

Regina started at the sudden exclamation and turned around to see a fishmonger dropping a four-foot cod on a silvery pile of its fellows. Two men, restaurateurs most likely, moved up to examine the fish.

"Watch your step, dear girl," Victoria said, pointing to the greasy mess on the concrete before them. In the mad rush of this night market, spills were inevitable and the rats were already feasting on what seemed to be cow's brain.

The wholesale market of Les Halles certainly earned its reputation as the belly of Paris. Sheltered from the night sky by a great steel and glass construct that gave it the look of a train station without tracks, it was here that the chefs, tavern owners, restaurateurs, and small market owners came to buy their goods for the day. The huge sides of beef being carried from carts by men of such strength they were simply called *les forts*, would end up on the *menus du jour* across the great city. Such was also the fate of tons of cheese, vegetables, fruits, fish and every other foodstuff imaginable. Everywhere buyers and sellers were arguing over the freshness, quality and price of goods. Along the outside of the market, small bistros ran all night. It was raucous, smelly and chaotic—in other words, alive.

It was not where Regina expected to find one of the undead.

"This way," Victoria said, leading Regina past a mountain of sweet-smelling melons from Provence and toward one of the many bistros. "Come along."

They made their way into the tight confines of the seemingly nameless establishment and took the rearmost of the three tables. The *patron* came out from behind the small bar, with a carafe of wine. "Two?" he asked.

Victoria nodded and he disappeared into the kitchen, remerging seconds later with two piping bowls of onion soup. Regina had identified it even before he set the bowls down, smelling the rich odor of the thick steam. She couldn't remember the last time she'd had a good meal.

Regina remember her clandestine excursions into the Cairene *souq* as a young girl. Les Halles reminded her of that, although all of it taking place at night, so the customers could make their meals ready for the day. It was not all bistro owners and inn-keepers making the rounds, however. Well-dress men and women were appearing in larger and larger numbers.

"They're coming from the theater," Victoria said, indicating a group of men in evening suits. "Here for a last drink and soup before heading in. Or perhaps to find amusement for the rest of the night." As if on cue, one of the gentlemen caught the eye of a woman walking alone and after exchanging a few words, they headed toward the alleys off the marketplace.

"Are we to find my mother among prostitutes, then?"

"No, not directly." Victoria lifted a spoonful of soup to her lips but took none into her mouth. "I would, however, ask that you stop this constant needling. Emma is dear to me as well, and I do not need to be constantly reminded of our cause."

"I'm… My apologies, Miss Ash." Regina hated herself for the stammering apology. She was aware, on some distant level, that her connection to Victoria was unnatural, but that did not prevent her from feeling the woman's ire like a hot knife. It did not stop her urge to do whatever it took to assuage that anger. And it did not prevent her heart from soaring when she saw Victoria smile.

"Nonsense, Regina." Victoria lowered her spoon back into the soup. "I am the one who must seek forgiveness. Your concern for your mother is understandable, only my irritation at it needs pardoning."

Victoria's hand brushed against Regina's jaw line and she had to fight not to lean into that soft touch. The velvet of the other woman's glove was smooth as a fox pelt. She realized she was holding her breath and exhaled; it came out as a quiet sigh.

"There, there, my girl," Victoria said. "We are here to arrange an audience with some others of my kindred who call Paris home. Just as in London, there is a prince in the City of Lights, and we must present ourselves to him."

Regina struggled to focus on memories and not on the proximity of her mistress. It had only been ten days since, in London, she had finally found her mother at a gathering of the kindred—*the undead*, she scolded herself for using Victoria's euphemisms—of London. They had been gathered by the prince of that city, who used the name Mithras. That meeting had been traumatic in the extreme. The prince had said very little, but his chiseled perfection had been very much like staring directly into the sun; an experience of searing beauty Regina had no desire to repeat. "Is that necessary?"

"I wish it weren't, but it is. Perhaps if we were just passing through…" Victoria's voice trailed off as she stared into the bustling crowd outside the bistro. Soon a tall, wide, bearded man emerged from the masses of the marketplace and entered. "Ah, here we are."

"*Bonsoir, citoyennes,*" he said in a clear, baritone

voice. He took a third chair and sat at their table.

Regina was once more thankful for the time she'd spent in Cairo learning diverse languages. Her parents had supported her hunger for learning, perhaps as a way to keep her content in the colonial home without much to occupy her, and had cheered her on through lessons in Latin, Greek, French and even a smattering of German. The latter had been hardest to find a teacher in. The Kaiser's subjects had scant presence in Egypt at that time, certainly not much in comparison to her own compatriots or to the French, but she had insisted on obtaining some lessons from Herr Mueller, if only to allow her to work her way through a copy of Heinrich Schliemann's reports on the excavation of Troy.

"Or should I say," the man continued in French, "welcome, visitors? I was surprised to received your letter, Victorine."

"I now answer to Victoria, Martin." At least to Regina's inexpert ear, her French was perfect, a lilting Latinate melody of slightly nasal sounds and just barely rolled Rs. "Victorine has been buried for many years, now."

"Never forgotten by those who loved her, however." His smile was wistful, and strangely feminine. "It is good to see you, whatever your name."

"Thank you, Martin." Victoria turned slightly and seemed to relax, but Regina still felt an electric tension in her. "Martin Fleury, my protégée Regina Blake."

"Enchanté, mademoiselle."

Regina nodded slightly. Victoria had not used her full title—as the daughter of a viscount she was Lady Regina—but that could mean many things. France had a century of to-and-fro behind it on the question of aristocratic privilege and had emerged only seventeen years before from its second imperial experiment into revolutionary fervor and then a third republic. Fleury had, she noted, first addressed them as "citizens," a practice only widespread in the most revolutionary circles. Perhaps he was not one to appreciate titles. "A pleasure, *monsieur*."

"I have," Victoria said, "a favor to ask of you, Martin."

***

Othman ibn Saleh al-Masri stood on the public gallery of the Collège Militaire and marveled. Gray hairs now outnumbered black on his head and his beard was almost entirely white. He had seen many a marvel, both ancient and more modern. As a younger man he'd watched the workers, under French orders, dig the immense canal from Port Said to Suez and the Red Sea. Living in Cairo for most of his sixty-two years, he'd gazed up at the pyramids of Giza and their guardian the Sphinx more times than he could count. He'd walked the citadel of Saladin and prayed in the mosques of Ibn Tulun and Al-Muayyad. Architectural and engineering feats were nothing new to him, God be praised.

Still, the iron structure he saw rising at the end of the Champs de Mars, just on the edge of the River Seine, was breathtaking. Four great curving legs, made of crisscrossing steel girders, rose to a height of fifty meters and there were joined by a giant platform of similar construction. Thereupon was a hive of activity and a labyrinth of scaffolding, as an army of workers pushed the tower ever further skyward. According to the local press, this was to be the centerpiece of the Great Exposition coming to Paris the next year, a three-hundred-meter marvel designed by an engineer named Eiffel. The same press was filled with critiques and qualms about the tower. It was a blight on Paris, some said, a terrible defacing of the city. Others predicted it would never be completed in time for the exposition. Construction had only started the year before and it was self-evident (the critics said) that such a structure could never be finished in so short a time. To Othman it was clear just how mistaken these nay-sayers were. Like the Egyptians, the Arabs and the Turks before them, like the British at this very time, the French were making a mark on the world. Some of his friends from the madrasa might call this an affront to God, a sign of pride, but architecture had always been close to Othman's heart. It was a natural instinct of man to honor God in the wealth of civilization. The French had much to answer for in their dealings with Egypt, yes, but he would not begrudge them this.

"A cathedral for the industrial age, I think." The voice, dry but strong, came from a bent-backed man making his way along the edge of the self-same terrace. He wore the black frock of a Catholic priest and used for support a cane made of wood as gnarled as he was. "I wonder if they will put an altar in there."

"Father André?" Othman's French, learned as a boy in Port Said, was accented but correct.

"At your service," the man said, intimating a bow with a nod of his head. "Mister Saleh, I presume."

Othman had long ago understood that many Frenchmen, just like their English counterparts, had difficulty with Arabic names. The man's pronunciation was passable, but he had arbitrarily decided that Othman's patronymic would stand as a surname. Othman's policy was usually to provide polite correction on this point, but given the information he wanted from this priest, he decided to let it pass. There were matters of graver concern to discuss. "Your humble servant. I come seeking the wisdom of Leopold of Murnau."

"Come," said the priest, "we will walk and we will talk about the undead."

***

Regina Blake used the writing desk in the sitting room adjacent to the bedrooms in the apartment they'd taken in the Hôtel de Guénégaud. It had now been close to a month since she'd been in Victoria's exclusive company and she'd almost fully adopted the woman's nocturnal schedule. Today, however, she could not sleep the sunlight hours away. Victoria had not called for her as they retired for sleep near dawn, so she had slept in the largely unused bed of the adjoining room. Cedric, the coachman, slept further down the hall. After only a few hours, however, unfocussed anxiety had won out over fatigue. She'd dressed and wandered the apartment.

Victoria had not left the hotel the previous night and asked that neither Regina nor Cedric do so during the day either. What under most circumstances would be a luxurious set of suites had become a gilded cage, one that reminded Regina all too much of her time at Bernan House. That grand County Durham mansion was the Blake family home and the symbol of the sorry life that awaited her as the marriageable daughter of a viscount. The Hôtel de Guénégaud, like the house of Monsieur Alphonse in Calais, was becoming its nocturnal counterpart, the symbol of the limitations of her new life. These were now the walls she couldn't escape—not unless she was willing to forego her mother, and Victoria.

As she had many a time in County Durham, Regina Blake put pen to paper and reached out to her closest friend.

My darling Jo,

I owe you, more than anyone, the truth. By now, I imagine you are at wits end with worry for me. No doubt Father and Malcolm have done their best to keep what they know from you, and I'm sure that, being men and thus prone to underestimating women, they have failed.

I never lied to you, Joanna. The full truth of the situation in which I find myself only became clear to me that rain-soaked day when you found me at your doorstep. Before then, I had blinded myself to the fact that Miss Ash, my protector, was something more than I understood her to be.

I reread my own words and I hardly recognize them, Jo. Can I, who argued so vehemently for plain truth when we were girls, have fallen into such half-measures? Last spring we had discussed the fear that Mother had fallen victim to some grave robbery. The truth is far stranger: she has risen from her grave and walks again, a step between breathing life and peaceful death. Nor is she the only one. Miss Ash exists in this undead state as well, along with many others.

I hear your questions already, my darling Jo. Why do I stay with this creature? I wish I had a simple answer to provide you. Or rather, I wish I had a simple answer that was truthful, for it would be easy to say that we have come to Paris seeking

Mother, because I am convinced she has been drawn into her unnatural condition against her will, and I long to free her. But that is not the entire truth, nor entirely truthful.

No, for as I sit here in this finely appointed apartment, I am constantly aware of Miss Ash's presence in the next room. I know she lies insensate and will until the setting of the sun, and some part of me awaits that event with bated breath. Do you remember our girlish fantasies about Cleopatra? Sitting on the shore of the Nile itself and imagining that queen who brought Antony and Caesar to their knees? A beauty who made empires tremble? Victoria is just such a creature, Jo, and I fear to leave her.

At last, this pen that has been dissimulating the truth, reveals it. Fear, that is the core of my life now. I fear leaving Miss Ash's side, but I fear remaining as well. With every passing moment I feel myself slipping further into her orbit and I understand, with greater certainty, just how far removed one such as she is from life. She does not breathe, Jo, and she survives off the blood of the living, off my blood. If this is true of Victoria, is my hope to save Mother just folly?

Pray for me, Joanna, and know I have not forsaken you.

Yours with love,

Ginny

The latest note, like the previous ones, had simply appeared on the desk of one of the brothers. Thomas Ventimiglio found it lying there in the morning, when he entered the library he shared with his three siblings overlooking the Rue du Chemin Vert on the Right Bank. They had made sure to lock all the doors and even taken the precaution to bar the windows on the third floor, but still whoever their benefactor was, he had no trouble stealing inside to leave his troubling notes.

The Ventimiglio brothers were all natives of the Parisian region, their father Benito having moved from Lombardy during the Second Empire. Thomas, the eldest, was twenty-two years old. Alain, the youngest, was seventeen. Benito Ventimiglio had died during the Commune, while Alain was still in his mother's womb, when the revolutionaries took out their frustrations on a priest of his acquaintance. Benito died defending a man of the cloth.

His widow, Adriana, raised her sons to honor their father's memory and to continue the tradition of service. Alain was baptized in Chartres, under the watchful eye of Father André Desosiers, a man of faith and fire. Adriana succumbed to tuberculosis in 1879, leaving the brothers as orphans. Father André saw to it that they were taken in to a church-run house and taught the illustrious history of their family.

Thomas and Alain—along with their brothers Christophe and Julien—learned that Ventimiglio men had served as soldiers in a secret army of Christ for generations. Their forefathers had been templars and their relatives remained Knights of Malta, Father André revealed. But their most sacred heritage was to stand against the devils who hid in the shadows, preying on the faithful. The Third Republic prided itself on reason and science, not superstition and religiosity, but the Ventimiglio boys were sons of the church through and through, and as Father André revealed the secret war a chosen few had waged throughout history, it never occurred to them to doubt. The armies of Satan were everywhere getting stronger, using the mask of rationality and pragmatism to erode the protective influence of Mother Church.

For the five years leading to the spring of 1888, the brothers had entered the fray one by one, becoming the strong arms of Father André. They had become soldiers in the Society of Leopold, a loose confederation of clerics and laymen dedicated to fighting back against the darkness. Actual confrontations with evil had been relatively few in those five years. Several debased men and women had suffered at the Ventimiglio brothers' hands and they felt confident they had broken up several covens of witches and dark spiritualists. In 1886, Father André had sent them to Bayeux and they had faced *something* in an abandoned house overlooking the Norman beaches. Thomas still woke nights with the image of a bone-white face dissolving into smoke.

So when the first of the notes had appeared, the brothers were not entirely unprepared. It was in a ragged handwritten script and declared: *A devil lurks in the cellar of the Auberge des Trois Moutons. Behind the siren.* Thomas and Christophe went to visit that inn on a Sunday afternoon. While his younger brother distracted the women tending the small desk with his fetching smile, Thomas crept deeper into the inn and found the cellars. In the rearmost, he spied a door painted with a faded advertisement for a brand of spring water that showed a mermaid drinking from a bottle.

The door was shut but he made quick work of the lock and found, in the storage closet beyond, what appeared to be the corpse of a young boy lying on a small cot. Unsure exactly what to do, he took the boy's cold body in his arms and headed upstairs.

Madness ensued. Partway up the stairs, the boy-thing suddenly woke from its death-like torpor and bared terrible fangs. The smell of cooking hair and flesh filled the air and Thomas, startled, pushed the thing away. It began to scream wildly. Meanwhile, the woman at the desk rushed into the room with a look of sheer terror on her face, as if this thing were her own flesh and blood. She grabbed it and covered it with her not-inconsiderable girth, but the screaming did not stop. In fact, it grew worse as the woman joined in.

Thomas and Christophe, who'd followed her in, saw why she wailed: the child-thing was clawing and gnashing its way into her flesh. She fell back and it used bloody nails and teeth, all needle-sharp, to dig into her chest. Thomas and Christophe had brought large knives and they used them to hack at the thing. Its flesh burned even after they split its skull in twain, filling the sun-drenched room with the smell of cooked skin and bone.

When the second note came, almost a month later, they were better prepared and since then had responded to each mysterious warning with military precision. Julien had been seriously wounded by a devil in the skin of a beautiful woman in June, and that had made them more cautious still. With the fourth—the most recent—they had doused the stairs leading up to the thing's apartment with whale oil and simply burned it out.

Thomas opened this new, fifth note, and read it aloud: "Devils live in the Café Thériaux, Montmartre." Thomas smiled. Alain had been speaking of the potential of black powder. Perhaps it was time to let him experiment.

Chapter Ten

They alighted from a carriage at the eastern end of the Place de la Concorde, one of the great squares of Paris. In its center stood the Luxor Obelisk, given to French King Louis Philippe by the Egyptian Viceroy fifty years ago. Regina had long hoped to see it in the flesh, and that she was at last doing so under the present circumstances only darkened her mood further. The grand square stretched between two long gardens, and formed a central point of an impressive axis that was clearly visible even at night. Gas and electric lights created a series of dotted lines heading off to the west, beyond the obelisk and along the sweeping boulevard of the Champs-Elysées toward Napoleon's towering triumphal arch. On the other side, on the path that Victoria, Martin and she were following, stretched the famed Tuileries Gardens and the Louvre Palace beyond it.

"It's as if the palace had never been there," Victoria said, her voice a hush.

"Ha!" Martin exclaimed. "You always had an attraction for that gilded façade. Personally, I think it's opened up the space, and anyway the fire was glorious."

They were discussing, Regina realized, the destruction of the Tuileries Palace that had once stood at the head of the gardens, between it and the Louvre proper. It had been Napoleon III's residence and seat of power—and suffered the wrath of the crowds during the communard uprisings at the beginning of the last decade. There was, indeed, hardly a sign of it.

"Was there no talk of reconstruction?"

Regina could practically feel the nostalgia waft from Victoria. She remembered their shared dream and wondered again what it must be like to see again a city one had known in another century.

"There wasn't much to rebuild, my dear. The boys of the Commune did their burning quite thoroughly. We were treated to the happy display of the blackened shell of the place until they tore it down a few years ago, though. Prince Villon wanted a clear view, I think."

The gardens were of that particularly French manicured style, all geometric shapes and right angles. Past the open, pebble-strewn first square (dominated by one of many large fountains) there spread out a forest's worth of trees arranged in a military order, forming perfect lines that marched toward the east where the burned palace once stood. Gaslights added to the rectilinear aspect, each point of luminescence forming one spot in a string of mathematical precision. Regina couldn't help but draw a comparison with Hyde Park, London's great public garden, with its naturalistic body of water and looping avenues. She had thought it ordered and tended, but the Tuileries showed what true, cold precision was. London seemed much more living, all of a sudden.

Instead of heading into the square and the mathematical woods beyond it, Martin headed south, where other lines of well-trimmed trees arced around the square. A sloping path led toward the central fountain, but he skirted it, heading instead for a long building standing between the gardens and the quays along the Seine. Once in the semi-privacy created by the building's shadow, he stopped and turned to Regina. "Tell me about your mother, Miss Blake."

Victoria tried to cut in. "I've already explained it all—"

"I wish to hear it in her words, my dear." His smile was hard. "Monsieur Villon and his entourage well remember my actions during the Commune. This is hardly a time when I would like to stick my neck into the guillotine."

"Then, by all means, find another person willing to introduce you in London once our business is complete," Victoria said. "I think you'll find Lady Anne and Lord Mithras even less welcoming of petty revolutionaries."

"There was a time when you didn't think our cause petty, Victorine," he said with cold disdain.

Regina felt a jolt of anger rise in her heart, a reflection of the same feeling boiling in Victoria, who spoke with barely restrained emotion. "And just how much have your grand principles accomplished, exactly?"

Martin's own anger was winning out and his voice, which had been quiet and melodious, became shrill. "More than any of the games Maximilien had—"

"Please!" Regina said. "It's all right. I'll explain myself. Lady Emma, my mother, became one of your kindred last Christmastide, in our home in County Durham."

"Yes…" Martin still had an edge in his voice, but it was losing its sharpness.

"I did not know it at the time, but her family is tied to the House Tremere, which I believe is a special case among your kind, yes?"

"Quite. Go on."

"With Miss Ash's assistance, I tracked down my mother last month in London, where I also met a certain Anton Wellig, the man who had…"—what was the right word?—"*remade* her. It became clear to me that she was no willing participant in the night society. She was his slave."

"For what purpose?"

"I do not know precisely, but nothing beneficial to her soul, I'm sure." Regina held back some details in her recital, of course. She had seen Wellig enact some dark art with her mother's blood, summoning London's Prince Mithras and even subjugating that creature's infinite will for a few moments. She felt those details were best left unsaid, however.

"And you seek to free your mother from this bondage?"

"Yes. Yes, I do."

He looked sidelong at Victoria but continued to address Regina. "That will not be easy, my girl. These Tremere warlocks are a dangerous lot, more so even than revolutionaries among the undead." A smile.

Regina released a breath she had been holding, feeling the danger pass.

Victoria spoke then. "And will this particular revolutionary help us, then?"

"At your service, *mesdemoiselles*." He bowed slightly and waved a hand back toward the main path into the Tuileries Gardens.

The walk from there to the Louvre Palace passed without Regina noting much other than the uncomfortably persistent memory of Martin's anger. Although he seemed to have become an amiable host once more, she could still feel echoes of the tension he had caused in her. It reminded her of her first nights venturing into London's night society last spring. In mere moments, these benighted souls could pass from intoxicating charm to terrifying rage, and it was all too easy to become their plaything. It was easier now that she could focus on her truer bond to Victoria, but the danger was still there.

She barely noted the manicured gardens, cast into lush green shadows by the combination of trees and gas lamps. The gurgling of fountains did no better to attract her attention and before she knew it, Martin and Victoria were leading her under the small triumphal arch that marked the entry to the great courtyard framed on three sides by wings of the Louvre Palace.

Regina had spent much of her life flouting the all-too-common sentiment that education should be the purview of the male sex. Although she had only limited formal schooling, her father and mother had provided tutors while in Egypt and she had avidly devoured libraries' worth of reading. Her especial love was the classical world, that period of Hellenistic flourishing when art, philosophy and statecraft seemed to have reached an imperfect but unmatched symbiosis. In fact, her secondary affection for the Italian Renaissance masters had much to do with their own love of the Greeks. Thus, when she and her companions entered the long gallery that ran along the Seine and formed the southern wing of the palatial complex, she knew to expect one of the important art collections of the world. For nearly a century, the Louvre had been the premier museum of Paris, displaying the great collections gathered by centuries of monarchs and occasional revolutions. Nevertheless, the sight of it left her breathless.

The gallery was essentially one enormous long room. Gas lamps and candelabras cooperated to push back the nighttime gloom, reflecting off the gilded arching roof some thirty feet above the ground. The two walls were completely crowded with paintings big and small, seemingly designed to interlock in just such a way as to leave not a square inch bare. Only the marble columns framing doors and windows interrupted the resulting mosaic of oil and canvas.

The hall itself dwarfed the people within it, but

they were there nonetheless. Martin led the way down the polished marble floor—reaching from wall to wall and all the way down the gallery, a surface larger than some London streets—and a manservant dressed in the manner of the previous century emerged from a side entrance to meet him.

Martin didn't stop, simply muttering, "Monsieur Fleury and guests." The servant bowed deeply in the overly stylized manner of his country, one stocking-and-hosed leg slipping behind the other and his head leaning deeply toward the ground. Martin, for his part, never broke pace.

There were others in the hall, including a few groups who seemed occupied with the admiration of one of the great canvases or another. A huge piece depicting bare-breasted Liberty on revolutionary battlements seemed to have attracted a few art aficionados, but Regina had the distinct impression they were more interested in watching to see who would come down the hall than in the merits of Monsieur Delacroix's brushstrokes. There were also other servants, universally dressed in throwback attire featuring ruffles and powdered wigs, most simply standing at their positions. Once, a man came calmly into the gallery from one of the tall doors leading into the central courtyard, carrying a silver platter with a sealed letter upon it. Regina was trailing her kindred guides by a good twenty paces by this time and the messenger passed within a few feet of her. He never acknowledged her presence or even glanced her way and she was left with the distinct impression that he might well have walked straight into her had she had the misfortune to block his way.

The gallery finally ended in heavy wooden doors, which two more automaton-like footmen opened as

Martin and Victoria approached. Regina caught up with them and slipped into the large, opulent lobby beyond. Made of the white limestone so common in Parris, the great room featured a broad staircase leading up to the second floor of the palace proper, as well as doors into other galleries. Artwork was present here as well, but in less ostentatious quantities than in the great hall they had just left. Instead, the beauty here was mainly architectural, the light walls contrasted with the polished brown-marble columns that held up archways framing the staircases. The floor, of a lighter marble with something of a pink tinge, picked up the light from hanging chandeliers, which also played off the classically inspired recessed statues overlooking the main landing. Regina had the impression of entering a Grecian temple and had to suppress a gasp.

"Bonaparte's architects had a flair for the monumental," Martin said, "even in staircase design."

"It's beautiful," Regina said, but Martin had already started to climb toward the first landing.

"Yes," Victoria said, "that it is." She placed her hand on the small of Regina's back to move her along as well, and the two women began their ascent.

Unlike the largely silent gallery, broken only by their own steps and the whispers of the few art appreciators, the stairs were redolent with sound—and with something more. The sounds began with the murmur-like din of too many whispers and resolved into a dozen overlapping conversations. The top of the stairs led to a large and open room, another gallery, although in the classical style of the lobby it overlooked. There, as many as fifty people were scattered about in small cliques, exchanging glances with each other and speaking with their compatriots.

But it was the tension under the conversations that

caught Regina's attention. It felt like the pregnant moment between the flash of lightning and the rumble of thunder, a time of absolute silence and impending roar. Regina felt the fine hairs on her arms and neck rise in anticipation of some danger unseen but still present.

Victoria felt it too and was scanning the room, searching for its source. Regina wondered just how the sensation had communicated itself between her and Victoria. Had this undead woman sensed her own unease? Or had it been the reverse—Victoria's awareness leaking into Regina's veins through the medium of the dark, cold blood she had sipped in Calais? And did the distinction really matter?

With no answers forthcoming, Regina concentrated her attention outward. Martin led Victoria and her toward one corner of the great room, where a white-marble Demeter gazed from an alcove between two dark-hued columns. Their position was not random, she intuited from the gaze of the sternly dressed clutch of women gathered around a divan set near a large window. The various cliques were ordered, although just how eluded her.

In London, Victoria had spent the summer guiding Regina through the layers of the night society. The girl had developed a sense of the social relations there, picking up on subtle cues and patterns of behavior over the course of several weeks and countless balls and soirées. She'd developed a working theorem of social behavior among the undead, in which those of lesser status seemed to orbit about those of greater status. Rivals took up opposite positions in a sort of gravitational balance. It had its limits as far as social models went, but it had served Regina well up to this point.

This gathering operated, she felt, by some other law. What had first seemed like static cliques quickly revealed themselves to be restless packs of some sort. As in London, kindred and their hangers-on seemed to share some traits in common—here men and women of archaic, aristocratic beauty; there groups of soldiers or sailors. She was very much aware that Miss Ash wore a beautiful black-rose cameo on her breast, which was mirrored in the one around Regina's neck and the ring on Cedric's finger. The lines of patronage seemed less strong, here, however. Individuals moved from one group to another, and in fact, no one seemed to stay still for very long. The more Regina paid attention, the more furtive glances, sudden tics and clenched fists she saw.

An image of caged predators played itself in her mind's eye. She was very much aware that she was potential prey wandering into this menagerie where she knew neither the lengths nor the strengths of the beasts' chains. Fear clenched at her guts and she covered it with words.

"They're afraid," she said in a low whisper. "Every one of them is afraid of something."

Victoria and Martin both glanced at her then. Although they wore nearly identical looks of almost-suppressed shock, she sensed pride behind Victoria's eyes as well.

"You always had exquisite taste, Victorine," Martin said. "It is uncouth of me to mention it here," he added, turning to Regina, "but I fear you have arrived at a difficult time for our fair city."

Nearly an hour later, the various footmen—all dressed in that same Ancien Régime style—heralded the arrival of their lord, François Villon, Prince of Paris and the Ile-de-France. They did so not with words, but with silent, subtle movement. One second they were all scattered around the room, each positioned as discreetly as possible. The next they had all turned to face, quite exactly, the hall's southern doors. It was as if each were a compass point suddenly and simultaneously finding true north. A moment later, the great oaken doors opened and Prince Villon glided in.

He was neither particularly large nor particularly small and he still managed to swipe the breath from Regina's lungs. He was not beautiful, at least not in the way Victoria was or Mithras of London had been when Regina had seen him at the beginning of the month. The monarch of the English undead had been male perfection, Apollo descended from Olympus to play his games. Where Mithras had been divine, Villon was sublime.

The French prince's wonder was in his movement, which elicited in Regina a sort of vertigo. Concentrating on him, she felt he moved slowly, languidly like a lover dawdling at his woman's bed. Every time she blinked, though, he was much closer than sense said he had any right to be. A distant part of her brain recognized some symptoms from her past exposure to the undead—others had been intoxicating in appearance, and she had once witnessed Victoria move quite literally faster than the eye could see—but those were quiet whispers among a storm of sensation. His beauty, she realized, was like that of a knife—cold, deadly and all –too enticing. In a benighted world where everyone wore masks of civility and station, she felt she might see straight into Prince Villon's soul.

She had the distinct impression that he had none at all.

He ceased his approach a good fifteen paces from them and although he looked in their direction, his lack of interest was so palpable that Regina had to resist the urge to glance behind her to see if he might be looking at someone or something else. Martin bowed only slightly but Victoria curtseyed, so Regina emulated her, although a beat late. The prince acknowledged this only in that he turned away and glided on to others. Their presentation was over, without a word being spoken.

Regina only noticed how silent the entire room had become in his presence when she heard her own exhalation.

None of them spoke until they had made their way back down the stairs, along the great gallery, and out into the Tuileries Gardens. Regina broke the silence. "What did you mean an 'unpleasant' time?"

He gave a ghoulish smile. "Why, child, someone has taken to hunting Parisian vampires."

***

The Parisian chapter house of the Society of Leopold, where Father André Desosiers agreed to lead Othman al-Masri a few days after their encounter at the Champs de Mars, was on the very chic Ile St-Louis. This small isle in the heart of the city was only a few hundred yards long and was just upriver from the somewhat larger Ile de la Cité. This last was quite literally the heart of the metropolis, the island where men had lived since Gaulish times. And it was there that the famous Cathedral of Nôtre-Dame rose in all its gothic splendor. Crossing the Pont de la Tournelle from the Left Bank to the Ile St-Louis, it was impossible for Othman not to gape at the cathedral. Seeing the great structure from the back, he could not admire its beautiful façade, true, but he instead was granted a view of its flying buttresses and the marvelous stained glass windows they permitted. Othman was a Mohammedan, but the very architecture spoke of the proximity of God, hallowed be His name. The rising steel of the Eiffel Tower seemed somehow lessened by this structure built before the age of industry.

The elderly priest had met him on the quay near the bridge. When Othman arrived, he had been haggling with a bookseller and vociferously accusing the man of being a Freemason. Father André had left the man's wooden kiosk with only one of the three slim tomes he'd been examining and so great was his consternation that he seemed oblivious to the religious wonder of the cathedral. "Damn that boy's eyes," he grumbled. "No respect."

The chapter house itself was in the shadow of the Church of St. Louis, tucked within one of the many quaint courtyards so characteristic of Parisian residential buildings, especially among the well-to-do. Father André used an iron key to unlock the gates keeping out the riffraff and the two men slipped in between the building façades and into the courtyard. The chapter house's door gave onto this little plaza and Othman wondered just what the neighbors who spied through their windows thought of the strange assemblage entering Number 12b Rue des Deux Ponts. *Perhaps this shadowy society owns the entire complex*, he thought as they ascended the tight stairs from the building's front hall and entered the second floor parlor.

Father André crossed to a large desk in the corner of the room and used another key to open a drawer. He fished around a bit and then brandished a stack of envelopes bound with string. "Your letters," he said. "I saved them all."

Indeed, Othman recognized the ivory envelopes he had used when writing to the enigmatic priest to whom his now-departed friend and ally Brother Nicholas had referred him. "I must confess," he said, "that your own letters remain in Cairo, under the protection of an ally."

The priest sat in a tall-backed chair near his desk before speaking again. "Brother Nicholas was too kindhearted for our calling, I think, but I valued his opinion. He spoke very well of you."

"Thank you. He had many compliments for you and your brothers in the Society," Othman answered.

"Good, now that the pleasantries are out of the way, let us hear your story."

Othman took a seat and began his recitation. "Emma, the Lady Blake, was a dear friend of mine in Cairo for several years. I instructed her children and spent many happy hours in discussions with her husband. It is my impression the Lady Blake, who died last winter, has risen from her grave."

"That," André said calmly, "is quite an impression, sir."

"I do not make it lightly. Lord Blake sent me a series of telegrams, speaking of being haunted by his departed lady wife. He also has received reports that her grave stood empty as early as last December."

"And you come to me for assistance in finding this damned soul?"

"Quite. I owe Lord and Lady Blake a great deal and I cannot stand idly by—"

"You realize," André interrupted, "that this woman must be destroyed? Sent back to her grave to face her maker?"

Othman swallowed. "Yes."

Chapter Eleven

The cabriolet Cedric had acquired headed south from the river and into the Montparnasse quarter. The crossroads with the quarter's eponymous boulevard roiled with activity despite the late hour, and the evidence of a burned-out building a little further down the street. Raucous music, banged out on a piano, came from two different open-air dance halls competing for patrons. Women in long skirts and men in pantaloons twirled and jumped to the tunes, to the cheers and laughter of those looking on, wine mugs in hand. Not even the beggars orbiting the crowd approached the carriage, however.

In the nights since their visit to the Louvre, Victoria and Regina had made a habit of visiting the city. The contrast with the weeks of virtual imprisonment in Calais and their first nights in Paris was stark, and Regina felt no small amount of regret for the lamentations she'd expressed to Joanna in her letter. She would have to write her again, she knew, to rectify that overreaction. They had thus far spent much of their time in the great gardens, squares and boulevards that Victoria had seemed so averse to at first. At night, these well-lit, well-ordered spaces were never quite unpopulated and although their interactions were limited to a few nods, Regina guessed she and Victoria were seeing parts of Paris's own night society, almost edging into its midst. She only hoped they would not take so long that all hope of finding her mother would be lost.

Regina stretched her neck to gaze at the lively crowd and felt the pulse of their festivities. She had only ever attended proper dances, but the scandal of nocturnal dance halls seemed an innocent transgression in light of the occult world she was uncovering. They were in all likelihood heading for the nearby Luxembourg Gardens for another nocturnal stroll and restrained interaction with Victoria's Parisian kindred. There every step would be controlled, masking the violence of undeath. Here, the dancers brimmed with life and expressed it with open glee. Regina longed to make that her own, to lose herself in their abandon.

"Are you looking to join the festivities, Regina?" Victoria sat deep in the carriage, away from the street and the people milling about.

"I— That is, no, of course not." Regina turned back to face her companion, although her ears caught the last crescendo of a dance and the accompanying hoots of delight from the crowd. "It's simply that, well, there's something attractive about life lived with such abandon."

"Be careful, Regina, lest you delude yourself. They may dance tonight, but they will toil tomorrow. Or beg."

"Yes, you're right. But they seem so happy just for the evening. It's intoxicating."

Victoria smiled at that, but said no more. The cabriolet continued along a large enclosed space, separated from the street by a tall wall of brick and plaster. Through a gate halfway down the barrier, Regina spied the shadows of gravestones. A slight mist seemed to hang over the night-darkened gravel paths separating squares of thin trees and sparse tombs, adding to the contrast with the cabarets only a few hundred yards behind them.

They circumnavigated the graveyard, which an engraved sign proclaimed the Cimetière Montparnasse. Several small gates along the east wall and a large opening on the southern façade gave Regina several more views of the burial grounds. It was, she thought, a macabre reflection of Paris itself. Well-groomed and rectilinear carriage paths lined by rows of low trees evoked the grand boulevards, while the tightly packed tombs reminded her of the bustling crowds. Indeed, each tomb seemed to be trying to outdo all others, with cherubs and angels abutting against obelisks and colonnades. The French did not abide by the reserved mortuary habits of Anglicans, it seemed.

"They've been moving the dead about since Napoleon's time," Victoria commented. "The old graveyards were too full, I imagine, so they've taken to building new ones or finding other creative ways to store the remains."

Regina let that last comment go without a response, knowing Victoria had more to say.

"Right here will do, Cedric." Victoria's quiet command to her mulatto coachman and valet brought the cabriolet to a halt before a house on the Rue Gassendi. The Left Bank had undergone less of the characteristic transformations of the Second Empire, so the streets here were not quite the straight avenues of the Opéra and others in the wealthier districts. Late at night and still close to the looming specter of the graveyard, even the street people of Paris seemed to have avoided this particular corner. There was no one to witness them but a stray cat mewling in an alley.

"I received a message last evening," Victoria said at last. "An invitation."

"We've been making ourselves known over the last few nights, I take it," Regina said. "Waiting for someone to approach us?"

Victoria smiled. "I have fewer and fewer secrets from you, my dear. I'd hoped an old acquaintance would get in touch, and she has."

"Why not seek this person out?" Regina asked. "As you went to Monsieur Fleury."

"I was unsure Clotille would welcome me."

"And now?"

Victoria smiled and descended from the carriage onto the cobblestone street. When, a few seconds later, Regina followed, they both headed into the alley with its feline guardian. Victoria only paused to give instructions to Cedric. "Wait for us here. We won't be long."

The alley, which Regina had thought only a short passage into a courtyard, quickly revealed itself to be the mouth of a veritable warren of hidden passages. She was put to mind of the Cairene *souq* she'd explored with such verve (and so scandalously) as a child, although the dingy limestone façades and the wet smell of waste here compared disfavorably to the sun-bright baked stone and spiced air of the Egyptian marketplace. Nevertheless, she knew well that these alleys could hide a great deal, and strained to see in the gloom. Once again, Victoria had neglected to provide illumination and although her preternatural eyes guided her easily in the half-light, Regina had to proceed with more caution than grace.

The dingy tabby who had greeted them at the alley's mouth seemed to find Regina's stumbling progress noteworthy. The cat circled the two-legged intruders, sometimes seeming to lead the way, at other times darting behind them to pursue some unseen prey. Regina, trying simultaneously not to fall into some puddle of wastewater, to be on the lookout for the aggressors who might be behind every corner, and to remain only a few steps behind Victoria, soon lost all sense of direction. She stole a gaze up at the stars winking in the small band of sky between the three- and four-story buildings around, but the constellations were of no help. Her brother Daniel had been the astronomer in the family, not her. Allowing herself a rare sigh of frustration, she looked back into the alley— and straight into a cloud of bloated, buzzing flies.

There was no warning. One moment she was looking up toward the sliver of sky and the next, the drone of tiny wings was filling her ears and dozens of round, heavy insectile bodies were pelting her exposed flesh. Drunk on some unknown diet, the fattened things landed on her neck, cheeks and face. They crawled toward her mouth, eyes and into her ears. She screamed and they flew into her mouth, causing her to choke and retch violently.

"Don't move!" Victoria's crisp voice, sudden as a whip-crack, chilled Regina. In a way both familiar and profoundly disconcerting, she felt the order in her very blood and flesh. Her muscles seized with the overriding desire to obey that imperative, the revulsion of the cloud of plague-flies be damned.

Regina forced herself to take shallow, even breaths between pursed lips. The tiny feet were like a thousand fine hairs growing on her, moving into the collar of her cloak and the sleeves of her dress. Panic and resolution both tugged at her. Desperate for any sense other than the crawling of the vermin, she forced open one eye. She instantly wished she hadn't.

Victoria was gone. Not absent, but the graceful beauty she had come to love stood transformed by a coating of black, roiling things. Light from some window-sill lantern cast a wan glow on the thousands of flies that had landed on her, becoming a second, diseased skin. Regina knew she too must be covered, but somehow the metamorphosis of that perfect alabaster flesh into a nest for a hive of vermin struck her even more deeply. She wanted nothing more than to grab Victoria by the hand and run away. But she had been told not to move.

Victoria, she realized, *was* moving. Despite the fact that she was capable of astonishing alacrity, she was walking carefully forward, acting as calm as a lady strolling in the park. Her hand dropped to her side, and without being asked, Regina knew to take it and step forward with her protector. A dozen slow, agonizing strides took them to a low door at the bottom of three steps from the alley proper. Victoria put her other hand on the latch.

"Have we passed your little test, Clotille?" Victoria's voice was quiet, barely a whisper above the buzzing flies, but it had its effect. After a few pregnant seconds, Victoria depressed the latch, swung the door inward, and all the flies took off into the gloom within.

Regina, suddenly released, let out a breath she hadn't known she'd been holding, and shook with a terrible shiver. "My Lord…"

"Prepare yourself," Victoria said. "There's worse to come."

The darkened entrance led into a dingy room with an open trapdoor in one corner. Victoria reached into her handbag and fished out a tallow candle, a small candlestick, and a box of matches. She lit the pale white thing and handed it to Regina. "You will need this."

I could have used it before, Regina thought, somewhat petulantly. *Maybe the flame would have kept the flies at bay.* She swallowed and realized that was possibly why she hadn't been given a candle before. Victoria stepped down the carved stone staircase that led from the trap door and Regina followed.

The stairs were extremely precarious. Descending

at a steep angle and in a tight spiral, they were slick with the cloying moisture of the underground. Twice, Regina stumbled and came close to falling. Victoria never wavered. The descent seemed to last an eternity, each circumference of the central stone pillar bringing the two women deeper into the underbelly of the city.

"There are miles of quarries under the streets of the Left Bank," Victoria said. "The city hollowed itself of limestone to feed its own growth. There's now an endless warren of tunnels that most Parisians are unaware of."

The staircase ended in a small, curving passage and if quarrymen had once carried limestone blocks through here, Regina had a hard time understanding how. The candle she held cast a wan light over a few feet of roughly carved stone and she had the distinct impression of movement just beyond that periphery of light. A few twists and turns later, the cramped passage opened up into a large open space, and Regina understood they had entered through an ancillary passage.

The main quarry was a towering space that swallowed the light of her candle and the echoes of her footfalls. She caught the suggestion of a curving roof several dozen feet above their heads and she had no hint of a far wall. This might be a large underground room or the beginnings of a broad tunnel running under Montparnasse and beyond. There was no way to tell, although the candle flickered in a light wind that indicated at least one other access to the surface.

"No light," came a sudden, raspy voice. Regina had just a moment to see a gnarled face before it blew out the small flame and darkness swallowed all. That moment was enough, however, to resuscitate the horror of the flies. The skin on that skull-like face was drawn and leathery, scarred by pox and boils. Its jaundiced eyes goggled from its head, pupils shrunk down to pinpricks. Its teeth, which Regina had glimpsed as it spoke that single order, were a snaggled mess of black and gray.

"Clotille," Victoria said. "Do we really need to play such games?"

The withered answer came from Regina's left and she felt the cold wind of sour breath on her neck. "Games are all that keep us sane," it said.

Regina wondered just how this cave-dwelling thing defined sanity.

"How very poetic of you, but I had hoped to avoid such histrionics here of all places." If Victoria was frightened, or even just nervous, she hid it very well. Her voice was a cool melody in the dank air, a calming lifeline for her companion. "If you are interested only in terrifying my protégée, then perhaps we had better leave."

A stillness followed, in which Regina had the impression of standing on the edge of an unseen abyss. And indeed, for all she knew, there was some medieval oubliette mere inches in front of her. Was it just her imagination, or was there a slight, dank breeze coming from that direction? Feeling panic rise in her heart again, she concentrated on keeping her breathing even and remaining still.

The sickly orange of a dirty oil lamp bloomed a few yards further into the catacomb and their hostess came into view. Dressed in a robe of gray linen, like a penitent monk of another age, her womanhood was only the vaguest suggestion of bony hips and slight breasts. A hood covered her face in shadow, but Regina remembered all too well the twisted horror that hid beneath. The wan light failed to illuminate much of the floor, and the sense of a yawning chasm still hung in the dank air.

"Why are you here, Victorine?" Her voice remained a grave whisper. "Tell me, then leave."

"I need your assistance, Clotille." Victoria's voice had lost its scorn but Regina could feel her revulsion like a vague aftertaste of bile—or was that Regina's own?

"What of it?"

Victoria crossed the distance between Clotille and herself in a half-dozen slow steps. Despite the uneven masonry of the catacomb, she moved with the grace of a prima ballerina. "We were once friends, Maximilien, you and I," she said once she was mere inches from the wretched woman. "I had thought we could still be."

Victoria placed her fine hand into the dark hood, presumably cupping Clotille's cheek or neck. The other woman's body language communicated the potency of this touch as she leaned into the hand like an orphan receiving its first, much-belated motherly love.

Revulsion, jealousy and anger fought a battle in Regina's stomach and the hint of bile became altogether obvious. Pins and needles bloomed just behind her cheekbones and she was certain she was going to be sick. How could Victoria bare to *touch* that thing?

"I remember," Victoria continued in a soft almost-whisper, "when there were no parts of Paris that could keep a secret from Clotille la Mouche. I cannot believe this is no longer true."

"Villon is not fond of sewer rats," Clotille said in a faraway voice.

"Tsk." Victoria removed her hand. "Prince Villon is madder than ever. Lost in his orgiastic pleasures, no doubt."

"You would know," Clotille said and Regina knew she was suddenly very much part of the conversation.

"Protégés and slaves are different things, Clotille," Victoria said. "Lady Regina is here because she requested my assistance, not to satisfy my own whims."

Regina crossed the shadowed room to join the two kindred women. She still dreaded an unseen gap, but the impulse to not be left aside was greater than her phobia. She made it to them without incident. "That's right," she said.

Clotille turned to face the newcomer in their circle. "And what do you then need my help with, little English rose?"

Regina swallowed, suddenly self-conscious of her accented French. Still, she told the reason for their arrival in Paris as simply as she could.

Victoria filled in a few additional details. "Monsieur Alphonse confirms that Lady Blake and Mr. Wellig came to Paris from Calais, but we have lost the trail here."

"This Wellig is a blood sorcerer, then?"

"Yes," Regina said.

"There is no guarantee they are still in Paris, you understand," Clotille said. This was a concern of Regina's, as well.

"Of course," Victoria answered. "In fact, I expect they are headed elsewhere, but I thought you might be able to uncover exactly where."

"I might," the wretch said. This had become, Regina realized, a negotiation—or had always been.

"And were there ever something I could do for you," Victoria said, "I would be happy to."

"You left us, you know." Clotille's tone took on a touch of its ire again. "You and Maximilien left the rest of us to pick up the pieces of your glorious revolt."

Regina sensed, through that strange conduit between them, rage roiling in Victoria's gut. Still, she showed precisely none of it, and instead sounded contrite. "I know," she said. "It must have been very difficult for you, Martin and the rest."

"Spare me your sympathy."

"Apologies never solve much among our kind, Clotille, but I hope you can understand that we had very little choice. The prince's men were going to stake Maximilien for the sun. We had to escape."

"He wasn't the only one to face Villon's ire. My Lucas burned for his role in the Fronde."

Victoria's suppressed anger was gone, replaced by genuine sadness. "I know. Maximilien did as well, you know. It took Villon a few years to catch us, but he did."

"You are still here."

"Just as you are," Victoria said. "We were fated to survive our men, perhaps. Or simply luckier than they."

"Perhaps." The wretch moved from side to side. "More than one man, in fact."

"You've lost another?" Victoria extended her hand again, taking Clotille's own in it. Except for the facts that they were two unbreathing creatures risen from their graves, and the whole exchange was occurring in a makeshift catacomb under the Parisian streets, it appeared to be a genuinely tender moment. "Tell me."

"His name is Mirabeau," she said. "Bertrand Mirabeau. A sometimes quarryman, sometimes thief. My…"

"Lover?" Victoria suggested.

Clotille smiled at that, and it was a horrible sight to see. "In a manner of speaking," she said, looking at Regina. "I share of myself and he watches the day. I care for him."

"He has been taken from you?"

"Sentenced to hard labor in the Santé prison. The superintendent of prisons is a worm named Levasseur who tortures the men daily and rapes the women. My

Bertrand calls out to me. You know the…"

"Yes," Victoria said. "He longs for you. But surely no prison walls can stop you, and certainly no bureaucratic worm."

"The prison. It is another's domain. He claims rights there."

She means feeding rights, Regina thought to herself. *A prison would be like a larder to one of…* She tried not to finish the thought, but it came unbidden… *their kind*.

"He will make Bertrand his own," Clotille continued. "Or make sure he is never mine again."

"And the prince does nothing," Victoria said.

"Nothing."

"Then I shall, dear Clotille," she said. "Then I shall."

***

The library in the Society of Leopold's Parisian chapter house occupied two entire floors of the building at 12 and 12b Rue des Deux Ponts. Othman's idle suspicion had been correct and the society—or at least its patrons—did own the entire residence as well as that facing it across the courtyard. The past few days had witnessed a prodigious growth in his understanding of the society itself and its methods.

Leopold of Murnau, the monk said to have founded the society in the early 13th century, was said to be the inheritor of a familial curse. Father André seemed less –than convinced by the details handed down through the centuries, but several testimonials claimed that the patriarch of the Murnau clan had, at some point in the Dark Ages before Charlemagne, made a pact with Mephistopheles himself. The parallels with the Faust story were, according to André, taken by some in the order as evidence that the Murnau legend was apocryphal and by others as proof positive that the

Faustian legend was the public face of a real case of infernalism. André had no doubt that the Devil had his agents on earth, but he seemed to find the idea of signed contracts and bills of sale for the immortal soul somewhat trite. A storyteller's convenience, he called it.

This recitation led to a long and fascinating discussion between the two men of Mohammedan and Christian views of the Devil. Othman spent several hours clarifying points about the figures of Iblis, the angel who refused to bow down before man, and of the shaitan, the most evil of the djinn born of smokeless fire.

When they finally returned to the original topic, André explained that Leopold had established the society to hunt down the agents of Satan—diverse witches, devils and creatures risen from their graves—with the support of the papacy. It was, in its day, an office of the Roman Inquisition. Othman brought up the excesses of that supposedly holy office, which in turn led to a discussion of the equally embarrassing zeal of several Arab conquerors and Muslim potentates, and risked degenerating into an all-too-familiar bout of religious accusations. Othman, who up to this point had been happy to find a Christian cleric open and interested in his faith and cause, finally said, "Can we but agree that men of every faith have often failed to live up to the examples of their prophets and of God?" André nodded and although tension remained in the air that evening, they eventually resumed their conversation.

The Wars of Religion, the Enlightenment, and the rise of anti-clerical revolutions across Europe had made the job of Leopold's society almost impossible to pursue in public. Thus they had retreated into the shadows, known only to higher-level bishops and the college of cardinals, and to those priests who had had reason to call upon their services. The Society had accepted lay people into its ranks, so long as they were faithful and true.

This recitation seemed to Othman flawed and incomplete, but having learned the lesson of their exchange on the issue of the Inquisition, he kept his reservations to himself. Regardless of its limitations, the Society had resources he could use to help Lord and Lady Blake.

"Tell me about these Blakes," André said.

"They came to Cairo in the 1870s. Lord Blake was—or is, I suppose—a military man, a colonel in the British army. He arrived when the khedive needed support from his new patrons, I believe. His family, Lady Blake and their two children, arrived a few years later when Lord Blake was tasked with staying on in Egypt."

"And before Egypt? Where did they live?"

"London, if I recall." Othman opened one of his small notebooks and scanned the elegant Arabic script there. "Yes, they met in London. I believe there was a contact with the undead then, although I only have a very few details. Lord Blake was reluctant to share, even when his wife became entangled with a cult in Cairo."

"Ah," said the elderly priest, "so there is a history of involvement. Interesting, then perhaps we should look at their own history. Where do they come from, these Blakes?"

"Northern England, I believe." Back to the notes. Othman had committed to paper much of what he remembered of the Blakes and what he could extract from his own journals and research in Cairo. That fastidiousness might bear fruit now. "Yes, Lord Blake's family owns an estate in a region called County Durham."

"And his wife? Who was she before becoming Lady Blake?"

"Hmm, yes." Back to the notes. "Her ladyship was never open about her past, but I have found a few papers that refer to her by her maiden name—they dated from before her marriage, I believe. Yes, 'Ducheski.' She was born Emma Ducheski."

"A Slav, then," Father André said. "Not English at all. Interesting. Let us see what we can find."

It took several long nights, but the chapter house's library did eventually give up several important—or at least suggestive—facts. Father André and Othman found assistance in Jean-François Hubert, an assistant to the master librarian. A bookish young man who had left the rectory after his sister had died while a member of a Theosophist society, he used his archivist's skills to fight the evils that had claimed his kin.

"Durham has quite a history," the boy said after an especially long day in the stacks. "There's more than a bit of the standard politicking over the local bishop's see before King Henry split from Rome. There were also several witch trials in the area. One Camilla Ewan burned there after being accused of cursing the women of Wolsingham to give sour milk."

Hubert consulted other tomes and then continued the tale. "We have imperfect copies of the annals of the now-defunct chapter house in Cork, but they seem to have investigated the case. This would be 1641 or so. The inquisitor who visited Wolsingham returned without solid evidence but recommended further inquiries. It's unclear if that ever happened."

Othman was impressed by the boy's thoroughness. "Any mention of the Blake family in all this?"

"None that I can find, but I do not have access to any reliable civil or even ecclesiastical records for the area. I have, however, found something of interest about the name Ducheski."

Othman leaned forward across the oak table where he had spread out some of his own notes and research, the better to hear. Father André appeared at his side, as if materializing from some other world.

"A Slavic name like that seemed unlikely to have a long history in North England," Hubert said, "so I consulted our records for the East. The Holy Church fought a long battle for the hearts and souls of the Slavs against the Greek and Russian schismatics and that generated a number of records, reports and testimonials over the centuries. Hungary was, in many ways, the cutting edge of these efforts and I think there may be something to be said for an effort to better organize all the ecclesiastical records from the period of Magyar expansion into what is now the Hapsburg Empire—"

"Out with it, boy." Father André was considerably less tolerant of Hubert's digressions than he expected others to be of his own, it seemed.

"Yes, well. There was a priest named Father Mikel who preached in the towns of the Olt Valley and in Romania in the fifteenth century. He made a record of several prominent families in the area who opposed his evangelism. Father Mikel was a member of our society and he believed that some of these Hungarians were in league with—" he looked to one of the books he'd carried with him to the table "—ah, yes: 'devils, Jews or other blood drinkers.'"

Othman could not suppress a smirk. "Judaism strictly forbids the consumption of blood, just as the Koran does. I'm afraid that that is a particularly Christian practice."

Father André looked at Othman askance but Hubert continued before the priest could take up the issue. "I doubt that Father Mikel knew much at all about the sons of Abraham, but he was fastidious in recording the names of those who opposed them. These included a variety of Slavic extended families and clans, including—and I quote—'the house of Krevacheski, also called Kruvetchski or Krucheski'"

"Or Ducheski," Othman said.

"I continue from Father Mikel's journal, translating of course: 'The men of this family are tinkers, blacksmiths and masons, and responsible for the construction of several of the castles and fortifications in these parts.' He goes on to describe an especially fearsome place inhabited by the last descendant of the once-great Vlaszy family. Ah, here he continues: 'One friar has told me that the Kruvetchski women consort with devils in the deep woods. They are witch-born, he says, and each one displays the third nipple reserved for her familiar. They bear babes withered like rotting apples and use their menstrual blood to fertilize crops of bitter herbs.'"

"Charming," Father André said.

Othman for his part was thinking of the strange ritual he and Lord Blake had interrupted three years ago in Cairo. They had thought they were saving Lady Blake from the hands of some mad zealot or even a sorcerer dealing with djinn, but could she have been a willing participant? Was it in her blood? Were the witch-born women of Hungary the ancestors of Emma Ducheski?

Chapter Twelve

"What do you know of the Santé prison?"

Victoria and Regina had returned to the Les Halles marketplace and this time their reception had been warmer. Martin led them into a nearby building, where he had set up something of a parlor and office on the fourth floor. The metal and glass structure of the covered marketplace glowed in the moonlit night and Regina could see the smoke of late-night cookfires and factories staining the sky. The parlor itself was of a utilitarian, even proletarian variety. No plush chairs and lush wallpaper of ivy trestles for Martin. Instead, a simple oak table and workbenches filled the room. The walls were bare plaster, save for one covered with a painted advertisement for oranges. It had the feeling of a makeshift space.

The Frenchman leaned against the wall near the faded advertisement before answering Victoria's question. "Not a place I would recommend spending any time, if that's what you mean."

Victoria smiled. "I was hoping for a touch more than that, Martin. I have it on good authority that we have a kindred who spends nights and days there."

He scratched at the patchy red beard that covered his jaw. "Not so surprising that. No one looks too carefully at deaths in that place. Caged meat, as it were."

Although she sensed that Victoria expected her to remain largely silent in this exchange, Regina could not hold her tongue. She'd spent too much time these nights saying nothing and this casual discussion of murder and exploitation was the last straw. "Perhaps you could save us your constant platitudes and be of assistance, sir."

Martin turned his gaze on her and for a long,

terrifying moment, she saw pure hatred there. It was as if fire welled up behind his eyes and every muscle in his large frame tightened in unison. There was a loud snap as the arm of the rough wooden chair he was using cracked in his hand. A slick sheen of pinkish sweat rose on his brow and Regina smelled blood in the air. She was quite certain she was about to meet her Lord and Maker and did not know exactly how she would account for her sins.

Then, like curtains being thrown open on a summer morn, the threat passed. A broad smile spread over Martin's face and he gave a hearty laugh from deep within his not inconsiderable belly. "Ha! Observant and opinionated, this one. Truly an excellent choice, Victorine. Oh, forgive me, Victoria."

"It is my own choice to be here sir," Regina said, covering her fear with more indignation.

This only made Martin redouble his laughter. "Wonderful! Truly wonderful!" He took a second to compose himself and then returned to his discourse, as if the play of rage and hilarity had never occurred.

"Let's see," he said. "The place is south of the Luxembourg, near the Hôpital Ste. Anne, I think." He drummed his fingers on the rough table, making a sound like a troupe of tiny marching soldiers. "It's new, too. They put it up just a few years before the Communards kicked out our second emperor—that would be fifteen, may twenty years ago. Not a happy place, as I understand it. I think they keep the prisoners under hoods or some such. It's pretty much a dumping ground for those not worth sending off to Brest or Guyana for hard labor in the *bagne*."

"And the matter of domain?" Victoria phrased the matter as if she were talking about property in an inheritance.

"Hmm, no. I don't know who hunts in the Santé prison, although whoever it is must do it with the sanction of the prince. He and his scourges keep a careful eye on such prime territory."

Victoria smiled. "And the chances of the childe of Maximilien d'Orsay gaining any information from Prince Villon or his underlings are nil."

"Less than that, I would say." Martin turned to Regina. "Anything you would like to add, my free-willed darling?"

Regina ignored the jibe. She had an idea. "Tell me, Monsieur, you do have friends among those who sell produce in this marketplace, I assume."

"You might say that I have many such friends."

"I wonder," Regina said with a casual smile, "might any of them know who sells foodstuffs to the prisons, then?"

***

The Santé prison was, it turned out, not very far from the place where Regina and Victoria had descended into Clotille's subterranean lair. It was in fact an easy walk from the walls of the Cimetière du Midi to the prison, something Regina felt sure only added to the strange wretch's dismay at being barred passage. Victoria's comment about Clotille knowing all the secrets of Paris spoke in that direction as well.

Regina took it upon herself to get as good a look at the prison as possible before they put their plan into action. Thus, while Victoria slept the day away in the Guénégaud on the Right Bank, she and Cedric crossed the Seine in the cabriolet, headed down the Rue Monge and the Avenue des Gobelins, before heading east along the Boulevard Arago toward Montparnasse—which would take them right past the prison walls.

And walls they were, rose-tinted plaster covering

masonry, and monolithic in the extreme. The prison complex formed a rough trapezoid, some 120 yards at the base (along Rue de la Santé where the gate stood) and 250 yards to a side along the large boulevard and smaller street framing it. The wall was a uniform two stories in height and uninterrupted save for the large gatehouse. From the street it was hard to see more than the walls themselves, of course, but the back two-thirds of the complex seemed to house the prison's main buildings, a huge four- or five-story structure set back from the wall. Regina could just see the meager windows of the cells on the top floor, set high in the wall so prisoners would see only a patch of dirty sky, not the world beyond their cages.

Along the larger roads, the sounds of pedestrians, horses, bicycles and all manner of other conveyances and street business drowned out any sound from beyond the wall, but when she made her way to the small street on the south side, she heard the metal-on-stone echoes of hard labor being done by unseen, but surely chained, hands.

She tried to remind herself that these men were thieves and killers to have ended up in such a place, but she could not call up the revulsion she needed. Her own actions over the last few months left too much room for self-accusation.

"Not much to see, I'm afraid," she said to Cedric once she rejoined him in the cabriolet. She'd walked the distance around the prison and left him waiting on Rue de la Santé. "Save for a great deal of wall."

"True, milady. At least from the ground, that is." The coachman then pointed across the intersection to the row of typical four-story Parisian buildings standing catty-corner from the prison. The building at the corner had painted across the limestone and plaster of its third floor *Chambres à la Journée*—"Rooms to Let."

Finances were hardly a problem for Lady Regina in general, and even on the run with an undead woman of mysterious heritage, she was well provisioned in coin. Victoria had also been very liberal with her own monies, which seemed to be rather bottomless. Regina suspected that there were several dukes, bankers and industrialists who, in exchange for the occasional pleasure of her company, ensured that Victoria Ash was never in want of wealth. Thus, it was not very difficult for Regina and Cedric to convince the proprietress of the hostel to let them have the fourth-floor room facing the prison. If this matronly woman—who introduced herself as La Pierrette—found it unusual to welcome into her grimy establishment a finely dressed young lady with an accent from across the Channel and a strapping mulatto man as a companion, she made no mention of it. In fact, once their ability to pay was clear, she repeatedly offered to get them the best room in the house despite the fact that she would have to expel the current occupant. "A writer," the woman scoffed. "It would be a pleasure to kick him out on his ear."

"That won't be necessary, Madame," Regina said. "Just the topmost room facing across the way, please."

The room was a tiny thing with only a dingy bed and a shelf for furnishing. The mattress, stuffed with the chaff of a textile factory in all likelihood, hadn't been cleaned for several revolutions, it seemed. A large dark stain sat in its center and the smell of an unemptied (or absent) piss pot was heavy in the air. The proprietress rushed to push open the grimy window to "give us some air" and thus disturbed a row of sickly pigeons from their perch on the dropping-spattered perch.

She did, nevertheless, reveal an excellent view of the Santé prison.

Regina paid her an extra stipend for privacy, which the woman swept up with an amazing alacrity. "Of course, Mademoiselle," she said and the bills disappeared into the folds of her apron. She closed the door behind her and Regina turned to the window.

"She may make some foolish attempt to rob us on the way out, you know," Cedric said.

"If so, she'll wait for the night when she'll expect us to be drunk or…"

"Distracted."

"Quite. And by then we'll be gone."

Cedric smiled broadly. "True. So, this prison." He turned to the window and Regina joined him.

The window was small and it was a tight fit for them both to gaze out of it. She found Cedric's proximity not at all unpleasant, but she concentrated on the prison itself.

The furthest section from them was the main building, rising four stories as Regina had observed from street level. It was not, as she had thought it might be, a single huge building the size of a train station, but rather a complex of five wings—two long ones running east-west and three short running north-south. Together they formed a large rectangle cut in half by the third north-south wing. This created two large courtyards, the ground of which was impossible to see from where they were since they were scarcely higher than the building itself.

The front third of the prison housed not only the large gatehouse but another large building. This one was three stories tall and so had been invisible from street level. It too had five wings, although they were arranged completely differently. Instead of forming a rectangle, they all converged on a central hub like the spokes of a wheel. The hub itself was, Regina thought, a manufacture of some sort, as it had two large smokestacks that were belching soot as from a coal-fire. One of the five spokes extended east from this building, linking it to the rear prison building. The other four spread out at 45-degree angles from the axis of the prison and the streets, forming a huge X. The westernmost quarter formed by these wings, and which fronted on Rue de la Santé, held the gatehouse and was devoid of prisoners. The other areas—significantly more removed from freedom—were devoted to exterior yards for work. Had it been only the wings that divided the space, the yards would have been quite large and although cut off from the free world beyond the prison walls, might have hinted at some mild liberty. To prevent this, the sadistically efficient architects had subdivided the space between the wings with more ten- or twelve-foot walls arranged to created dozens of small, cramped yards shaped like cheese- or pie-wedges.

"My god," Regina whispered as the implications of imprisonment revealed themselves to her. To be in such a place was never to see beyond a dozen yards. The sheer claustrophobia of the complex sent a shiver down her spine and made her clutch the man next to her.

"And to think," she said, not looking at Cedric, "we are attempting to get into that place."

***

Mathieu Roupil was a wholesaler who purchased from farmers in the Seine Valley southwest of Paris proper. He had managed to prosper over the last decade by marrying two of his daughters to the sons of prominent farmers in the region, sealing familial compacts that led to cooperation in bringing produce to market. He had been traveling into Paris twice weekly to sell vegetables, meats, eggs and other goods (variable by season, of course) in the great market of Les Halles for the past five years. Roupil had made a tidy profit for one of his station in life, becoming not bourgeois but at least well positioned among part of the rural classes. He owned no great estate and his family had certainly not been aristocratic during any of the monarchical or imperial régimes of the past century. Republicanism had done him well, however, and as both a Protestant and journeyman in the Freemasonic lodge (Eastern Rite) located in the town of Meudon-sur-Seine, he was a staunch supporter of the Republic and its supporters.

This support, and the friendships he made at the lodge, had resulted in some profitable patronage for Monsieur Roupil. In Meudon, he was seen by many as a future candidate for mayor, and he had also gained several lucrative governmental licenses. One such license was a contract to provide produce for the vast concrete and limestone belly that was the Santé prison. He was not alone to feed the hundreds upon hundreds of men spending days and nights there, but he and his relatives were responsible for the entire supply of legumes and much of the cheese. They also provided wine and liquor for the guards in a system so routine it hardly qualified as black-market goods.

On the damp morning of 29 August, 1888, Roupil, five of his workers, and a nephew he was hoping to cure of indigence thus paid an entirely expected visit to the prison. They made their delivery early and the small, weak sun had barely begun its futile attempt to dispel the autumn clouds when their three large carts were allowed through the prison gates from Rue de la Santé. Guards with long guns were up on the walls that framed the space through which the carts passed before heading through a second and a third gate. This last was to the side and brought them not into the guardhouse proper, but to the access-way to the kitchens and stores in the southwestern wing.

Several guards, in black uniforms and armed with sabers, met them at the large oak doors leading to the unloading area. Roupil's workmen drew the doors open and then started unloading the barrels of pickles, bushels of carrots, cases of beans, and wheels of cheese they had this morning. Roupil himself chatted with the chief watchman, who confirmed that the regular order was being filled. The man, who had probably been asleep no more than a half-hour ago, did this by vaguely looking at the assembled carts, glancing at some paperwork, and nodding. They could, Roupil knew, be unloading cases of gold ingots and barrels of black powder and the man wouldn't notice.

A group of prisoners, all in drab gray shapeless work suits, arrived to complete the unloading and carry the goods deeper into the complex that was their world for the duration. Most seemed strong in the way of sailors long at sea—wiry muscles hanging on an underfed frame. They had been relieved of their shackles to make their work easier, though that wasn't always the case. Despite the fact that these men were in the Santé for the long haul, he preferred dealing with them than coming across an accused man jailed while awaiting trial, or a man serving a short sentence. Men in either of those categories were forbidden any and all contact with fellow human beings, in part on the pretense that they should not be recognized as former inmates once they regained their liberty. Roupil wondered if the social reformer who had thought of that policy understood what it meant to spend a year in absolute silence and isolation, forced to wear a burlap hood over your face on the rare occasions the jailers saw fit to bring you out of your cell.

Roupil had a healthy respect for the idea of poetic

justice. Something of a historian, as all supporters of the Republic must be in the approach to the Revolutionary's centennial year, he thought often of the story of Robespierre, that petty tyrant who had perverted Revolutionary justice—properly aimed at the aristocrats and priests who had robbed the people for centuries—and instituted the Reign of Terror. That he had ended up facing the same guillotine blade to which he'd consigned Danton and other Revolutionary greats was a beautiful example of well-deserved justice.

He could only hope the same force of history would sweep up the "reformer" who'd decided on complete isolation for many in the Santé. Perhaps he would end his days deaf, dumb and blind.

Roupil, buoyed by his thoughts, left the Santé with a smile on his face.

***

Regina finally decided it was safe to move from her hiding space two hours later. She had been tucked into the false bottom of a large crate of carrots and it was the cramp in her thigh that finally told her to move. The cramp had come twice already and faded in the face of her perseverance, but this time it refused to leave, despite the fact that her leg was otherwise entirely numb.

Martin's contact, a wholesaler named Roupil, hadn't batted an eye at the prospect of smuggling people into the city's newest prison. That had surprised Regina, even though this whole enterprise was her idea. She'd expected resistance, for surely were they discovered, Roupil would at the very least lose his business and might well expect to end up behind the prison walls himself in short order. She'd even been trying to think of ways to convince the man, perhaps using the incentive of monies drawn from her father. Martin had simply sat the man down and said gently, using his Christian name, "Mathieu, I'd like you to do this for me." The man had nodded and set to work.

This was the same loyalty she'd seen in Cedric when presented with the idea of heading off across Europe on a mad quest. Not the curt "yes, ma'am" of the long-suffering servant, but an enthusiasm at the prospect of service. Of, Regina realized in the long hours in her carrot crate, being of use. Was it something in the nature of these kindred of the night society, these immortals seemingly frozen between breathing life and still death, to engender such loyalty? It would go a long way toward explaining their ability to exist alongside the daylit world without drawing its attention.

Regardless, the plan had worked. There had been only the most casual inspection of the foodstuffs, and after a nasty bit of jostling as they were carried to the stores, the stowaways had arrived deep inside the Santé. It was now, by Regina's reckoning, still short of midday. If they were to move before the cooks came for supplies for the long process of preparing the evening meal, they had better start now.

With a hefty push, she dislodged the horizontal board at the base of the crate. She'd feared she'd be unable to do so, but it came loose just as Martin had said it would. The nails keeping it in place were weak, it seemed. She then scurried out of the false bottom. It was as tight a fit getting out as it had been going in, and she was very glad to have shed her woman's clothes for a simple prisoner's shirt and pants. Mannish, certainly but that was the whole point. She squeezed through the opening with nary a quarter-inch to spare. This was the main reason Cedric had not come along on their clandestine journey—he just could not fit in so tight a space.

Once out, she assessed where they were. The stores were as Monsieur Roupil had described them: a giant room divided by wooden racks set to carry various supplies and foods. The ground was cold stone and the ceiling a good twenty-five feet up.

Roupil had not mentioned the windows, however. Victoria had been very explicit about not taking the next step by the light of the sun. "The darker, the better," she said. But instead of the pitch dark of a cellar, the room had dim light provided by a row of small windows placed at the top of the walls. The glass there was dirty and yellowed and each cast only a pale square of light, but Regina guessed that Victoria would not be pleased. Still, the light was dim and no direct sun hit the area where Monsieur Roupil's delivery was stored. Regina was deep in shadow and so were all the crates, barrels and other packages.

Time for the next step. Regina reached back into her hidey-hole and pulled out the bundle of clothing stuffed in there. She unrolled the heavy linen jacket, in the same undyed prison gray as her shirt and pants, thus exposing the short metal pry bar she'd placed there. With the tool in hand she went to the large barrels standing a few yards down from the carrots, six of which were stenciled with the words CORNICHONS ROUPIL, indicating that they contained the merchant's pickles.

Regina did her best not to think about the implications of her actions, about what it meant to believe that this part of the plan would work. Both Victoria and Martin had assured her it would not be a problem and she had little choice now but to believe them.

Despite the deep shadows, Regina could see reasonably well—well enough that she wondered if her vision might not have grown more sensitive from all the time she'd spent wandering the night over the last months. She found the one barrel where the stenciling had been poorly done so that the merchant's name was blurred and smudged, seeming closer to BOODID than ROUPIL. Thanking grace that this barrel was both right side up and did not have another resting atop it, she used the pry bar to break the seal around the barrel's top and then pry the wooden disc out.

Regina knew basically what to expect, but her heart sank, her head swam, and her stomach churned nevertheless. The barrel was full to the brim with liquid and curled up within it, completely submerged, was Victoria Ash.

Regina's senses seemed to be working in some accelerated fashion because the image of Victoria seared itself into her mind in less than a heartbeat. Victoria was entirely nude, her pale skin almost glowing in the dim hint of light. Her face was upturned and her mouth open just a touch, as if slack-jawed. One arm was awkwardly tucked behind her back and one of the legs was similarly stuck under her in an odd angle. Regina realized that she'd heard the prisoners rolling the barrels along the concrete floor and the thought of being stuck in there as it turned was enough to jolt her into action.

Not really thinking about the strength it would take or the resulting noise, she pulled on the barrel to tip it and thus sent the water and Victoria pouring out onto the concrete floor. The water—and water it was, not the vinegary brine in the real pickle barrels—came out in a rush and spread out. Victoria tumbled out in a mass, her limbs splaying. This revealed dark purple bruising all across her rear and thighs, the result, Regina realized suddenly, of pooling blood.

Regina hurried to her and turned her over onto her back. The rough concrete had left bloodless scratches in her perfect flesh. Regina stopped, realizing suddenly and finally that this was not the drowning woman her instincts had told her it was. Victoria was not gasping for air, fighting for life or any such thing. She appeared to be exactly what one might expect to find after sealing a person, naked, into a barrel of water and leaving her there for five or six hours: a water-logged corpse.

Another wave of panic-backed nausea hit Regina and she had to close her eyes and turn away. *I knew it would be like this*, she thought to herself, tasting bile in her throat. *I know what to do.*

Once she felt strong enough she opened her eyes and turned back to Victoria, who of course had not moved. Gripping the dead woman's jaw, she forced open her mouth. A bit of water flowed out and Regina saw that there was a pool of it in Victoria's throat. She also noted the woman's teeth. The gums and lips were drawn back and the teeth seemed unnaturally sharp, most especially the long canines. These were the teeth of a predator, Regina knew.

"I know what to do," Regina said aloud this time. Taking the pry bar again, she drew its edge across her own palm, raising a painful welt. Unsatisfied with her work, she pushed the edge of the bar forcefully into the welt and drew it along her palm once more. The welt burst and red points of blood began to rise along it. She waited a minute for some good-sized drops to form in her palm and then tipped them over Victoria's still-gaping maw.

The blood drops hit the water in her mouth, dissolving into a pinkish brine. When the third did so, the corpse—Victoria—spasmed once, coughing up a lungful of water onto her bare neck and chest.

Then, a full minute later, when Regina was feeling

the edge of panic returning to her nerves, Victoria's eyes fluttered once, twice and then open. The whites were not their usual color, but a jaundiced shade like that of curdled cream. The irises were a cloudy gray and the left was visibly more dilated than the right. The usually emerald green aura around them was pale and worn, like dried spinach.

Victoria shifted onto her side, dragging her limbs as if they were made of lead.

"Carefully," Regina said, unsure of how one addressed a woman in the midst of returning from the dead. Or the undead. "Slowly, now."

Victoria made a gurgling sound and pulled herself into a kneeling position, her forehead resting against the ground in a perverted kowtow. When she drew her legs under herself, she didn't raise them and Regina heard the rough sound of skin tearing on the concrete. Victoria seemed either unaware or unconcerned by her nudity and as her back arched in another convulsion, she pushed her bare bottom and exposed sex toward the girl. Sickly splashes accompanied the next few convulsions as the undead woman emptied her lungs and stomach of the quarts of water in them.

Regina noticed that the bruised flesh on Victoria's rump was paling by the second. Blood was reentering her system, moving her limbs and—hopefully— awakening her mind.

After the last of the heaves, Victoria remained immobile for several minutes and Regina could not bring herself to say or do anything. The resurrected Victoria then rose into a kneeling sit, threw her head back, reopened her eyes—and screamed.

The scream was a raw thing that lacked in volume but spoke of tortured vocal chords and a terrible fear. She collapsed onto her back and it seemed to Regina as if she wanted nothing more than to sink into the concrete she was now futilely clawing at with one hand while the other rose to fend off some unknown attacker.

"Miss Ash!" Regina exclaimed and jumped to her side. "What is it? What?"

"L- light…" Her voice was a raspy whisper. Regina saw panic on her drawn features and twin lines of ruby tears were running from her eyes and down the sides of her face. "The light…"

Victoria was seeing the pale, grime-filtered rays of sunlight coming through the high windows and playing across some of the beams of the storehouse. They were still in deep shadow, but Regina suddenly understood that just the sight of the day was enough to awake animal panic in her patron. She dragged Victoria across the floor and into the wooden racks behind the pickle barrels, where there was no way to see the sun or any of its glow.

Here it was dark enough that Regina could barely see Victoria's silhouette. She didn't have to, though, as the woman cleaved to her like a babe to its mother, shaking with fear. "There, there," Regina said.

Then Victoria's hand clasped itself around Regina's neck and sharp teeth bit into the artery in her neck. Weakness and ecstasy danced through Regina as this fearful thing drank her own strength in greedy gulps.

Darkness darker than night rose up to claim Regina. Despite the fact that she knew she was huddled on the cold ground in the deepest corner of the storeroom, she had the sudden sensation of falling.

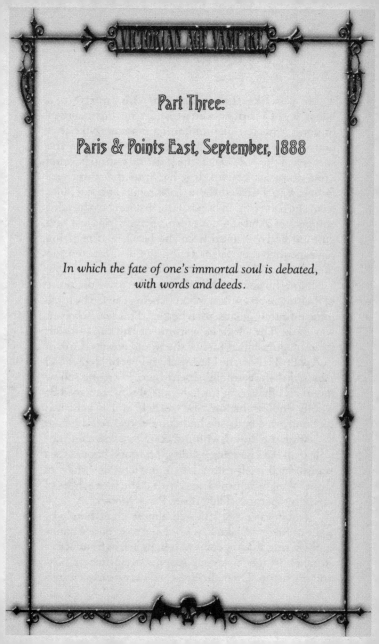

Part Three:

Paris & Points East, September, 1888

*In which the fate of one's immortal soul is debated,
with words and deeds.*

Chapter Thirteen

It was like the ocean. Not the constrained buoyancy of a bath or even a clandestine dip in a river or pond. This felt like something immense, like that morning five years past when she had floated in the silty sea of the Nile Delta, the knit and cotton bathing dress doing its best to drag her into the water and failing. She'd floated there, looking up at a sky bluer than she'd ever thought possible, listening to the faint snippets of Arabic—counterintuitively musical and guttural both—carried from the beach and reaching her ears when they deigned to break the surface tension of the water. She'd been at peace then.

Now, however, was different. There was the sense of floating in an endless space, of being carried by some force infinitely greater than herself. This sea, however, was dark. The glorious warmth of the sun—which Egyptologists called Ra but she would always think of as Apollo-Helios, the blazing charioteer of Homer and Aeschylus—was totally absent here. Even the sallow moon and flickering starlight was absent, replaced by woolly, endless shadow. She was cold and an ache was blooming in a body she hadn't quite realized she had.

With the slow dawning of consciousness came not only pain but emerging solidity. The dark, buoyant sea transformed itself into a harsh, unyielding surface of stone. Weight returned, and with it the first echoes of memory. Victoria. The prison. Paris. *Mother.*

Panic was next, followed almost immediately by sight as Regina Blake's eyes opened to expose a dance of flickering shadows and wan light across a surface of stone and timber. A deep gasping breath came next and she sat up. Then, dizziness and very nearly a return to the black ocean of unconsciousness.

It was the voice that kept her from fainting.

"There we are," it said in French with a peasant inflection and an echo of some other Latinate tongue. "Your girl returns to us at last."

Regina's eyes eventually found their focus and she assessed the situation through the haze of fatigue and muscular aches that lay across her mind and body like a heavy blanket. She was dressed in the simple woolen prison clothes she'd brought with her, and her womanly legs felt strange in the scratchy, mannish trousers. She was in some sort of cubicle, sitting on a rough wooden bench or pew, where she had been lying until she awoke. There were plaster walls on either side of her, but they did not reach the ceiling. They did, however, restrict her view to the scene straight ahead of her. That, it turned out, was a Mass, although surely not a holy one.

Indeed, the cubicle gave her the view of a stone altar with a large crucifix behind it and a mad priest before it. The man wore a threadbare robe in a pale gray, although it seemed almost dark compared to his ashen skin and impossibly light blond hair. An albino, perhaps. The hair was long and unkempt, falling over his drawn, high-cheeked face and framing eyes that seemed to flicker between blue and black. There were candles, also—tall, unseasonable paschal ones in tarnished miters arranged haphazardly about the altar.

Regina took all this in without saying a word. The fact that the priest was smiling at her stole any will to move, much less speak. She had the distinct impression that this particular cleric was most versed in last rites.

"The beating heart has room for such complexity," he said to her, "a testament to God's favor upon the sons and daughters of Seth and Noah. Those walking in the line of Caine struggle with a simpler, more honest nature. Although a more beastly one."

"And you," came Victoria's voice from somewhere beyond the plaster dividing walls, "are intimately aware of the Lord's favors, I assume?" Regina released muscles she hadn't realized she'd been tensing. The fact that Victoria was free to speak, still living—if that term had any meaning for one such as her—raised Regina's spirits.

"You mock, Miss Ash," the priest said, "Fear not, my nights of claiming to understand the intimate details of His holy work are in my past. Such was the hubris of youth."

"Then what do you preach, father?" Regina asked the question as simply as she could, mostly trying to carry forward this conversation so that she might have time to grasp just what was going on here. His references to "nights of claiming" instead of days meant he must be the kindred they had been looking for— assuming they were even still in the prison—but beyond that Regina had little idea of what had transpired since Victoria had clamped onto her neck. As long as this man kept talking, she had a chance of finding out.

The priest smiled wider. "I share only the wisdom God has seen fit to bestow upon me. I guide the flock to accept that God loves them and that His love is all-powerful and ineffable."

"I can't imagine there is much evidence of love in this place," Regina said.

"Then the boundaries of your imagination are unfortunately limited, young girl," he said. "But I can see that is not so. As I said, you are a complex creature, one who denies that which she knows. Would you be here were it not for love?"

"I…" The flippant response died in her throat as she thought of her mother, for whose sake she had embarked upon this mad quest. And of Victoria, for whom she'd felt such panic upon seeing her unmoving in the barrel, corpse-like. Was that not love?

"You begin to understand," he said. "God's love is everywhere, especially in the darkest places, for He created those as well."

"Not the Devil?" asked Victoria from her unseen position elsewhere in this chapel.

The priest glanced to his left, confirming that Victoria was somewhere in that direction, and gave the light laugh of a benevolent parent explaining some simple fact to a child. "You have no idea, I think, just how much blood has been shed over that very same misunderstanding. Zoroastrians, Albigensians, Bogomils, Nestorians: they all fell into the easy hubris that God is simple and fallible, that He somehow let His creation be perverted by some equal adversary. Ahriman. Satan. Lucifer. They failed to understand that it is we who are imperfect, not Him. It is not God who has fallen, but us, both kindred and kine."

Regina had heard that expression—"kine"— before in London. It was a term used to refer to those not brought into the night society, something the undead called the living. In London it had seemed dismissive, almost derogatory. In this cleric's speech it somehow took on a reverent quality. The conversation was transforming itself again, from a mere way to forestall whatever came next, to a ray of hope— although a faint one.

"Does that mean…" Regina began, feeling as if her tongue had grown woolly, so reluctant was it to form clear words. "That is, Father, if both kindred and kine have fallen, can they both be redeemed?"

"Of course," the priest said without hesitation.

Regina felt as if she had been trapped in a sooty, smoke-filled manufacture and was now emerging into a green, sunny pasture, her lungs filling at last with fresh country air. If redemption was possible, then the mother she loved was not lost.

"I'm sure many would say that our earthly nature is a clear sign of our damnation," Victoria said.

"Beware of the laziness of misguided Calvinists," the priest said. "It is wholly possible that God determined our election at the dawn of time. Even if He did not, He surely knows our fate, for all knowledge is His. Those who claim, however, to be able to deduce our fate or election here on Earth are fools. If the Cathars' pride led them to believe they were more perfect than God, the Calvinists' leads them to believe they can see as clearly as He."

"So we all have hope to be saved?" Regina tried and failed to keep the excitement out of her voice.

"Yes. Eventually, we all must face our Lord and answer for our sins." He walked toward Regina then, a beatific smile on his face. "Do you have sins you wish to confess, child?"

She wanted, with almost every fiber of her being, to say yes. She longed to drop to her knees in supplication, to empty her mind of the mad race into the shadows her life had become. Was there a single sin she *hadn't* committed in the last year?

Still, something inside her told her to hold her tongue and she did. That something felt cool and smooth, like silk or marble. It was like a pressure felt at an instinctual level. *Don't*, it said. *This is a snare designed to trap you tight.*

"Well then," the priest said, "perhaps another time." He took a few steps back and addressed the room.

"We should retire to other quarters to discuss the matter of trespass, I think."

"Yes," said Victoria—and Regina realized that her cold instinct spoke with Victoria Ash's silk-smooth voice.

***

The cleric's name was Father Anatole and the Santé prison was, it seemed, his abbey. The small chapel in which Regina had awoken was used during the day for the prayers of those prisoners in isolation, the walls existing so they would not see anyone but the priest tending to their souls. At night, the undead abbot used it as a space for private sermons to those chosen for special revelation.

By all appearances he had a terribly acute sense of all the goings-on within the prison walls. That was how they had been discovered, apparently.

"Your arrival woke me from my slumber, Miss Ash," he said. "I was happy to see that my novices were able to find you and Lady Regina before anything unfortunate happened. The light can appear in the most unexpected places."

Having seen Victoria's unholy terror at the sight of wan and distant sunlight, Regina, when she overheard this comment, had little doubt that it implied a threat. Her cold instinct—with Victoria's voice—gave another nudge: *You see?*

She did.

Not that Father Anatole treated them shabbily. Once he led them out of the dour little chapel, they found themselves in the long halls of one of the prison wings. Without being able to glance outside, Regina had no way of knowing just where they were in the enormous penitentiary, but she thought it likely that they were in the central wing, surrounded on all sides by more parts of the prison, invisible from the outside and the most removed from freedom.

They passed several prisoners in the halls and each wore a long cowl that prevented him from seeing much of anything. They extended unmanacled hands to the walls to use as guides, moving in near silence. Near because as she passed the men, Regina invariably heard a musical mumbling coming from them, the sound of prayers meant for God's ears only.

"Where are the guards?" she asked. Indeed, as they progressed down one hall, up a flight of stairs, and along another passage, only hooded prisoners were anywhere to be seen.

"At prayer," Anatole said. "Those whose lot it is to watch over the penitent must first understand their own sinful natures. Otherwise this whole enterprise is but hypocrisy."

Victoria joined the conversation. "And the novices you mentioned?"

"Most are also at prayer. That is, after all, the entire object of isolation, to give one time to face God free of distractions. In past ages, monasteries served this purpose, but their great flaw is that they required the willingness to enter them. The penitentiary system avoids this flaw by drawing in those who exhibit sins and giving them the necessary conditions for repentance."

"This place," Regina said, "seemed more like a dumping ground than a place of spiritual rebirth."

Anatole smiled beatifically as he ushered them into another room on the second floor, its windows shuttered tight. "Alas, you are often right. That is in fact the prime example of the hypocrisy I mentioned afore: guards, wardens and administrators who see their charges as so much chattel and fail to recognize that they too are sinners."

"Let he who is without sin cast the first stone," Regina said.

Anatole nodded. "Yes, the answers are there for them, if they turn to God."

"And if they do not?" Regina asked.

He gave a nod to the simple chairs scattered around the room, indicating that Victoria and Regina should be seated. "Then the Grace of God cannot protect them from the wages of their sins."

"They become prey for the redeemed, then?" Victoria asked, having taken the seat furthest from Anatole's, and thus placing Regina between them. "A convenient arrangement for the redeemed, but hardly one that encourages guiding sinners to salvation."

Regina saw a flash of red anger play itself across Anatole's pale face. Blood suddenly filled disused veins and the harsh light of the room's gas lamp reflected off his hard eyes. It was a moment before he responded. "You reduce the soul and its redemption to simple things, Miss Ash. Seek to understand before you criticize."

Victoria looked away for a moment, and when she returned her gaze to the priest—and thus to Regina— it had softened considerably. "Accept my apologies, father. I have seen too many use honeyed words to entrap. I do not trust easily."

"One without hope cannot be saved," he said, "but I understand your reservations. Sin is a chameleon, wearing the countenance of salvation, education, or liberty with ease. Be wary, by all means, but do not abandon hope. We are not in the Inferno yet."

Regina felt an electricity passing between Victoria and Anatole, and it caused a chill tingle to run up her own spine.

"My protégée," Victoria said, "has seen one dear to her entrapped and fears for her soul. Might we hope you could provide instruction in the manner to protect her from damnation?"

"One cannot seek salvation from God on another's behalf, my child." Anatole said this looking at Regina, but she felt the words carry through her to the unliving woman behind her. "One must first seek it for oneself."

"Then," Victoria said, "might we stay here, nonetheless? To search for it?"

Regina felt lightheaded, as if balancing on a vertiginous escarpment, aware of the beauty and wonder of the scenery, and the yawning danger of the fall. Might this be a step toward salvation for Mother? Might it be one for herself?

Anatole smiled. "I would be honored."

***

"Father Anatole teaches us that penitence is the key," Paul said, giving Regina just a hint of his infectious smile. She had become aware of Brother Paul, on her second night at the abbey, and a week later they were almost inseparable. A tall, black-haired fellow, he'd brought her an evening meal of pork sausages and boiled vegetables, and introduced himself as the man who had discovered Regina and Victoria after their botched intrusion into the prison's stores. He'd seemed neither upset by their presence nor worried that she might resent him having discovered them.

Truth be told, she hadn't been. Her stomach was rumbling and she was very much glad for the company, seeing as Victoria had retreated into directed prayer with Father Anatole soon after sunset. They'd chatted amicably much of that first night and repeated the exercise every night since then. He had become her guide in the abbey and was slowly, she knew, becoming something of a spiritual guide as well.

This night, they had sat side-by-side as they listened to Father Anatole's sermon in the chapel. He had warned of a great Judgment coming, and of the peace all sinners must make with their souls before that night. "Redemption," he'd said, "like all true sentiments, begins in the heart and travels throughout the body by means of the veins and arteries. This monastery can be the heart of a new, redeemed body, if you will be its blood and veins."

Regina, without realizing just what she was doing, had clasped Paul's hand in her own. If only this were true, might she bring relief to her mother's hopeless soul? When she'd noticed her hand in his, she'd looked up at Brother Paul, sure he would be shocked by her forwardness. Instead, she found him looking on toward his abbot, smiling, and holding her hand peacefully. Now, with the sermon over, and there being several hours still until pre-dawn prayer, the two of them had retired to Paul's cell to continue their conversation.

"But feeling sorry for a sin doesn't erase it, does it?" Regina asked, sitting beside Paul on the metal-framed bed.

"The point isn't to erase a sin, Ginny," he said. "And regret is not the same thing as penitence, it is at best an intermediary step. First you acknowledge your sin. Then, regretting it, you must make penance. Finally, you must accept Christ's forgiveness. Can you do that?"

"I… I don't know, Paul."

He took her hand in his. His palms were rough but warm. "I take my name from the Apostle, Ginny, do you know his story?"

"The conversion on the road to Damascus."

"Not quite," Paul said. "St. Paul—or Saul as he was before that point—saw the Savior on the road to Damascus and went blind. His conversion, his acceptance of Christ's mercy, only happened after three days in darkness. Then, his sight restored and his heart redeemed, he took the name Paul and began his evangels. Do you see the distinction?"

"The conversion wasn't instantaneous," she said after a moment. "Redemption takes time."

"Indeed it does, and effort as well. Can you take the first step? The admission of sin?"

She was silent for several minutes longer. "I've disobeyed my father. Lied to him."

"Very good." He squeezed her hand and pulled her somewhat closer to him.

"And," she continued, "I've sinned… in the flesh." She swallowed. "I've lain with a man not yet—that is, not my husband. And a woman, too. I've drunk her blood and given mine to her." Tears were running down her cheeks, but she barely noticed them, so heavy were the words in her throat and in the air.

"Where do you think the sin lies in these acts, Ginny?"

She looked up at him through bleary eyes, perplexed. "Well, they're not proper… that is, the Bible says—"

"Sins are not acts, Regina," he said, cutting her off with a kind, forgiving tone. "Sin is a spiritual matter. The physical aspect is secondary, irrelevant. The martyrs who disobeyed their pagan parents' orders to sacrifice to false gods were not sinful in their disobedience. Those who take the Eucharist are not sinful for drinking blood. The man and woman who mate are not sinners for the act."

"But—"

"The sin is in the thought and the intention, Ginny. Who you take as a husband, whom you disobey or obey, and why you do so, those are the distinctions that matter to God. Those are the things for which your soul must account."

Regina faltered in the warm silence of this man's smile. There was no harsh judgment in him, only loving acceptance. His open heart compared so favorably to all those she had thought loved her before. Her mother, who kept dark secrets from her; her father, who pushed her away when she needed him most; Malcolm, who revealed himself to be a part of the night society as well; Victoria, whose love was a sharp and fickle thing. Could she really hope to find such peace in this place?

"Come," he said after a few pregnant minutes. "It is time to return to the chapel for prayer, and then sleep. Your resolve will come in its own time."

***

Malcolm Seward's train from Calais arrived at the Gare du Nord in the mid-afternoon of September 9th. He had never been to Paris before and the city was, to his mind, disorienting in the extreme. Although not quite the metropolis that was London, this was more a factor of its ongoing transformations than any lack of size. Paris had gone through spurts of renovation in the 1860s, through war and revolution in the 1870s and now through a variety of new changes. A Universal Exhibition was in the offing and public works were everywhere under construction. This all made it difficult to navigate the city without a guide.

Thus, it was late at night before he made his way to the doors of the Maison de Tunis on the Left Bank. Twice he felt sure street toughs had chosen him as their evening's prey, but he'd so far escaped any fisticuffs. Perhaps they'd sensed some desperate edge to his stride.

Having seen the darkness that inhabits the night, he was less than intimidated by ruffians of a more mundane sort.

The door to the shabby four-story boarding house was shuttered and locked, hardly a surprise at half-past-midnight. There were plenty of other businesses open for patronage up and down the street and the sound of merry-making, cheap wine and cheaper women reached his ears. Part of him longed for release, be it in the bottle or the boudoir, but he had other matters to attend to. He pounded on the door with his fist.

When that had no effect, he pounded again and added a loud call of "Hello in there!" to his arsenal. The shutters moved slightly as someone undid the door behind them, then they too parted. A swarthy face more than filled the gap.

"*Quoi?*" the face asked.

Lt. Seward had served in Egypt and picked up a bit of French there, but it was a poor and broken thing. The fatigue of the journey and the reemergence of his morbid dreams conspired to erase what little vocabulary he had mastered. "*Je…*" he began, fighting to regain some ability to communicate. "Monsieur Othman al-Masri," he said.

"You look al-Masri?" The clerk's English was better than Seward's French, and certainly than his Arabic, but not by a great deal. "Him not here."

"What? But this is the Tunis House… the Maison de Tunis, yes?"

"Yes, Maison de Tunis. No al-Masri here." The man waved vaguely in the direction of the street. "*Parti.*"

"He left? Is that what you mean? When did he leave? Where did he go?"

"Gone two week," the man said.

Seward fished in his pocket, coming out with a few French coins he'd obtained in Calais. He hoped it would be enough. "Where?"

"Rue des Deux Ponts," the man said, snatching the coins lightning-quick. "*Numéro douze.*"

He closed the door with a slam, leaving Seward in the darkened street, to wonder, *Where the devil is the Rue des Deux Ponts?*

Chapter Fourteen

Paul had spent the day working in the prison laundry, so he smelled of raw soap when he came to visit Regina that evening. A flickering candle covered the small cell—once correctional, now monastic—in a yellow light. When he sat next to her, she noticed that the skin of his hands was pink and raw. She took his digits in her own hands and felt there the residual heat of scrubbing in scalding water.

"Poor thing," she said, holding his hand against her cool cheek.

"It's nothing, Ginny. How are your reflections progressing this evening?"

Regina pushed back from the small desk that they had brought into her cell the evening before. There were several sheets of paper covered in Regina's elegant, tight script placed next to a soft leather bible. The single candle, an inkwell and a simple pen completed her study equipment.

"Well. It's been several years since I last read the Vulgate."

"The Bible was not part of your life outside, Ginny?"

She smiled. "Of course it was, but we are Anglican. Our church teaches the gospel in English and uses the text commissioned by King James."

"Of course," he said, letting his hand linger on her cheek. "And you read the Latin text…"

She leaned into his hand, allowing him to cup her cheek, and closed her eyes to concentrate on the feel of him. "In Egypt, when I learned Latin. It was one of the main texts we used, along with Ovid and Virgil."

He slid closer to her, causing the bed to creak slightly. Her hand touched his leg, which was taut under the raw fabric of his prison uniform. She breathed in and caught the mannish smell of him under the soap-scent. She realized just how much she missed the smell of another living person. Victoria was scented with perfumed oils and occasionally the copper-tinge of blood, but never the slight acidity of life.

"Who was your teacher," he said, glancing at the pages of notes, "to have schooled you so well?"

She opened her eyes and was not startled to find his face close to hers. "An Arab man, Ibn Saleh. He instructed me in Latin, Greek and several other subjects."

"A Mohammedan?" His voice had become a whisper.

"Yes. He spoke very eloquently of his faith." Without realizing it, she matched his hushed tone and advanced herself ever so slightly. When she spoke again, her lips were almost touching his. "More so than most priests I've met, in fact."

"Fascinating…"

Paul's breath was shallow and warm, and he too leaned forward slightly, making his lips touch hers ever so slightly, like the faintest of sea sprays carried by a coastal wind. The contact sent pins and needles through Regina's flesh, and a lightness into her head.

He pressed forward into a real embrace, his lips parting hers and his hand slipping behind her head to pull her to him. A light moan of pleasure escaped her throat, and her body pressed against his. Her hand wrapped around his back, trying to maximize the contact of living flesh. Their embrace lasted a second, a minute, an eternity. Her head swayed with the intoxication of the moment.

Then he pulled away. She reopened her eyes to find a confused expression playing itself across Paul's features. He seemed to be in pain.

"I…" He stood up and pointedly made distance between them. "I can't, Ginny…. Father Anatole…"

"I understand." Her expression matched his, the longings of her heart battling with the realities of her situation. "But you… that is, these past weeks I've come to see things so differently…"

He smiled, but it was a smile full of longing. "God be praised, but the bonds of flesh… that is, only in matrimony sanctified by the holy father's church…"

"I see," she said, crestfallen. "Could I ever be accepted? Into the church?"

The fog lifted from his eyes. "Ginny! Of course you can. The blood of the Savior can feed all the repentant." He crossed to her and clasped her in his arms. "To seek redemption as you have, it is a miracle!"

Laughs of joy bubbled from her. "Thank you, Paul. Thank you!"

"I will discuss your conversion with Father Anatole tonight, Ginny." He held her at arm's length so that he could look into her eyes. "You're embarking on the greatest journey, Ginny. You will be saved!"

"Can you stay with me tonight?" she asked, quietly. Then, "To pray?"

The longing on Paul's face was palpable, and it was as if an invisible tether were drawing them together. "Would that I could, darling Ginny. I have rounds to make among the penitent and then to aid Father Anatole in tonight's sermon."

"I could—" She stopped herself. "No, go. I'll be fine here with the words of God."

"I… Perhaps tomorrow night, once I've talked to Father Anatole."

"Oh, Paul…"

He kissed her, frankly and truly. Then rose and walked to the door. Before leaving he turned to her. "My soul soars, Ginny. Truly."

***

Lt. Malcolm Seward had found the house on Ile St.-Louis, at 12 Rue des Deux Ponts two days after his unsuccessful attempt to find lodging at the Maison de Tunis. That first night, without any shelter forthcoming, he had camped under a small footbridge and known that God did indeed look out for his soldiers, when the storm that had been threatening turned into nothing but a mild drizzle. Exhausted from his journey but well aware of the dangers of dozing outside in the foreign city, he floated in a half-slumber that reminded him of those horrible nights during the Sudanese expedition. In fact, his awareness of the cobblestone alley in which he'd crawled merged with dream images of the arid landscape beyond the Upper Nile Valley. On top of that mélange, his mind added half-glimpsed bull's heads, and the sun somehow split to became the eyes of Captain Ellijay, reminding him of his duty to the Queen and to his brothers in arms. He woke with a start, surprising the young girl who had been trying to liberate the contents of his pockets and his traveling bag.

"What? No!" He pushed at the child, who was dressed in a simple, dirt-stained dress, and she went sprawling. He stood up and raised a hand as if to strike, sending her scampering off. He thought it odd that she didn't speak a word or even scream out. Only the pitter-pat of her clogged feet on the cobblestones filled the dewy, gray morning.

That day had been taken up with finding proper shelter and securing a map and directions. He'd hoped to make it to the address that same evening but was dismayed to find that one of the locals had sold him a bogus or outdated map. By the time he returned to his rooming house near the Porte de Clignancourt, he'd wasted another day.

When he finally found the address, he was half convinced that this Othman of Lord Blake's was a wild goose for him to chase. He'd been about to turn tail when the door opened a crack and a wizened face peered out. Seward was surprised to see a priest's collar peaking out under the man's sagging chin.

"*Oui?*" The man's tone was distinctly unwelcoming.

Seward struggled to get a grasp of his paltry French. "*Je recherche… un homme…* Othman al-Masri?"

"*Vous avez la mauvaise addresse,*" the priest said and moved to close the door. Seward was quick enough to hold it open with his strong arm, though.

"Wait! Sir, father… *mon père… je suis…* a friend… *de* Lord James Blake?"

"You 'ave zee wrong address, *monsieur,*" the priest said in accented English a hundred times clearer than Seward's French.

"But I was given this address… that is…" Sudden inspiration hit Seward. "That is, I walk the path of St. Eustace, father."

There followed a long minute of silence, in which the priest simply stared at Seward and the young lieutenant held his ground. Neither spoke, until the priest finally opened the door. "*Entrez,*" he said.

From that point on, things were much easier. Seward understood that these men were members of that self-same Society of Leopold that Sister Mary-Elizabeth had told Colonel Blake and him about. He did discover, however, that whereas Mary-Elizabeth's

Bible implied the society to be a grand order run from Rome, the men here seemed to be more isolated. Seward discovered this when he asked whether Father André—the priest who had greeted him—might summon help from Rome to deal with the situation. He'd just given a dour "*Non*" as answer.

"Such is not the way of things," the house archivist Jean-François Hubert explained sometime later. A younger man, his English was virtually unaccented. "Several times during its history, our society has come close to destruction because the forces of darkness have been able to hunt its members down. We operate secretly, and only a few of us have even a vague image of the society as a whole. Each chapter house is largely on its own."

Seward, Hubert and the Arab Othman al-Masri formed an unlikely triad, but they bonded very quickly upon the lieutenant's arrival. As it happened, al-Masri and Seward had crossed paths before, though the lieutenant had not noticed the man then. It had been on one of Seward's visits to the Blake house in the Garden City of Cairo when the family lived there and he was serving under Col. Blake's command in the 12th Hussars. Seward had taken the man for an Arab house servant and paid him little heed. Al-Masri, however, had taken note.

"Lady Regina spoke very highly of you when I was her teacher, Lieutenant." The Arab wore the white robe so typical of Egyptian men, and Seward had a strange case of déjà vu, as if this were Cairo and the world of horror he'd uncovered in the last year was but a dream. "She said nothing improper, of course, but I sensed you had captured her young heart. That is a precious thing, Lieutenant—the love of a girl."

"I understand that, sir. That is why I am here, in

the hopes of saving Lady Regina from the clutches of a…" the word caught in his throat, "… a *devil*." He went on to lay out some of the details of Regina Blake's experiences as he understood them. He was as forthright as he thought reasonable, remembering Capt. Ellijay's imperative for discretion. He certainly did not reveal the existence of the Taurine Brotherhood, nor his own bloody initiation therein. He did discuss the disappearance of Lady Blake and the murder of the maid Mary at Bernan House last winter, as well as the strange comportment of the Ducheski family as a whole. He related most of what he knew of Victoria Ash and the fact that Lord Blake and he had searched her London house. He left out the death of the pretty young maid there.

"We found this letter there, and this is what brought me here." He handed over the letter in Regina's hand and scrawled over by the maid. "I don't understand the nature of the defacing, but the handwriting in the letter proper is Lady Regina's."

"Indeed," al-Masri said as he looked it over, "I would recognize it anywhere. She is in Paris then, with this Miss Ash. But there is no address, and I can't make much else out." He passed the letter on to Hubert before continuing his discussion with Seward. "But where is James? I would have expected him here."

"I left him to seek permissions and make arrangements to come here, and when I next returned to Monroe House, he was gone," Seward answered truthfully. "Lord Blake had left a note that he had found some new way to find Lady Blake. He did not elaborate." The note had mentioned Vienna, but Seward saw no reason to tell anyone but Capt. Ellijay that.

"The Hôtel de Guénégau!"

Young Hubert's exclamation surprised both Seward and al-Masri, and they gaped as the archivist held the defaced letter aloft and raced to his desk. He put the sheet down and took down a heavy leather-bound book that seemed to contain papers of many different colors. They approached and found the book to be bound letters from a certain Baron François Gaupin.

"Gaupin was a friend of the society's for many years," Hubert explained as he madly flipped pages. "He died fighting the Prussians during the war, but before that, he was an habitué of many of the *hôtels particuliers* across Paris. Many of them print their own distinctive stationary for the use of those taking apartments there. Including this one." He triumphantly flipped a page, revealing a letter written on a paper that was the same pale green as Regina's. Both also displayed a faint imprint of the letters HG. The bound letter also listed the name and address of the hotel in question:

HÔTEL DE GUÉNÉGAU
RUE DES ARCHIVES
IVE ARR. PARIS

***

"When the reckoning of Gehenna is visited upon the children of Caine and the brood of Seth faces its enemy on the field of Armageddon, we will all be made to answer for an existence of sin. The last son of David's line shall emerge from the lake of poison called Wormwood, and the Last Day shall become the Final Night. This will be Judgment. Who among us will be ready for that accounting?"

The chapel was full, prisoner-cum-initiates filling the isolated cubicles and prayer boxes, each cut off from the others but with a view of their spiritual guide standing at his simple altar. Father Anatole had been speaking for over an hour, switching from French to Latin and back again, with occasional forays into what Regina thought might be Catalan or Provençal. His long blond tresses formed a wild curtain of hair about his face, and a zealous fire burned in his shockingly blue eyes. He was beautiful.

Brother Paul, serving as his aid in the service, stood to the right of the altar, his head bowed and his hands grasping a Bible bound in cold iron.

"The patriarchs of the blood will rise from the earth, and the angels of light will descend from the sky on that terrible, sacred night," Anatole continued. "None will be able to hide from them, and none will be able to mask their sins. Those found wanting will be consumed, body and soul along with the rest of the base, physical world.

"Only the saved," he continued, "those who have accepted their sinful nature, passed through their period of penitence, and grown redeemed, can hope to see the gates of Heaven yawn wide for them at last. We here, in this house built by man to punish and used by God to redeem, we take these steps."

A palpable sense of pride floated across the room, each of the hidden penitents taking a moment to reassure themselves that they were walking the true path. This bubbling of that most insidious of sins evaporated with Father Anatole's next words.

"Do not think we have done enough!" he exclaimed. "We are not assured passage into the love of God. We have not earned our place among the powers and principalities yet! Every night brings another test, another challenge we must face. Only on that Final Night will we know whether we have been true to our words and our lord! So know that you are still a sinner, and seek out the crimes unaccounted for, the indiscretions unadmitted, the blood spilled without repent."

The other penitents were hidden from her view, but Regina felt sure that they were all swaying as she was, buffeted by the rebuke from this creature attuned to the ineffable. She felt tears welling up in her eyes.

"But rejoice!" Anatole extended a hand toward Regina's cubicle. "Tonight another soul begins its quest for redemption. Tonight a woman becomes our sister."

Regina felt the pull of his gaze like an invisible current and rose from her pew. She took eleven steps forward, stopping when she was less than a yard from the stone slab that served as an altar. On it was a tin cup, a dark red-brown liquid within it. Father Anatole dipped the middle finger of his left hand in the liquid and its tip came up bloody.

He looked directly at her. "Do you seek anointing in this, our church, sister?"

Regina spared a glance at Paul, who was still clutching his iron bible but was now looking intently at her. She looked back at the unliving preacher in front of her and said, "I do."

"To take this step," Anatole then said, "you must first shed the prideful name given to you by a sinning world. Your once-father named you Regina, Queen of the World, a defiance of the place of God. Your new mother, the church, gives you the new name of Agnès, Lamb of God. Do you accept it?"

"Yes," she said, without hesitation.

"Then accept this anointing as a first step on the long road to redemption." Anatole daubed his bloody finger on her forehead and cheeks. "Now, Agnès, turn to face the congregation."

She turned around and gazed out at the semi-circle

of tight cubicles and niches, seeing dozens of faces looking at her with joy and even reverence. Her gaze fell on one face in particular, one of pale alabaster skin, framed by coppery-red hair, and marked by jade-green eyes. Victoria was wearing a simple shift, much like the one Agnès had been given, and her hair was tied back in a severe bun. Still, she was beautiful, and Agnès could hardly hold back her own sobs when she saw a ruby tear of blood run down that flawless cheek.

Chapter Fifteen

Seven of them went to the Hôtel de Guénégau the next afternoon. Malcolm Seward and Othman al-Masri had not met the Ventimiglio brothers before that morning, but Father André assured them that they were stalwart and reliable men of faith. Seward thought them a little rough, especially young Alain, but he'd known many soldiers who made up for their lack of social grace in courage under fire, so it was ready to make allowances. Also, none of the four brothers spoke a word of English, so he wasn't privy to any of their conversations.

Othman, however, understood almost every word (all save those swallowed by their occasionally indecipherable accents). He was not reassured. The eldest, Thomas, seemed at least dedicated and focused, but the others were less reassuring. Christophe, one of the middle brothers if Othman guessed right, was a slick charmer who made the Arab's skin crawl. He made polite comments to Othman's face and then stole looks of disdain to his brothers, assuming them to be unseen. The other two brothers, Julien and the insufferable Alain, were at least open in their hostility. Julien, who sported a raw scar on his neck, seemed unable to let more than a few minutes pass without some comments about pagans, the "dark races," or the deviltry of Mohammed. Othman refused to rise to the goad, but he hoped that the fates had a suitable justice in store for this man some day. Alain, the youngest and most worrisome of all, didn't speak at all. He just stared at Othman and cracked an evil smile every time one of his siblings mentioned an especially gruesome bit of violence. "You mus' understand," André said in accented English, "the fight requires soldiers, and soldiers are not innocents."

Othman just smiled, nodded and hoped for the best. If they were to rescue Lady Regina, he decided, they would have to get to her before these brothers.

When their large carriage stopped before the hotel on the Rue des Archives just after 4:00 p.m., Seward led the three younger Ventimiglio brothers into the building, despite the language barrier separating them. Othman followed Thomas to the back of the hotel.

Thank the Prophet for Seward's presence, he thought. *Perhaps all is not lost.*

*** * ***

Brother Paul brought Agnès along with him on his visits to the penitents on the evening following her anointing. He said he was ministering to those penitents under his special care and wanted her to come along. She jumped at the opportunity.

"Your decision to enter into penitence," he said, stopping in the long, darkened hallway of the central wing of the Santé prison, what she had come to think of as the abbey. "It's simply marvelous, Agnès."

She smiled and raised a hand to touch the crusted blood that still marked her forehead and cheeks. There were few opportunities to wash in the abbey, but she felt that even had she scrubbed constantly over the last twenty-four hours, the marks of her conversion would somehow still be visible.

"I couldn't have done it without you," she said.

"Nonsense," he said, covering the telltale glow of pride, "I but showed you some passages to examine. You found the truth in the Gospels yourself. If anybody, it's Father Anatole you should thank. This is his holy work."

"Of course. But it's you who has acted as my guide,

Paul." She stepped closer, and the heat of the lantern he held matched that in her breast. "My beacon. Without that…"

"Shh," he whispered, touching a finger to her lips. "It's you who—"

She pulled his hand away and kissed him, unable to take more words when she longed for a more meaningful exchange of spirit. The flare of skin-on-skin was a pale but meaningful approximation.

They both broke the contact, simultaneously stepping back from the abyss of longing as much for the sake of the other as for themselves. Still, the lingering sensation of his lips on hers, of her arm on his chest, remained a quiet, persistent invitation to return to the edge.

"We should continue on," she said, hoping she meant his ministerial rounds and not the route of the flesh. "Before the dawn comes."

They headed further down the corridor, passing cell after cell. Entering one of the many austere stairwells, they climbed to the topmost level, the only one to receive even a touch of sunlight, and headed toward the cells of those under Paul's special care.

"How is it that Father Anatole keeps the profane world out of the abbey?" Agnès's question came shortly after they'd reached the top floor. "Do not the various administrators and guards ask questions?"

"God grants tools to his chosen minister," he answered. Agnès thought he'd say no more, but after a long pause, he continued. "For one thing, Father Anatole has acolytes who serve him in the rest of the prison, but more importantly is the power of redemption. Erasing sin is impossible, but a sinner confronted with one such as Father Anatole will believe a great deal."

Agnès said nothing, but her mind went to the effects Victoria and her kindred had had on her in her life before arriving at the abbey. If they could twist her heart and cloud her judgment, what could a soul like Anatole's not do? Were he to have told her the central wing of the prison was disused, would she not have believed it with all her sin-stained heart?

Paul stopped before a large iron door that seemed like all the other large iron doors to the cells on this floor. His hand rested on the heavy bolt, and he turned to Agnès. "My darling, penitence is a difficult process. It can even be painful."

Agnès swallowed. "Like the blindness of St. Paul."

"Yes," he said with sudden energy. "Yes. Truly confronting our sins is the supreme effort. It was in this very cell that I had my three months of blindness."

"Days," she said. "Three days."

He smiled. "Would that I had the soul of an apostle, to have found my peace in so short a time. No it was three months from the time my sinner's eyes closed to the time I was ready to accept the sacrament." He threw open the bolt with a loud metal-on-metal sound. "Still, I hope that my own ordeal has left a mark in this room, so it is here that I minister to the best of my students."

Agnès stepped forward and into what at first appeared to be a bare, if large cell. It was likely originally a group cell for those sentenced to communal labor, for it was easily three times the size of the restrained little room in which she'd spent the majority of her new life. The only features she could see included a small pile of what she took to be some form of kindling and a window high on one wall.

She was looking up toward that small square of cloudy night sky, vaguely remembering what the sun had been like (for she had never known it in her new life), when she saw the man. He was hanging from a chain or rope tied around his feet and secured to some unseen hook or bar in the high ceiling. Immobile in deep shadow, he seemed somehow to have too many appendages.

"This is Sebastien," Paul said upon following Agnès into the room. He brought the lantern with him, and its light revealed a stark scene. The man, if he could be called that, was indeed hanging from a heavy rope tied to his ankles, passing over a beam in the ceiling and coming down to be tied to a hook in one wall. Other ropes bound his legs and arms. His flesh was a sickly gray in color, as drawn and shabby as cracked leather. It was also pierced with at least dozen wooden stakes or sticks. His mouth was bound with a gag of rope and cloth.

These details came into sharper focus as Paul, demonstrating a strength that belied his lean frame, slowly lowered the man. He retied the rope so that the man dangled a few feet off the cold dirt and stone ground.

"Sebastien served a creature of darkness before he arrived at the abbey. He has yet to accept the truth of his sins." Picking up a couple of the sharpened stakes in the corner, Paul beckoned Agnès over to the hanging man. He handed her one, and she noted it was roughly hewn but serviceable.

"His endurance is a phenomenal impediment to his acceptance of penitence. I last visited him a week ago, and I hope he may be ready to at least accept his new name before God." Paul reached behind the man's head, causing him to spin slowly on the axis of the rope. Paul steadied him and untied his gag. The rope fell to the floor and with agonizing slowness, the man spit up the wadded cloth that had been stuffed in his mouth. It was stained red and yellow with blood and bile.

"What is your name, brother?" Paul asked, kneeling to look him in the eye. "Your name?"

The man took what seemed like an eternity to answer. Agnès expected him to thrash, but apparently he was well beyond that. He took a few ragged breaths, and the shafts piercing his flesh shifted, making audible sounds of scratching across bone. One puss-caked eye managed to open, showing a yellowed orb with a brown iris and a pinprick pupil. His lips, cracked and covered with burst cankers, moved several times before he could manage audible speech.

"Mi…ra… beau…" he whispered. "My… name… is… Bertrand… Mirabeau…."

Paul stood up and looked at Agnès. "You see the bind the monster has on his soul. To think there are creatures who use parodies of the sacraments of blood to tie souls to them is a great sadness to me. It makes a mockery of Father Anatole's holy work."

Agnès nodded.

"Sebastien," Paul said turning back to the hanging man. "Let go of your pride. You must, for the sake of your soul."

And with that, he plunged a stake into Bertrand Mirabeau's open eye. The man's ravaged lungs managed only a raspy scream.

"This is holy work," Agnès said.

***

Cedric Nathaniel hadn't had more than an hour's sleep in the last two weeks. Ever since Miss Ash and Lady Regina made their way into the prison and promptly disappeared, he'd been what could delicately be called troubled. In the forty-five years since Victoria

Ash visited Jamaica and enticed the emancipated mulatto son of sugar-trader Jonah Nathaniel to become her coachman and more, he had never felt quite this way. There had been absences before of course. Miss Ash had traveled from Savannah to New York without him in the spring of 1847 and ended up staying away until the autumn of 1850. That had been a terrible loneliness, but Cedric had kept the sense that somehow she was well and that some night she would either return to Georgia or call for him. There had also been dangers, of course. During the War Between the States, they had escaped the burning of Atlanta by an uncomfortably close margin. That had led to a mad flight north, dodging Yankee soldiers and some of Miss Ash's kindred as well. Like all wars, this one was used to settle a great deal of old scores, and it seemed a goodly number of creatures caught between life and death wished to see a world without Victoria Ash in it.

They got their wish, at least in part. Cedric and Victoria had made it to Halifax and then crossed the Atlantic in the hold of a leaky ship and found shelter of a sort in England. Throughout that terrible passage— a reverse echo of the slave ship's course that had brought Cedric's mother's forefathers to Jamaica at the end of the seventeenth century—he had feared that they would sink to the depths of the ocean. But still, he had been physically close to Miss Ash and certain that whatever fate had in store, they would face it together.

There had also been the jealousy of course. Cedric had fed on the black, delicious blood in Miss Ash's perfect veins off and on for decades, and it had given him many gifts. Strength, yes, but also beauty that would not fade. Cedric Nathaniel would celebrate his sixty-ninth birthday on the next Christmas Day, but he neither looked nor felt more than the twenty-four he'd been when Miss Ash had found him. Those four decades had given him ample time to realize that his mistress's affections were more diverse than his own. For a few precious years, he'd felt as if he were her favorite, and he still remembered those as the best of his life, despite the difficulties of being a free man of color (especially one seen in the company of a white woman) in a slave society like antebellum Georgia. Then other protégés and favorites had come into their circle. At first he'd been insanely jealous and had even murdered one of his rivals one bright October morning, using a heavy rope to secure a large stone to Terrence Rome's unconscious body before throwing him into the Savannah River. Eventually that had faded. Miss Ash was kind to her protégés and lovers so long as they were appreciative of her, and Cedric found that if he only waited long enough, his rivals either earned her scorn or found their own path out of her bed. He had not shared a relation with Miss Ash that an outsider would think of as sexual in a generation, but to him the simple consumption of her dark blood was the most erotic pleasure known.

This time was different. Different because he was isolated from Miss Ash by the thick walls of the Santé prison and by a widening gulf he could feel within himself. His mistress was facing a real challenge, one that resonated in the parts of her that were always with him, and there was little he could do about it. He had promised to wait for her, not to intervene, and he would not break his pledge to the woman he loved as the sea loved the sky. Every night brought greater conviction, however, that his inaction would cost her existence and hence his own (for what would life be without her?).

He had taken to spending a good deal of time in the small servants' common room located on the top floor under the eaves of the hotel. The staff and the servants of other guests would gather there for quick meals and to exchange gossips and stories. Miss Ash had taught Cedric French in the early years of their relationship in preparation for a social season spent in New Orleans, so he was able to hold up his end of the conversation. Cedric's skin-color seemed less an issue here than in London—and was clearly less so than in Savannah—but he was not fool enough to think the various maids, menservants and valets color-blind. Still, the idle talk helped pass the time.

He was, therefore, headed for that room, carrying a pot of coffee to share with the closest thing he had developed to a friend in the hotel—a rake-thin porter named Hubert—when he spotted Lt. Seward entering the building. Cedric had only crossed paths with the lieutenant a few times in the last year, when Lady Regina had entered into Miss Ash's confidences, but he made it his habit to remember all those who might have a grudge against his mistress, and Lady Regina's purported fiancé was definitely on that list. Still, Cedric's immediate reaction was not one of threat. Instead, he thought that perhaps Seward might provide a way out of his quandary. If he told the lieutenant where Regina was, then maybe—

Then Cedric saw the other men, and he knew that things would take a much uglier turn. There were three that he could see, all with the same ugly look about them. Two entered the hotel on Seward's heels, and the third posted himself at the door, his hand resting all too obviously on the weapon concealed under his three-quarter-length coat.

Cedric put the tray he was holding down on one

of the steps and rushed up the stairs. His own rifle was under lock and key in a footlocker in their apartments, but if he could get to the back staircase, he might escape before these men caught up with him.

He never made it. The fourth of the ugly men was at the top of the stairs.

Chapter Sixteen

"Sister Agnès," a familiar voice said from the doorway to her cell.

Looking up from her desk, she felt relief wash over her like a cool wave. *Victoria, at last.* It had been two nights since her visit with the recalcitrant Mirabeau, and Victoria had been absent since then. *In private contemplation with Father Anatole,* Paul had said.

"Come in, please," she said as calmly as she could.

Although she was wearing simple prison clothes like the rest of the people behind these walls, Victoria Ash still moved with the grace of a ballerina. Despite the simple shift and tight bun, her beauty was intoxicating. The mundane movements of closing the door behind her, crossing the small cell and sitting on the rough cot were somehow inculcated with perfect poise.

"Agnès," she began, but stopped when the other woman practically threw herself in her arms, as a child would to its mother's breast.

"Oh, Victoria!" She clasped tightly to her, taking comfort in the proximity. "Please, don't call me by that name. It will surely drive me mad."

"But…"

Regina felt tears of relief welling in her eyes. These last few nights had been excruciating, watching every word, every act, until she could get to Victoria. Wearing the half-mad religion of the abbey as a mask, her conversion an act of desperate theater she feared would at any second be revealed. But it had all been worth it. "I found Mirabeau," she said. "If we can free him, find a way to escape…"

She stopped speaking when she realized Victoria

had grown stiff and unresponsive. She looked up at the green eyes in which she had once lost herself, and they seemed very distant indeed.

"Oh, Agnès," Victoria said.

"Regina," she whispered. "My name is Regina."

"You see my sister," came a third voice, masculine and enrapturing. Father Anatole was standing at the door to the cell, even though Regina was sure Victoria had closed it. He wore an expression of quiet concern that matched Victoria's all too closely. "She piles sin upon sin. Making false testimony before God."

Regina looked back toward Victoria, who was nodding slightly. "No…"

"Yes," Anatole said. "While you bore false witness in the house of God, while you eschewed the careful counsel of Brother Paul, Sister Madeleine has taken the steps toward acceptance of her sins and the search for redemption."

"Madeleine?" Regina looked at Victoria.

"Victoria is gone," she said, her eyes getting more distant with every passing second. "I have submitted myself to God at last."

"No," Regina said, standing upright, turning on Anatole. "How dare you—"

"Silence."

His one word hit Regina like a hammer blow, stealing her voice and the very will to form words. In that instant, looking into the radiant blue of his irises, she glimpsed the infinite zeal there. A zeal so strong it had reshaped a prison into a mad abbey. So strong it had retooled Victoria Ash into the ghost of a person called Sister Madeleine. So strong it would not stop until the whole world was brought to God under its ministry.

"Now sleep," he said. And she did.

***

Some bond within Regina broke while she dreamed that night and through the following day. Images of Victoria haunted her slumber, mad hall-of-mirrors images of the undead beauty shattering again and again. Regina herself, slipping and sliding into the emerald lakes that were her eyes only to resurface and find the water frozen over, transformed into creamy, flawed jade-colored glass.

When she awoke at last, her bed mat was soaked through with her cold sweat. The rough linen blanket had long since found its way to the ground, and her skin had a sheen of moisture all over it. Her hair was soaked through.

She moaned slightly as she moved, feeling aches in every part of her being. She found the tallow candle on her small desk after some stumbling, and when she lit it, she realized that her Vulgate Bible, her notes and all her writing instruments were gone. Even the chair was missing, leaving the desk naked.

Her menstrual flow had come during the night, and she realized with a start that this was her cycle's first manifestation in several months. A wave of nausea rose within her, and she wretched in the wooden bucket in the corner of the room. There was blood in her vomit.

She barely made it back to the cot before collapsing again.

***

The next time she awoke, she felt certain that Victoria—or Madeleine—was watching her. She expected to see her standing over the cot when she opened her eyes and was startled to see another there.

"Hello Agnès," Paul said, his voice full of gentle

concern. "I've washed you."

And indeed, Regina felt clean. The mat under her was dry, and the soft cotton sheet covering her was cool and comfortable. "Thank you," she said.

"It was… That is, no thanks are necessary." He looked away.

Regina moved to sit up and felt the fabric of the sheet move against her chest. She was nude, she realized, and the implications of Paul having washed her finally dawned in her somewhat addled brain. Fear rose in her, for she remembered Mirabeau's fate at Paul's hands, but illicit pleasure rose as well. A bead of sweat formed on her sternum.

Somewhere far away, she felt something shift, an attention grow keener. An instinct told her Victoria must be right behind her, but she knew that her gaze originated from further afield. The undead woman's senses were keen enough to watch over her protégée from whatever privileged position she had taken at Father Anatole's side. Regina felt like an caged animal in a menagerie, there to amuse watchers on the other side of the bars, and revulsion gnawed at her. It only augmented the tingling that was covering her skin with goose bumps.

Apparently aware of the rising charge in the room, Paul rose from the cot. "I should leave you."

"Does Father Anatole know you are here?" The guilt in his eyes answered her question

She slowly sat up, the sheet slipping from her like a stage curtain revealing a forbidden spectacle. Somewhere, dull green irises focused, and an emerald flaw formed in them.

"Agnès…"

"My name is Ginny. You used to call me that, Paul." She extended an arm to touch his thigh, feeling distant eyes bore into her. "Please don't leave."

"I... I can't." He stepped away from her and toward the door.

A desperate chill twisted her innards. Everyone in this God-forsaken abbey was in Anatole's demented grip, from this conflicted man to Victoria herself. She'd thought the undead beauty somehow invulnerable to the lunacy surrounding them, but she wasn't. Regina was truly alone in this church of the mad. No one was going to free her. It was up to her.

"Paul," she said, standing up to reveal herself fully. "You don't want to leave."

He wanted to say something, perhaps, but the sight of her seemed to steal his tongue. She took encouragement from that and approached, moving languidly, like a cat. The stone floor was cold and hard under her soles, but heat rose through the rest of her. The sense of being watched intensified with every movement, until by the time she reached her man, she could imagine Victoria sitting in Anatole's chambers, her eyes focused on her protégée.

"Ginny," he said at last, "I mean, Agnès—"

She kissed him. Not in the way of a betrothed woman, as she had several nights before, but acting only on pure, physical desire. She imagined herself to be as Victoria had been in London, or better yet as one the wasp-waisted concubines at Merritt House. Her tongue slipped into his mouth, teasing at his own, and she pressed her naked flesh against his rough woolen prison clothes.

She moved her kisses to his throat and explored his body with her hands. She felt his taught muscular frame under the rough fabric and found the swollen evidence of his own ardor. She was the bull-woman, the harlot she had played for her once-beloved

Malcolm Seward at Victoria's behest on that pure, physical, sinful night which had cost her virginity and very nearly her life. Here the risks seemed greater still— all of which only fanned the flames of her own desire.

"Ginny…" he moaned.

"You want this," she whispered in between bites of his bitter skin. "You have since I first came here."

"Merciful God…"

"They say you can't have me." She pulled open his shirt, exposing his well-muscled chest. Her mouth moved to his nipple, surrounded by a delicate ring of hair. She nipped at it, making it stand erect and summoning gasps from him.

"A sin… you…"

"Yes," she snapped, plunging her hand through his waistband to grab his stiffened member. "I'm a sinner, Paul. A sinner."

His hands had found her, one stroking her rump and the other inexpertly groping a breast.

"You can't save me, preacher." She moved her mouth up his chest and neck, to the side of his face, so she could whisper in his ear. "You can only punish me."

"Yes!" Releasing his pent up savagery, he picked her up and slammed onto the rough wooden desk a few steps ahead. She felt a flash of pain as her back knocked over and snuffed out the single tallow candle, plunging the room into tight, hot darkness. "Yes," he grunted again.

In the absence of light, the violent coupling became an incongruous collage of sensations. The burn on her back, made raw by the friction with the rough wood of the desk. The sudden, painful penetration. The smell of sweat and blood. The pulses of pleasure as she bucked her pelvis to meet his grunting thrusts. Her own moans, so much rawer and wilder than in the intoxicating bliss of lying with Victoria.

And Victoria. Without the distraction of vision, Regina's sense of her erstwhile protector sharpened. It was very much like she was sitting in the room, her green eyes ablaze, the heat of needlessly circulating blood raising a blush of life to her pale flesh. Her sharp teeth peeking from behind parted lips.

"This is what you want," Regina said to the apparition, not caring if the man plunging into her with savage zeal thought she was addressing him. "This is what you love best, isn't it? To watch, to feel the pleasure through me. This is what I gave you. This is what you can have again."

"Yes," Victoria said an eternity later, both far away and close at hand.

Regina felt the pleasure, like a dark rapture, wash from Victoria to her along whatever eldritch connection existed between them. Her back arched in response and her climax rose with it, starting as a far-off tingle and washing over her in wave after wave of explosive pleasure. She screamed her ecstasy and felt the man who had invaded her release his seed.

He collapsed atop her momentarily, but was soon pulling himself off of and out of her. His breathing was harsh and heavy, laden with anger and guilt. Regina moved and felt the burns, cuts and splinters on her back like the lashes of a whip. She heard him open her cell door, and she stumbled to the cot. She felt blood and ejaculate drip from her. She collapsed on her side. She was only vaguely aware of the door opening again several minutes later.

"Anatole will not be pleased, darling girl."

She turned over and felt the soft and too-cold touch of unliving feminine skin slide over hers as the cot creaked to accept the burden of a second occupant.

"Victoria," Regina whispered.

"Yes," she answered. "I'm here. Sleep, darling."

Regina drifted into slumber, feeling the aches and pains recede and Victoria's arms envelope her protectively.

"Thank you," Victoria whispered just before sleep took the girl.

Chapter Seventeen

The affair of the Santé prison and the night of September 15th and 16th, 1888 would be something of a scandal that autumn and through to the spring of next year, when the Great Exposition and the exile of General Boulanger would eclipse the matter. Street rumors, newspaper headlines and long-winded assemblymen all seemed to outdo each other in hyperbole and fantastic details, so the true story would never fully emerge. Nevertheless, in years to come, the consensus would be that shortly after 1:00 a.m. on the morning of the 16th, anarchists, foreign agitators or Boulangists (depending on whom you asked) detonated a large amount of explosives on the Boulevard Arago, running north of the prison. The explosives—likely barrels of black powder or sticks of dynamite—were concealed in a cart that seemed to be stacked with vegetables or other mundane items (accounts varied). There was also evidence that said anarchists managed to plant some further explosives in an underground drainage sewer that ran under the prison wall. The result was an explosion that shattered windows across the street, woke residents and livestock from sleep for miles around, and created a substantial hole in the impressive northern wall of the prison.

The explosion apparently sparked a panic among the prison guards and a riot among the inmates, more than a few of whom seemed to be engaged in some nighttime work detail for which no viable explanation was ever forthcoming. Several fires broke out, and enraged prisoners took it upon themselves to liberate still more inmates, using tools or stolen keys to break open cells across the penitentiary. The guards, reinforced by local gendarmes and soldiery responding to the explosion, managed to quell the outbreak but only with the force of arms. For upward of an hour, chaos reigned in several parts of the prison. No official body count ever emerged, but even conservative estimates put the number of guards and prisoners killed that night in the dozens. Some spoke of upward of one hundred dead.

What never emerged was the role played by the two priests newly assigned to the prison, who managed to convince a few guards to help them open two subsidiary doors on the south side of the prison. This allowed the Ventimiglio brothers and Malcolm Seward—the "men of action" of Paris's Society of Leopold—to go in pursuit of their prey.

For Victoria Ash and Regina Blake, trapped inside the prison and its undead abbey, the chaos provided the cover for escape. Alone in the small cell that had been Regina's home—or rather that of "Sister Agnès"—the two of them acted in a rough harmony. Jumping at the opportunity to avoid the admissions that hung in the air around them, they both went to the cell door. Regina half-expected it to be locked tight, but Victoria had come in, so it must be open.

"Your lover left the door open when he left," Victoria said with equal parts jealousy and spite. "Shame makes men forgetful."

Regina hated her at that moment. *Does she even realize what I've given up for her?* The answer bloomed in her mind like a poison bud. *No, but I don't know what I've forced her to surrender either.* She did her best to shake off these pointless recriminations and concentrate on the tasks at hand.

Chaos was already gripping the abbey. "The Apocalypse is upon us!" some overexcited novice yelled off to the left, and that chorus was taken up by others. "Fire in the watchtower!" another yelled.

"It's madness," Regina whispered.

Victoria smiled darkly. "Father Anatole is reaping what he has sown. Come, maybe we can get out in the mess." She started down the corridor, leading Regina into the nearest stairwell and making to head down, toward the ground floor.

"No," Regina said. "We have to get Mirabeau."

Victoria stopped short, an uncomprehending look on her face. "There's no time. We have—"

"We have to get Mirabeau," Regina said and promptly headed up the stairs. After a moment Victoria followed. They were not the only ones using the stairwell, however, and two panicked novices pushed past them heading down as they made the last turn before the top-most landing.

"They'll kill us all," one exclaimed, shrilly. "Hurry."

Regina kept going, redoubling her speed up the last of the steps. Questions of who and why found no purchase in her mind. Her only concern was that if someone was killing people in the abbey, they had to get to Mirabeau before the killers did. The dread of losing her last chance of finding her mother kept her legs pumping until she emerged in the high-ceilinged corridor of the top-most floor.

Further down the hall, there were two men holding rifles. They wore neither uniform nor insignia, but they were clearly working together. Indeed they raised their weapons in unison and just before they fired Regina had the strange insight that these killers must be related.

They have the same nose, she thought.

In the instant before jets of smoke and lead exploded from the rifles, though, something else hit

Regina full force, collapsing her as a swift wind would a house of cards. No, faster. As if she had been pulled down rather than pushed. One instant she'd been staring her death in the face, the next she was flat on he ground, Victoria's strong arm keeping her down.

Victoria, who'd been a full half-flight behind her a second ago.

Regina looked up as best she could and could see the two men readying to fire again. The one to the left, slightly younger she thought, was working the bolt-action on his carbine. The other one was faster and was already aimed and ready. It made very little difference. Where Victoria had been—right next to Regina—she suddenly wasn't. Instead there was a blur of motion that reminded Regina of the swing of her father's saber in fencing practice, a dissolution of the solid object into a suggestion of speed and movement. That blur was Victoria, who covered the distance to the faster of the attackers in less than an instant.

The whole scene took on the slow-motion staccato that occurs in the moments before tragedy, but still Regina could not quite follow Victoria's movements. One instant, she was raising the gunman off the ground one-handed—the thought that such strength in a lithe woman was unnatural flitted through Regina's mind, but there was too many unnatural things to bother with such trivialities. The next instant, the man had slammed into his brother as if thrown by a high-ocean gale. The two collapsed in a heap, and Victoria who was suddenly further down the hall, turned to face them.

Regina had lifted herself into a crouch by this time and it occurred to her that Victoria had drawn the men's attention away from her. She began to move toward what she hoped was Bertrand Mirabeau's cell.

She'd taken three steps when the slighter of the two men, the younger one, drew a long knife and tried to get up. Victoria's eye locked on him and everything changed.

In County Durham, when Regina had been a young girl, there had been a problem with rabid dogs. Barely eight years old and much more inquisitive than was thought proper for her sex at any age, Regina had peered over a low hedge and watched when the men of the house had responded to an alarm raised by the cook: a dog in the vegetable garden. It was a border collie, but disease had transformed the skillful herder into a mad thing. All its muscles were tensed, its eyes were wild, and foam dripped from its bared teeth. It had been, for the young Regina Blake, the single most frightening thing she'd ever seen. A second later, her father's gun had put the creature out of its misery, but that wild thing would haunt her dreams well into womanhood.

Victoria looked a hundred times worse.

Her chest convulsed as if she were going to vomit and she spewed forth a terrible hiss of hatred. Her green, lustrous eyes disappeared into hard black slits in a contorted visage. Fangs more terrible than any dog's revealed themselves when she drew back bloodless lips. Her hair seemed to billow out like the fur of a hissing cat and a sense of menace so palpable it felt like a hot, maddening wind blew from her. Regina knew Victoria in ways difficult to explain. Despite the time in the asylum and the previous night's emotional trauma, she felt a lingering empathy for this undead woman. Regina also was neither the cause nor target of this dread, predatory gaze. Still, she felt as a condemned woman in the terrible instant between the gallows' door dropping from beneath her feet and the noose snapping tight around her neck.

For the knife-wielding man who was the subject of that gaze, the effect must have been all the worse. Indeed, he stood still save for a terrible trembling as that initial hateful hiss washed over him. His knife slipped from his grasp and clattered on the ground, and the sour smell of urine filled the air. Victoria made the slightest movement forward and it was enough to provoke a scream from the man and snap him into panicked, scrambling, life-preserving flight.

He brushed past Regina in his escape down the hall and that goaded her into motion as well. She did not turn tail and run back the way she'd come, however. Instead, gripping onto the same reserves of courage that had carried her this far in her mad journey, she took another ten steps toward Victoria, reached the open door to Bertrand Mirabeau's cell, and slipped inside.

She found the man in a heap on the floor in the center of the cell. The ropes that had bound him had been untied, and it seemed that some of his wounds had been tended to. His flesh was still a savaged mess of cuts, punctures and welts, testaments to the holy work he had suffered.

"Monsieur Mirabeau," she said, kneeling at his side. "Can you hear me?"

He answered with the faraway voice of delirium. "I… I kept faith…"

"Yes," she said. "Yes, you did."

"Where!?" Victoria's voice was tainted and twisted by rage, and it hit Regina like a slap. She turned to see the undead woman raising the remaining, and larger of the two gunmen, off the ground by his thick throat and pressing him against the heavy stone wall of the prison. The monstrous visage she'd worn a minute ago had faded, but her anger was still palpable. "Where did you get it?"

Regina took the few steps to the cell door, still wary of this woman who could be both siren and gorgon, it seemed. "What?"

Victoria raised her free hand, her left, and Regina could see the heavy band that was clutched there between thumb, index and middle finger. It was a large pewter ring, a man's, inlaid with onyx that formed a black rose. Regina recognized the pattern, and well she should. Before arriving in the Santé, she'd worn the same pattern on a cameo around her neck, onyx and mother of pearl. Victoria too had worn such a piece, hers being the most well-made of all and acting as the template on which the others were based.

In the night society of London, Regina had discovered that the undead made use of such symbols and patterns to mark those in whom they had an interest. It was an echo of the stories of a lady's favor carried from medieval times and the sensibilities of the Order of the Garter perhaps, although with a far darker reality underlying it. Cedric Nathaniel had worn this ring on his left hand.

Therefore, Regina well understood why Victoria was so adamant to uncover the band's path from her coachman and companion's hand to that of this man—for Regina could clearly see, as he uselessly grasped at Victoria's extended arm around his throat, the gash and chaffing on his ring finger, from which Miss Ash had forcefully removed the ring. The man, however, made only half gurgles in response to Victoria's questions.

"He can't breathe," Regina said, getting close enough to take the ring from Victoria's hand. It had blood on it, but she couldn't be sure whose.

Victoria released her grip and the man slipped

down the wall, his knees not quite taking his weight. He stopped, leaning back against the stone, gasping. "Father... save... me..."

It was, Regina thought, perhaps more terrible to see Victoria's features now than when she had turned her hate on this man's brother. Her face, which had been hard and angered, softened like a flower petal unfurling for the sun. Her eyes became limpid pools of emerald and her hair crimson ringlets framing alabaster skin. It was terrible because Regina knew, in her deepest core, that it was not real. Knew, not only because she had seen and felt just how easily Victoria could play with the emotions of the living, but also because she could still feel a distant echo of Victoria's true self in her veins. She's shared blood with her and that bond, although weakened, still afforded her an insight. What she felt there was not even vaguely reminiscent of the kind, seductive expression now cascading off Victoria's face. It was ice-cold hatred.

"What is your name?" Victoria stepped closer to the man so that she almost enveloped him.

"Tho... Thomas. Thomas Ventimiglio."

"Such a musical name," she said, using the same hand that had left angry welts on the man's throat to gently stroke his cheek and travel down his chest. Regina could feel the erotic heat building between the two like a head of steam. "Where did you get that ring, Thomas?"

"F—" He stopped short as Victoria's hand found the swelling between his legs. "From the African... At the Hôtel de Guénégau..." His breaths were short, shallow things.

Regina's hope for Cedric died, and she felt the hate in Victoria grow icier still.

"What happened to that man, Thomas?" Victoria's

eyes never left Ventimiglio's. Her right hand touched his face while her left worked into his trousers to stroke there. "Where is he now?"

"He... He wouldn't answer our questions."

"No? Go on."

"It... ah... took all day and night for him to... ah... tell us..."

"Mmm, yes."

"He was so stubborn... Once he said the San... ah... Santé , we had to..."

"Of course you did, but what? What did you do, Thomas? Tell me, please."

"He was a sinner... ah... ah... and I used the gun... it was... ah... justice.... Father said..."

"But you took his ring?"

"It was so... ah... beautiful...."

"Thank you," Victoria purred. "I should perhaps reward you for your honesty. I could make it feel so good that you would welcome the ebbing of life, Thomas."

She brought her lips close to his and Regina, standing not two steps away felt memories of when Victoria had touched her flesh with those lips and the teeth beneath them. The pleasure had been pure and overpowering and she was, for an instant, jealous of Thomas Ventimiglio.

Then there was the wet, fleshy sound of overripe fruit being crushed, and a look of shock, pain and betrayal snapped onto the man's face. Victoria then plunged the thumb of her right hand into his left eye, all the way to the second joint. His legs gave way altogether, and he slid down the wall until he was sitting. During the slide, Victoria's bloody thumb popped out of the socket and her left hand came loose from his trousers, clutching the gory remains of his genitalia.

"I don't think you deserve that," Victoria said before licking the blood from her right thumb and dropping the wet mess from the other hand . She bent down and calmly rifled through his pockets, looking (Regina guessed) for any other souvenirs the man might have taken. She found a leather wallet and searched it. Out of it, she drew a carefully folded, but shabby piece of paper.

Victoria said nothing, but seemed perplexed as she unfolded the paper and glanced over it. She slipped it into the single pocket of her shift and closed her eyes.

Regina thought she should do something, but when Victoria's eyes opened again, confusion had turned to anger. Not the icy hate of a minute before, but a white-hot rage that triggered a self-protective instinct in Regina and made her recoil. It was good that she did, because she suspected that Victoria, once she had bitten out Thomas Ventimiglio's throat and feasted on the blood of the wound until there was none left, might well have turned on her had she been close at hand.

As it was, Victoria remained over the man's corpse until Regina emerged with Bertrand Mirabeau in tow. The man was a heavy weight for her to bear, just barely conscious, unable to support himself. Victoria had left her animalistic feast by the time Regina had taken the few steps to reach the cell door with the man and moved to help. They reached the stairwell and made their way down, Victoria assuming the full weight of the man.

"We have to find a way out," Regina said, immediately chiding herself for stating the obvious.

"If we escape the abbey," Victoria said, showing no sign of strain at bearing a man twice her size, "we can get to the front gate."

They reached the ground level and turned left, the right-hand way starting to fill with smoke. The central wing of the prison—the abbey—connected to the others at both ends, so they should still be able to make it. They passed by the side passage leading to the chapel, and Regina heard a familiar voice.

"No," Victoria said, but Regina was already heading down the hall.

"Wait for me at the abbey door," she said.

***

Regina found Paul in the chapel itself, screaming incoherently as he overturned the rough stone altar. When the thing refused to shatter upon falling over, he yelled at it like a maddened child.

Then he turned on Regina. "You!"

He advanced quickly, with such violence in his gaze, that Regina recoiled. He caught her in the corridor outside the chapel, grabbed the scruff of her shift and pushed her against the wall. His strength was tremendous and she felt trapped, the breath being pushed out of her chest.

"Paul…"

"He's gone, Ginny! Father Anatole is gone!" Expectorate flew from his mouth and hit her face. "God is punishing us, he said! For our sins!"

"He's…" She struggled for air with which to speak. "He's mad, Paul. You can escape him."

"You've damned us all! You've damned us—"

There was a loud detonation, and the side of Paul's head exploded in a bloody spray mere inches from Regina's face.

He slumped to the ground, only half-releasing his grip on her shift. Regina had to forcefully extricate herself from his dead hands before looking around.

Malcolm Seward was standing at the end of the ground-level passage, which she knew led to the courtyards facing the small street to the south of the prison. A smoking pistol was in his extended hand, testament to his skillful shot into Paul's temple.

"Thank providence," he said once he'd crossed the distance between them. "I thought I would never find you. We must go before they seal the prison again."

He took Regina by the hand, dragging her from Paul's savaged form, blood and brain matter still clinging to her dingy clothes. A storm of emotions raged through her heart, paralyzing her for the time being. She focused on the destroyed face of Father Anatole's acolyte and saw in the shocked gaze there a chimerical amalgam of men: the man she had lain with, whose flesh had merged with hers. The man whose touch had been the instrument by which she'd freed Victoria, and hence herself. The smiling torturer who had driven stakes into Bertrand Mirabeau's flesh and plucked out the man's eyes. The gentle man who had spoken to her of salvation and the immortal soul. The bloody corpse already attracting flies.

The jumble and juxtaposition was dizzying. But then, Regina realized, so much of her life had become an unholy union of desire and horror, of love and rage, that Paul fit all too well. Images of the recent past rose up within her. Her mother become the instrument in some vengeance she did not quite understand. Herself entwined in an erotic kiss with Victoria Ash, a woman who by rights should have gone to her rewards centuries ago. Malcolm, his chest bare and his lips smeared with ox-blood, straddling her, entering her during an arcane ceremony. Raising the knife…

"No!" Suddenly, terribly aware, she twisted from his grasp. "Get away from me!"

"Darling?" He looked momentarily dumbstruck before impatience, even anger, overtook that. "We have to be quick." He reached to grab her again. "There'll be time—"

"Don't!" She pulled away again, causing him to stop in his tracks. "What is the Taurus Club?"

Perplexed, he dropped his hands to his side. "What? What are you talking about?"

"The Taurus Club, Malcolm," she spat. "I know you've been involved since before Christmas. I saw your medallion."

He left hand rose to the point on his sternum where a medallion about a chain might hang. Regina had no doubts that one in fact did. "I…" he stuttered. "It is a social club, for military officers, and—"

"And the chamber, Malcolm? What about the chamber in the basement?"

Confusion turned to shock. "What? How do you—?"

"It was me, Malcolm." She advanced on him forcing him to backpedal until he was up against a wall in the hallway. "I was the bull-woman."

From far off came the sound of gunfire. The guards had gotten to their armory and were using lead shot to get escaped felons and purported anarchists sorted out. Neither Regina nor Malcolm noticed.

"You…" He swallowed and stepped back so that he was pressed against the wall. His left hand rose to his own throat. "But I…"

"That's right Malcolm," she hissed. "You took me and then drove a knife across my throat."

"But…"

"And, God forgive me, I was even tempted to go back with you when you found us at Dover! I wanted things to be as they were, but they can't be. They can't! My heart is dead, Malcolm, and you killed it!" Tears were running down her face, and her blood was pumping at speed. Through the blur of her vision, she didn't see the iron portcullis of anger and cold rage slam down across Malcolm's features until it was too late.

"Whore!" he screamed, pushing her away from him so she tumbled onto the hard ground. By the time she looked up, he was pointing his pistol in her face and screaming further invectives. "Do you know what I've gone through for you? You worthless little tart! If that was you in the club you were begging for it and got what you deserved!"

"I deserved a knife across the throat?"

"You seem well enough now," he spat back, "although that doesn't have to remain so."

"Go ahead," she said, "finish your work, then. Be a good little soldier for Ellijay and the rest."

Rage still twisted his features, but he hesitated.

"I met him at a nighttime gathering on the Westminster Embankment, along with your friend Pool."

"Tony?" The anger seemed to falter.

Memories of the event popped through Regina's minds like sepia-toned daguerreotypes: meeting with Lady Anne Bowesley, the seneschal of London's night society. That stern beauty presenting one Captain Ellijay as a kindred of hers and his protégé Lieutenant Pool. The questions that had led Regina to take the place of the prostitute hired to act as the bull-woman for the ritual of Malcolm's initiation into whatever lay at the core of the Taurus Club. "Have you ever seen your dear Captain Ellijay under the light of day? Ever?"

The gun wavered.

"Ask yourself why not, Malcolm. Do you even know who you've become?"

The gun fell to his hip and his shoulders slumped. He looked down at the ground. "Use the door at the bottom of the southernmost stairwell," he said.

It was Regina's time to be confused. "What?"

"They've unlocked it. You can get out that way without being seen, but you have to go now.".

"Malcolm…"

"Quickly!"

Regina picked herself up and headed down the hall to meet Victoria. Just before she turned the corner, she glanced back and saw Malcolm collapsed on his knees, his body wracked in sobs. She kept going.

Chapter Eighteen

That it was less than a mile from the walls of the Santé prison didn't prevent the Cimetière Montparnasse from being a world apart. It was near dawn, only a few hours since their escape from the confines of the abbey, and Regina had a sense of the anxiety roiling in Victoria.

They had crept through the streets from the prison to the cemetery, avoiding the panicked residents and gendarmes reacting to the explosions and fires at the Santé. All the while, the inner beast Victoria had unleashed on Thomas Ventimiglio seemed frighteningly close to the surface. Still, they were here, carrying the mutilated form of Bertrand Mirabeau down the central carriage path of the cemetery, through the band of trees that marked the edge of a tomb-field and among the tightly packed stone monuments and gravestones. Both women wore the simple shifts they'd had on for the last—what had it been, weeks? Neither said anything.

Victoria propped Mirabeau on one of the graves, a slab of gray granite inlaid with pillars and sporting two cherubs. The man, his eyes poked out by Brother Paul, and wounds still seeping from where stakes had been pounded into his flesh, made a shabby addition to this display of necrotic ostentation.

"Come out," Victoria said in a voice seething with barely suppressed rage. "Now!"

That anger sent jolts through Regina's own spine, but genuine apprehension, even revulsion, eclipsed the faint echoes of emotion carried through the eldritch bond between them. Victoria was here stripped of the seductive aura that had once bathed her at all times, but without the pure blood-rage of a few hours ago to replace it. This was the undead creature stripped bare, just an unliving shell full of anger at the night that had imprisoned it. Regina suppressed the urge to run from the graveyard and not stop until she was back in the arms of someone who truly loved her. She did so with the chilling understanding that in all likelihood no one still fit that description.

"Come out, you leprous hag!" Victoria spat. "I have your pet for you."

A shiver ran up Regina's spine, culminating in her skull and sparking the animal sense that something was lurking behind her. Unable to fully acknowledge, much lest resist, the urge to do so, she spun on her heels to face the unknown danger. Where her instinct told her to expect a predator several yards away, she found a ravaged, boil-ridden face mere inches from hers.

"Hello, little Englishwoman."

Regina yelped and stepped back, assaulted by the sight of this wretch and the spoiled-milk smell that surrounded her like a shawl. She felt the twin blooms of shame and anger in her cheeks. "Clotille."

The wraith-like creature seemed to have little time for an exchange with Regina, however. Clotille slipped past her, the feel of the creature's scabrous flesh proving her all too solid to be naught but an apparition. That this creature was kindred to Victoria seemed impossible to Regina—as it had when they'd ventured underground to meet her—until she turned to see the two of them at once. With the terrible madness and violence of the escape fresh in her mind, Victoria no longer seemed to her so far removed from a withered undead thing like Clotille. *The wretch only wears her death more openly*, she thought.

"Bertrand!" Clotille advanced to cradle the wounded, blinded man lying on the ornate tomb. "What have you done to my Bertrand?"

Victoria was faster than the withered crone, however, and deftly blocked her way. "Not yet, Clotille. First, I have some questions."

"My Bertrand…" The woman's already nasal voice rose in pitch to the whine of a child.

"I'm more interested in this," said Victoria, throwing a folded parchment at Clotille, who caught it by instinct.

"What?" She unfolded the paper and looked at the writing that must have been across it. Regina's eyes, despite her time locked away from the sun, were not as night-honed as those of the undead. She did recognize the paper as the one Victoria had lifted from Ventimiglio, however.

"Victorine," Clotille said in that same whine.

"Do you recognize the writing, Clotille?" Victoria asked, ice in her vice. "I do. I seem to remember a remade street girl so proud of having acquired letters in her new existence that she always sent messages in pithy notes."

"But…"

"And I remember receiving one of those same pithy notes several weeks ago, telling me she wanted to meet me, telling me to come to the catacombs near this very cemetery to meet her. Didn't I, Clotille?"

"You can't prove anything."

The blow came so quickly that Victoria's arm was nothing but a blur. Before Regina had even registered that something was happening, the slap of perfect alabaster hand against putrescent cheek was reverberating off the nearby tombs and Clotille was on the ground. Regina, moving without thinking, crept further up the thin space between two tombs, using them for shelter but also to get a better view of the confrontation.

"Do you really think so?" Victoria was saying. "Villon and his sycophants are all desperate because of the havens your witch-hunter friends have burned. This mess at the prison will only add to the chaos. Anatole knows you wanted his man, do you really think they won't all jump on the chance to be rid of you?"

Regina had almost reached her position when Clotille, still crouching, looked up, her face contorted by rage and red streaks of blood-tears seeping from her jaundiced eyes. "You whore! What right do you have to come here after so long and question me? You and your pig-brained Maximilien left us to hang! To hang!"

"Don't dare lecture me about those nights, hag! Do you even remember what happened? Maximilien playing his games with nobles and parliamentarians, whispering here and there, confident they would dance to his tune. When the revolts came, where were his allies? Carrying torches and stakes just like the rest!"

"It could have been—"

Victoria continued without losing a beat. "And now you do the same with these witch-hunters! How long before we're all put to the pyre?"

"Those who burned deserved it," Clotille spat in a whisper. "Petit Jean in the Auberge des Trois Moutons betrayed me…."

"Did my Cedric betray you, Clotille? He died at their hands too. And the prisoners in the Santé? How many have died tonight because of the madness you've started?"

"I didn't send them after you," Clotille said, her voice softer. "That was—"

"That's the whole point, you wretched little hag!

Once you start them burning, they won't stop when it's convenient for you. They won't ever stop."

"Give me my Bertrand."

Regina glimpsed the impression of movement. With the blood pumping through her veins, the darkness of the night, and the trauma of the escape, she wanted nothing so much as to believe that Victoria had simply trotted from where she was to the spot right next to Bertrand, her left hand clamped tightly around his exposed neck. A part of her that had become inured to the preternatural world she'd sunken into, however, told Regina that Victoria had again moved faster than any creature had a right to, that she'd crossed the distance quite literally in the blink of an eye.

"Why should I give him to you?" Victoria tightened her grip on the man's throat.

In that instant, Regina saw what would unfold with a daylit clarity. Clotille, angered, would choose the easiest victim through which she could strike at Victoria. Although there were two living souls and two undead in the graveyard at this moment, Regina and Bertrand would soon be joining the corpses six feet below them. "Stop!" she screamed, aware that Clotille had already vanished from sight in order to strike.

Victoria faltered and released her grip on Bertrand's throat. She stared at Regina, questioning and then surprised.

Regina felt the calloused hand grasp her neck and bright spots of pain danced at the edge of her vision. Clotille was there. "Wait," she said, "please." The pressure ease, but only slightly.

"We came to Paris to find Mother," Regina said. "Madame Clotille asked us to find Mirabeau and we've done so. The rest is meaningless."

"Cedric," Victoria said in a voice of ice, "was not

meaningless."

"You've already exacted vengeance, Victoria." Ghastly images of only a few hours ago floated before Regina's eyes. "A man lies dead for the crime of his murder. Do you really need to see Bertrand dead, too?"

Victoria said nothing but removed her hand from the prostrate man's throat. He emitted a low gurgle.

"And you, Madame Clotille," Regina said, closing her eyes since she could not turn to face the hag, "will snapping my neck solve any of your problems? Just tell us where my mother and her keeper went and we will take the next train there. No one need know about the notes."

Clotille's voice was raspy and all –too close to Regina's ear. "You would do this?"

Victoria gave a slight nod. "Paris is dead to me," she said. "If you are fool enough to throw yourself on its pyre, so be it."

The pressure on Regina's neck released and she risked a look back. She was greeted by the unsettling view of Clotille's face, covered in warts and smeared with blood and dirt, seeming to dissolve into a wisp of smoke before she vanished altogether.

"Vienna," said a voice out of the empty night. "They went to Vienna by train."

***

"It was God's will."

Father André would repeat that sentence several times in the days that followed the chaos at the Santé prison. It served him as a bulwark against the despair that threatened to grab him. Thomas and Christophe Ventimiglio both died in the strike against what they had determined to be a nest of devils in the Santé. Alain, the youngest brother, was as good as dead, having fled from his brother Thomas's side and thus blaming himself for the loss of his elder. In addition, he found his nights haunted by the image of a terrible, monstrous woman, all fangs and claws and bloodlust.

André saw to it that friends in the church took care of him for the rest of his days, none of which would ever again include a peaceful night's sleep. It would be years before he simply woke in a sweat, instead of screaming for the protection of Christ the King.

Othman al-Masri suffered a break in his left arm that night. A panicked gendarme had attacked him with a baton while he lurked outside the prison waiting for Seward and the Ventimiglio brothers. He thanked God and the Prophet that the policeman had been satisfied to see him collapse and had immediately taken off after others.

Malcolm Seward was a haunted man after the events in the prison. For the first day, he simply insisted on being left alone and walked the Parisian streets to clear his head. Eventually he came back to the chapter house on Rue des Deux Ponts and gave André and Othman the news.

"They'll head for Vienna, now. I'm sure of it."

Chapter Nineteen

The Grand Express d'Orient, the luxury Paris-to-Constantinople train operated by the Compagnie Internationale des Wagons-Lits, left the Gare de l'Est at precisely 7:30 p.m. the following Tuesday, September 18th. It was chilly and overcast and with the equinox approaching it was fully dark by the time the train pulled out from under the great steel and glass frame of the station and headed along the Right Bank of the Seine and out into countryside.

The train, featuring all the latest appointments and a level of luxury unheard of in travel except in the finest transatlantic steamers, was the subject of much admiration across Europe and even into England. Regina had, several years ago, read Mr. De Blowitz's *An Excursion to Constantinople* in translation, an account of the first trip of the Grand Express in 1883. The train had been the subject of much excitement among the French and English in Cairo, who saw in it a perfect complement to the canal at Suez, making it possible to travel by train to Constantinople and from there by ship to the Indies, all without needless circumnavigation of either Europe or Africa.

Regina had been somewhat disappointed to learn that the first trip had not, in fact, made it all the way to the Ottoman capital by train, needing to use diligences and ships to complete the last leg of the journey. Even now, she'd noticed from the schedule when they had boarded, the train went only as far as Varna on the Black Sea, using a special ship to complete the last stage to Byzantium in almost a full day. Everywhere, there were notices that work on the final rail link was underway and it seemed only a matter of months before the Grand Express was truly complete.

Regina did her best to keep these idle thoughts in the forefront of her mind as the train sped toward the German border. Anything to distract her from the month-long horror that her stay in Paris had been, and from the prospect of entering yet another city of the undead. *Please, dear Lord, let Mother be safe*, she thought for what seemed like the thousandth time as the train pulled out of the modest station at Bar-le-Duc. *Please let this horror have an end.*

They had the two rear-most sleeping compartments of the second of the two sleeping cars in the train to themselves, so there was very little activity outside the doors. The other passengers were mostly sleeping away the night, and if not, might head for the dining car located in front of the sleeping cars. Regina and Victoria had peace and quiet from the others aboard, and they gave it to one another as well for several hours.

Mr. Nagelmackers, founder of the Express, had become rightly famous for the smooth ride of his trains and Regina was sorely tempted to put pen to paper. Still, she didn't, for the turmoil of her emotions seemed too powerful to be contained with simple words. She sensed Victoria's presence through the wood-paneled wall dividing the two compartments and she found an echo of her own confusion there. Liberation from the hidden abbey inside the Santé had cost them both greatly and Regina felt as if she were adrift on an ocean of doubts and fears.

She must have surrendered to fitful sleep, because when she next became aware of her surroundings, Victoria was sitting on the opposite bench of her compartment, visible in the faint light of the compartment's lantern. Clearing the fog of sleep from her mind, she looked out at the blackness of night speeding by on the other side of the car's window. "Where are we?"

"Germany," Victoria answered. "We'll be in Strasbourg within the hour, I think."

Regina, more as an exercise in distraction than out of any real concern, tried to remember the specifics of the schedule without consulting it. Through the Rhineland and into Bavaria throughout this day; Austria and their destination of Vienna by midnight of the next night. Then what?

"I owe you my thanks, Regina." Victoria's voice was devoid of much of its habitual melodiousness, tinged with fatigue or even defeat. "Without your actions, I might never have left the abbey."

Words died unborn several times in her throat before Regina could speak. "Much of me wanted to stay as well. Father Anatole offered..." She couldn't say the words.

Victoria could. "Hope. Redemption. Salvation."

"Yes. But at too high a price."

"I didn't think so at the time. I was all too glad to surrender myself for the comfort he provided. It can feel so good to put the leash around one's own neck."

Salty tears escaped from Regina's eyes, rolling down her cheeks to find her lips and bead on her chin. "Yes," she said, looking into the dead green eyes part of her still wanted to love. "It can."

"Do you remember our conversations about the rules of my kindred's night society? Last spring, in London?"

"The iron law of secrecy," Regina said after a few seconds.

"Yes. We hide our existence, our nature, our actions from the eyes of the day. We pretend to be just bored aristocrats or," she waved vaguely at the compartment they rode in, "ordinary travelers. We masquerade as the living."

Regina nodded, unsure what to say.

"To drop that mask of secrecy is a serious matter indeed," Victoria continued. "It is tantamount to treason among us, and punishable in the most severe manner possible."

The madmen who'd set the prison alight came to Regina's mind. If there were even a few more of those zealots scattered about, then this iron law of the undead made all too much sense. Still, even in her relatively limited experience, she had seen several instances of the living and the undead rubbing shoulders without uproar. Indeed, given that Victoria and her kindred slumbered during the day, they almost certainly needed breathing attendants and aides to watch over them and to carry out certain tasks.

"You all seem to skirt the edge of treason with some regularity," she said. She was conscious of Victoria's delicious—and terrible—proximity. Her own chest heaved with shallow breath and she was very much aware that the other woman's did not move a whit until she took in air to speak.

"That, I suppose, is part of our nature," Victoria said with a smile. "We cannot exist without kine, but to spend time in their proximity is to risk revelation."

"A paradox."

Victoria smiled, suddenly, fleetingly mirthful. "Yes, quite. You have the soul of a philosopher, my darling Regina. Maximilien would have been quite fond of you, I think."

The echoes of a shared dream floated through Regina's mind. "Your… father? That is, the man who made you?"

"My sire in the blood, yes," Victoria answered, choosing her preferred euphemism, evidently. "And before that, my lover, my protector and my master."

"Master?" A chill traced Regina's spine.

Victoria smiled again, this time without joy. "Love is ever a complex thing, but never more so than among my kindred. Emotions are malleable things to many of us, including such potent things as love and hate."

Regina remembered the way in which, in her first exposures to the undead, she had been battered by the terrible charisma and sensuality of the creatures. The air itself had felt intoxicating that night. Matters had only gained some focus when Victoria had agreed to take her under her wing, to make her a protégée, a process that had involved an exchange....

"Blood," she said aloud. "It's a matter of blood."

"Yes. There are other seductions, but the drinking of our blood is perhaps the most potent one. It creates a growing affection in the drinker with each sip, so much so that soon enough she exists for little else but to please her master."

Regina's head swayed. Victoria had sipped of her blood many a time now, but how many times had the reverse occurred? Three, four times? More? Horror and revulsion rose from the pit of her stomach and she slid along the plush bench away from this undead thing, finding the train car's wall in only a few inches. And yet, the green of Victoria's eyes, the slope of her neck, the intoxicating stillness of her veins and flesh, all called to Regina with a palpable force.

Memory-images flashed in her consciousness like the glimpses of tortured countryside illuminated by lightning on a storm-wracked night. Herself, naked and slithering up Victoria's cold body to find her mouth. Victoria's wrist, slit and welling up black blood that smelled of copper and turned earth. The overwhelming, orgiastic sensation of the woman's needle-sharp teeth puncturing her own flesh.

Regina could not decide if these recollections were repulsive or alluring, whether guilt or longing was quickening her pulse and spreading pins and needles across her skin. Both at once, most likely.

"You see," Victoria said, her voice soothing and compassionate. "Every sip tightens the bond, until the doubts and confusion are utterly erased."

"It isn't mutual. The bond. To you, it is just... I am just *nourishment*."

Victoria's eyes dropped to her own lap and for several long seconds only the rhythmic *rat-tat-tat* of steel wheels passing over the seams and gaps between lengths of track filled the pregnant silence in the compartment. When she raised them again, Regina saw the glimmer of sympathy that was there retreat behind an emerald-cast armor of determination.

"No," Victoria said. "The bond isn't mutual. Living blood doesn't create such an attachment. That is left to the vicissitudes of the heart. You have never been simple sustenance, however."

"A convenience, then. A servant, as you put it in Calais." A realization dawned on Regina then. "Cedric, too? And Theresa, your lady's maid?"

"Yes."

"For how long?"

"Theresa has been with me for only a few years, but Cedric..." She looked away again, and dabbed at a single pinkish tear that had escaped her right eye. "He had been my man for a good deal longer. Since a good many years before your birth, I'd guess."

A new wave of nausea bloomed in Regina's guts. "I don't understand... You, I understand that age...

but he breathed as a man... He wasn't..."

"The blood does more than bond the heart, Regina, or don't you remember that night on Pall Mall Street?"

She did indeed. Terribly wounded—at Malcolm's own hand!—she'd thought she would die, but upon drinking deeply from Victoria's wrist, she'd survived. In fact, the savage wound at her throat had healed as if it had never been. Her hand went to her neck, feeling for a scar that was not there. "Immortality?"

"Of a kind, but only with a regular intake of blood. I myself was Maximilien's companion for half a century, but had he abandoned me, the years would have quickly taken their due."

"But he died, truly died. Or was that a lie you told Clotille?"

A hard, cold spark of anger appeared in the blackness of Victoria's pupils and reverberated into Regina. She felt as if she were looking down the barrel of a gun, so real was the sense of sudden, imminent danger. She should apologize, she felt, but did not.

"It was no lie," Victoria said, her voice failing to conceal that same rage. "He has been gone for a great deal of time, but by then I was as you know me."

"Undead."

"Yes."

"Did he love you, this Maximilien?"

Victoria's anger ebbed, revealing a melancholic shore. "I... I think so, in his way. When he was gone, the bond that his blood had forged in me died as well, and I was left adrift. One instant I missed him more than anything. The next I was cursing him to hell. He had used me, and for that I hated him, or I wanted to hate him, perhaps. But I had loved him without condition or question and could hardly remember a time when it hadn't been so. To lose that certainty was more painful than anything."

"You still don't know, do you? How he felt about you?"

The two tears that traced Victoria's cheeks now were frankly red, trails of blood as rich as from any artery. "No. And I never will."

"How can you have done this to me, then? To Cedric?"

"By necessity. It is how I exist, my darling. By doing what I must to survive and trying, as best I can, to limit just how monstrous I become. I've tried to be caring and watchful of my protégés, to love them as best I could, and to always be aware of the chains I have wrapped about their hearts. I have not always succeeded in that, I fear."

Petulance bloomed in Regina. "Have you *ever* succeeded?"

"If you have truck with others, who treat those to whom they feed their blood as chattel to be used and discarded without compunction, you may find yourself reevaluating your opinion. Remember the footmen at the Louvre, for instance."

Regina felt her heart softening and swallowed the terrible doubt that this was just a symptom of Victoria's blood. "They were as automatons."

"Fed on blood and their wills entirely subjugated without care."

Regina had to admit that Cedric had never seemed to be such a soulless creature. Diligent and loyal, perhaps, but also intelligent and charming. "Paul, and Father Anatole's acolytes. The blood sacraments. They were slaves too, but he seemed to care for them."

"More than that, even," she admitted, "and that is what made me vulnerable to his arguments. He truly believed, I think, that he was saving their souls. The idea that my blood could be a salvation, a benefit to you, to Cedric."

"Paul certainly seemed to take pride in his status, to feel he had been drawn up from the morass of a sinner's life. Although I wonder if poor Mr. Mirabeau would agree."

"Indeed. In the end, it was just another form of bondage, was it not? One that offered the certainty of salvation in exchange for liberty."

"Liberty does not appear to play a large role in your nocturnal society, Victoria."

She nodded. "No, it does not. Philosophers make much of liberty, but it is an elusive, even phantasmal thing in practice. Even in your daylit world."

"You don't need to convince me that freedom is not an easy thing to come by. We live in an imperfect world, no doubt. That does not condone enslavement and exploitation, however."

"I hope that in poor Cedric's case I gave him at least some compensations for his freedom." Victoria held up a hand to stave off the objections already burgeoning on Regina's lips. "And I cannot undo that which I have already done, that which I needed to do for my own survival. But you are correct: Bondage remains bondage regardless of how soft the chains or how gilded the cage. Your actions to free me from Father Anatole's sway reminded me of that more than any words could."

"I'm glad."

"This still leaves us with the matter of secrecy."

"The iron law."

"Yes. To have shown you what I have—it requires your absolute discretion."

Regina swallowed. "Enslavement."

"In the usual manner, yes. The bond of blood eventually becomes so strong that the risk of betrayal is minimal." Victoria moved from her bench to Regina's and placed her hand on the living woman's neck. "But after these last weeks, you of all people do not merit such a fate. I have lived it and would not impose it on you."

"A quandary then."

"There is, I'm afraid, only one other true solution."

Regina's blood ran with ice and she suddenly, desperately wanted to flee, some animal part of her belatedly screaming in alarm. That same animal inside, however, could not leave the gaze of the more powerful beast evident behind the cold emerald of Victoria's eyes. It was like awaking to find a lion perched at the foot of her bed—a beautiful, wondrous sight that was the prelude to carnage.

Victoria's voice was nearly a whisper when she spoke next, the ivory needles of her long canines peeking from behind her ruby lips. "The secret must become your own," she said.

Victoria's hand, still on Regina's cheek, slipped back to her neck and pulled forward with a terrible force. Simultaneously, she leaned forward herself, bringing her mouth to the living woman's neck and the artery lurking under the flesh there. For Regina, the familiar eroticism of the feeding rose like a hot wind from within her, blowing away the detritus of her worries and fears. Over a blissful few minutes, the world was nothing but the waves of pleasure keeping time with the rocking of the train car.

Then, when she was certain she could take no more, the black, icy waters rose after the orgiastic heat. As it had in the day they had infiltrated the Santé prison, the numbing sensation closed in on Regina's senses. Fatigue swept over and through her and she should, she knew, have simply surrendered to unconsciousness. Instead, some small spark of her mind remained aware enough to feel the chill enter her veins and capillaries, grip her bones and organs. Her mouth grew dry, filled with nothing but the shriveled leather of her own tongue. Her heart's beating, at first so potent with fear and pleasure, slowed first to a relaxed pulsing, then to a slow throb, and then to weak contractions so far apart they hardly seemed to emanate from the same organ. A black fog crept into even this last iota of sense and she felt herself pulled far away from her cold, unmoving body.

Unbidden, a fragment of Virgil came to her in those last, eternal moments before all went black. The Sybil's warning to Aeneas before entering Hades:

The way to the Underworld is easy;
Night and day lie open the gates of death's dark kingdom;
 But to retrace your steps, to make your way out to the upper air—
That is the task, the hard thing.

Epilogue:

London, Mid-September, 1888

*In which one pattern begins to form
and another is revealed.*

The Highgate Asylum had a bevy of peculiar visitors the night of September 16th. Dr. Gerald Watson Scott, director of the facility, welcomed them with the unquestioning attention of a servant who was used to dealing with those whose stations far exceeded his own. Miss Parr, whom he trusted implicitly, had arrived with the guests, and that was enough introduction for him. He returned to his bedchamber on the top-most floor of the asylum, locked the doors and shutters tight, and went to sleep without giving the visitors walking his halls another thought. He hoped sleep would come quickly, and most of all, he hoped it would not rain.

Two floors and several rooms over, attendants were laying an unliving monster of epochal age into a large bed. Mithras, the prince of London's unliving host, a creature of unsurpassed power, will and age, was deep in a slumber from which none seemed able to wake him. Lady Anne Bowesley, his seneschal, was left to deal with the consequences.

She felt the tight pinch of tension between her eyes—present since that disastrous night in Sydenham over a month ago—building into a throbbing pain.

"He should be safe here, Your Grace," said Nicholas Pine, one of the attendants along to aid in the transport from the house on Piccadilly where the prince had spent most of his recent nights.

"His Royal Highness does not require your prattling concern, Mr. Pine." Lady Anne's voice was taut and cutting, like a whip-crack. "He simply requires your obedience in these matters."

Pine swallowed, a leftover habit from the years before his entry into the night society. "Yes, Your Grace. Of course." Bowing slightly, he retreated into the hallway and left the room to his betters.

"You may leave as well," Lady Anne said to the other man who'd helped place Mithras into the large bed. This one was not her kindred, but a ghoul, and he knew his place. He muttered something that might have been "Yes, ma'am" before retreating. He never looked Anne in the eyes, and she paid him no mind.

The most infuriating part of it all was, of course, that the insufferable Pine was not altogether wrong. The prince *did* require the safety of the heavy walls of this house of the mad. Miss Parr had personally assured Lady Anne that the asylum was safe. She claimed it as her domain and had made sure that none other had any interest in it. Despite her tiresome suffragette proclivities—as if the vote were somehow significant!—Miss Parr was nothing if not thorough, so Lady Anne had decided to trust her judgment in this matter. Prince Mithras would stay here for the time being, safe from the sun and prying eyes behind stone walls and steel shutters.

None of which did one whit to resolve the larger issue of why the prince has slipped into catatonia. *At least he is quiet now*, Anne thought. Another woman might have felt guilt for such feelings, for taking comfort in her lord and protector's incapacitation. Not Mary Anne Bowesley, who had no time at all for guilt. And regardless, insensate slumber was clearly better than the raving dementia that had periodically gripped the prince over the past month. Or the destructive hungers he had exhibited over the same period, for that matter. No, compared to that, she welcomed the quiet that had reigned in him since the last manic incident, in the pre-dawn hours of September 8th.

"Miss Parr."

Juliet Parr, who had been in the antechamber going over the details with Nicholas Pine, opened the door to the room and walked in. "Yes, Your Grace?"

Anne did not turn around. Miss Parr was sporting jodhpurs and a short riding jacket tonight, another example of her tiresome, mannish ways, and Lady Anne did not feel like laying eyes on her. Parr had served well as sheriff of North London these last few years, but now there was a troubling amount a hubbub in one of the areas under her jurisdiction.

"What is this business in Whitechapel?"

"A pair of murdered prostitutes," Parr answered without losing a beat.

"Bawdy girls die all the time," Anne said without the faintest hint of compassion. "Why in God's name am I hearing whispers about it in proper circles? *The Times* is full of it. Am I to believe that some fool named Mr. Harris would see the Home Secretary involved? In the murder of *prostitutes?*"

"It seems these murders were carried out with unusual brutality, Your Grace. Dissection and evisceration. The coroner, a certain Mr. Baxter, is leading inquests into the deaths, and the press seems in want of sensation to write about. Mr. Harris is a member of a local vigilance committee that is calling for the government to post a reward for the murder's capture."

Lady Anne felt the ache in her brow redouble. "We have enough to concern us this autumn without the prattling of such riffraff. Do see to it that this doesn't become a distraction."

"Of course, Your Grace." Miss Parr took a step back, ready to return to more immediate affairs. She stopped when Lady Anne raised a hand. In it she held a folded fan of the palest ecru.

"Captain Ellijay has made some progress in the matter of Miss Ash and her protégée," the seneschal said. It was a simple statement, pronounced without needless anger. The implication was clear enough without the hyperbole: Ellijay had done what Miss Parr had not.

"Indeed? I'm surprised he did not see fit to share

such information with General Halesworth or I."

Her back still to Miss Parr, Anne allowed herself a tight smile. *Not everyone reports to you or your fellow sheriff, little man-girl,* she thought. Letting that pleasure pass, she spoke in a businesslike manner: "His sources report that Miss Ash has left France and is headed for Austria. For Vienna, more precisely."

"Our suspicions about the Tremere—"

"Would seem confirmed, yes."

House Tremere was a cabal of vampires built along the lines of the various Masonic and Hermetic secret societies that were such the rage at the time. They practiced an arcane form of ritual that earned them monikers ranging from the cautiously respectful (thaumaturges) to the scornful (witches). They were also said to receive orders from a secretive council of elders headquartered in a lavish father-house in Vienna. This earned them the reputations as schemers and usurpers. Prince Mithras had never made secret his enmity toward these blood-sorcerers, and Lady Anne's suspicions had fallen on them as soon as His Royal Highness had fallen into apparent madness. But until now, evidence had been very difficult to come by.

"I believe," Anne continued, "that it is time I had another conversation with the local representative of our sorcerous kindred. Perhaps you would be so kind as to arrange a meeting with Dr. Bainbridge."

Juliet Parr faltered for less than a second, but she was not a woman prone to hesitation, so from her, a second felt like an hour. "I'm afraid Dr. Bainbridge has left London for the Continent, Your Grace."

There was a loud snapping sound.

"Then, *perhaps* you could inquire as to when he might be returning," Anne said. "Forthwith."

"Yes, Your Grace."

Once Miss Parr had closed the door to the antechamber behind her, Lady Anne unclenched her fist and let the shattered remains of her favorite fan fall to the ground.

***

Hesha Ruhadze found what he was looking for in the early hours of the morning of September 17th.

That night was his second visit to Merritt House, a fine private home on Park Lane in Mayfair, since his arrival in London with Mr. Beckett in tow. Ruhadze had stolen away from his hostess, the delightfully shallow Lady Merritt, to watch the night sky from the thin balcony on the top-most floor of the large house. There was a good wind blowing up at this level, and such things were needed to make proper obeisance to the Lord of Storms. He whispered a prayer in the old language and dropped a few grains of sand he had personally collected from the depths of the Libyan Desert on the winter solstice of 1844. They slipped from the coffee-and-cream-colored skin of his palms and caught on the wind, blowing west over the house's gardens and into Hyde Park beyond.

As far as gestures of faith went, this was no grand ceremony. Although the effort of collecting the sand had been considerable, this was not a ritual that would attract much attention. Just a few mumbled words in a foreign tongue and a bit of grit on the wind. Any proper Englishman watching would have assumed that this "simple African" was just playing with the night air. It certainly did not compare to the grand rites performed by the greatest priests. This was not the sacrifice of the sixteen hundred pilgrims, when Ankhesenaten—blessed by his name and memory—was said to have blotted out the hated sun itself with the ashes of all those who gave themselves over to Set. No, those heady nights were centuries past now, and Hesha had simpler needs. This was but a quiet affirmation of the freedom of his soul and a humble prayer for aid.

And, as it turned out, a prayer that Set answered.

Hesha watched the grains flow over the gardens below with keener sight than was possible in life, focusing in the glinting shards of silicate as they rushed into the night. When the last one disappeared even from his eyes, he kept gazing, taking in the rare panorama afforded by his vantage facing the expanse of the park. The bulk of the city was to his back, but still he got the impression of the size of this new Babylon. His colleague Halim Bey had chosen well when he decided to serve Set in this place. The Western Desert was far off, perhaps, but not the greed, pride and gluttony that were such useful tools in eroding the chains of social compact that enslaved the world. It was a surprise, Hesha Ruhadze thought, that no other Setite had set up practice in this city.

And then he saw it. His gaze had descended to Lady Merritt's private gardens almost directly below him. By the standards of great estates outside the city, they were not terribly expansive, extending behind the house for perhaps twenty yards. In this claustrophobic capital, however, where such a space could have housed dozens of well-to-do residents, they were a tremendous luxury. What made them truly special, however, was the fiendish hedge-maze that covered most of the space. Tall walls and tight, curving passages occasionally opened up into small clearings centered on burbling fountains, most of which drew their figures from classical themes. There were no easy passages, but few outright dead-ends, making the maze perfect for illicit seductions and feedings. Lady Merritt prided herself on providing ample flesh for her distinguished, undead guests to feast upon.

The pattern of the maze was devilishly hard to determine from ground level. From Hesha's vantage, however, it stood revealed. There was a central clearing without any fountain or statuary, and it was almost completely surrounded by a hedge-wall. To enter the circle required using a slight passage that formed a zigzag of sorts directly facing the house. To Europeans eyes, the zigzag likely would seem just another geometric flourish, but Hesha saw there the posture of a monarch on a throne in hieroglyphics, with the center clearly serving as an oversized and featureless head. Hedge-walls radiated out from the central clearing, connecting it to each and every other clearing. These were all smaller, and they featured the fountains and statues. Because these radiating links were walls and not passages, there would be no way to determine these connections from within the maze. The pattern was clear from above, however, and it was one Hesha Ruhadze recognized.

The hedge maze at Merritt House was a representation of Kemintiri, the Thousand-Faced Daughter of Set.

About the Author

Philippe Boulle is the managing editor of White Wolf Fiction, and thus spends far too much time thinking about vampires and other things that go bump in the night. He is the author of a variety of roleplaying games, **Tribe Novel: Red Talons**, and the science fiction novellas *Heavy Gear: Crisis of Faith* and *Heavy Gear: Blood on the Wind*. He lives in Atlanta, Georgia.

Acknowledgments

My thanks to copyeditors Diane Piron-Gelman and Carl Bowen, whose thoroughness makes me look so good. Also, to Pierre H. Boulle and Adam Tinworth for looking over manuscripts of **The Madness of Priests**. And, as before, to Sara for, well, too many things to list here.

Victorian Age Vampire™ Trilogy
BOOK THREE: THE WOUNDED KING
by Philippe Boulle

Book Three:
The Wounded King

GRAVE SECRETS REVEALED

Regina Blake is reunited with her mother at last, but it may be too late to save either of them. Amidst the glories of Hapsburg Vienna, the two women are subject to the wiles of the Tremere warlock with only the vampires Victoria Ash and Beckett as dubious allies.

A return to London only makes matters worse, as an undead prince dips into madness and threatens to take the Empire with him.

Can Regina hope even to survive, much less prevail?

ON SALE IN APRIL

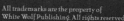

Dark Ages™
Clan Novel Series

The War of Princes Rages On!

Vampiric pilgrims head into Western Europe only to face the priests and knights with the strength of God on their side. Meanwhile, stories of Caine spread like wildfire. Has the Third Mortal returned at last?

The 13-part epic of vampires in the Middle Ages continues as the golden city of Constantinople rises from the ashes and pyres of the Inquisition light.

BOOK FOUR
SETITE™
by Kathleen Ryan
On Sale in February

BOOK FIVE
LASOMBRA™
by David Niall Wilson
On Sale in April

BOOK SIX
RAVNOS™
by Sarah Roark
On Sale in June